GREYHOUND

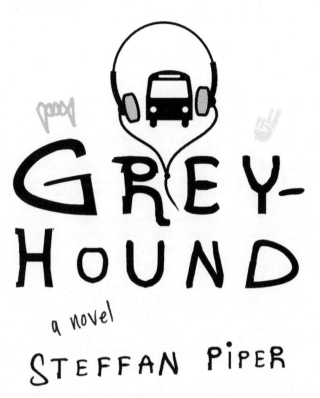

GREY-HOUND

a novel

STEFFAN PIPER

PUBLISHED BY

amazonencore

PRODUCED BY
MELCHER
MEDIA

Text copyright © 2010, Steffan Piper
All rights reserved.
Printed in the United States of America

10 11 12 13 14 15 16 / 10 9 8 7 6 5 4 3 2 1

Published by AmazonEncore
P.O. Box 400818
Las Vegas, NV 89140

Produced by Melcher Media, Inc.
124 West 13th Street
New York, NY 10011
www.melcher.com

Library of Congress Control Number
2010901885

ISBN-13: 978-0-9825550-9-5
ISBN-10: 0-9825550-9-1

Cover design by Ben Gibson
Interior design by Jessi Rymill
Author photos by Steffan Piper
Complete versions of the poems referenced in this novel can be found in
The Collected Poems of Langston Hughes, published by Vintage in 1995.

SUSTAINABLE
FORESTRY
INITIATIVE

Melcher Media strives to use environmentally responsible suppliers and materials whenever possible in the production of its books. For this book, that includes the use of SFI-certified interior paper stock.

The bulk of what you are about to read is true.
Certain names, places, and characterizations of certain people have
been adjusted for the sake of fiction and telling a compelling story.
Any unintended likeness is coincidental.

DON'T BELIEVE WHAT YOU HEAR, DON'T BELIEVE WHAT YOU SEE,
IF YOU JUST CLOSE YOUR EYES, YOU CAN FEEL THE ENEMY ...

—"ACROBAT," U2

CIRCA 1981

CONTENTS

GREYHOUND
SCHEDULE DETAILS

LOCATION	ARRIVES	DEPARTS	LAYOVER	SCHEDULE
Stockton, CA	03:55am	04:05am	:20	1443
Modesto, CA	04:45am	04:50am	:05	1443
Merced, CA	05:35am	05:40am	:05	1443
Madera, CA	06:15am	06:20am	:05	1443
Fresno, CA	06:50am	07:30am	:40	1443
Bakersfield, CA	09:25am	09:45am	:20	1443
Pasadena, CA	11:40am	11:45am	:05	1443
Glendale, CA	11:56am	12:01pm	:05	1443
Los Angeles, CA	12:25pm	02:00pm	1:35	1364
Riverside, CA	03:10pm	03:20pm	:10	1364
Palm Springs, CA	04:20pm	04:30pm	:15	1364
Indio, CA	05:15pm	05:25pm	:10	1364
Blythe, CA	07:20pm	07:50pm	:30	1364
Phoenix, AZ	11:10pm	12:01am	:50	1364
Glendale, AZ	12:20am	12:25am	:05	1364
Flagstaff, AZ	02:55am	03:45am	:05	1364
Holbrook, AZ	05:20am	05:25am	:05	1364
Gallup, NM	06:55am	07:10am	:15	1364
Grants, NM	08:25am	08:30am	:05	1364
Albuquerque, NM	10:05am	11:10am	1:05	1364
Tucumcari, NM	02:00pm	02:30pm	:30	1364
Amarillo, TX	05:20pm	06:50pm	1:30	1364
Elk City, OK	09:30pm	09:40pm	:10	1364
El Reno, OK	11:00pm	11:05pm	:05	1364
Oklahoma City, OK	11:40pm	12:10am	:40	1364
Tulsa, OK	02:00am	02:30am	:30	1364
Joplin, MO	04:35am	04:40am	:05	1364
Mt. Vernon, MO	05:10am	05:15am	:05	1364
Springfield, MO	06:00am	06:45am	:45	1364
Lebanon, MO	07:35am	07:40am	:05	1364
Ft. Leonard Wood, MO	08:20am	08:25am	:05	1364
St. Louis, MO	10:50am	01:10pm	2:30	1684
Indianapolis, IN	06:35pm	07:10pm	:35	1684
Columbus, OH	10:45pm	11:45pm	1:00	1684
Pittsburgh, PA	03:10am	03:30am	:20	4692
Altoona, PA	06:45am	06:45am		4692

1.

The skin across my face was taut and smooth like plaster. My eyelids wouldn't close, and I felt frozen in place, like a fixture. I was stretched out across my small twin bed like an old wooden toy, hoping I wouldn't fall asleep. Staring out across my room, I couldn't keep my eyes off the two suitcases that were neatly packed and sitting against the wall. My mother had seen to it that everything was ready to go, especially me. Just after the nine o'clock news, I was very abruptly herded off to bed wearing an old pair of pajamas that I was probably sporting for the very last time. Almost four hours later, I was still awake but fully dressed. I already had on my puffy brown windbreaker that had gotten to be a little too short in the sleeve and my brown rubber shoes that were only a buck fifty at the secondhand store, bought at the beginning of the school year. The rest of my clothes were haggard, dull, and as thin as the wallpaper of my room.

Staring at the ceiling of my bedroom, I watched the headlights of the cars passing on the street below. The shadows of the tree branches and the window frame brushed above me in a tangled gray mess. My mother and her new boyfriend, Dick, still hadn't come back from going out for drinks, just before ten. I kept telling myself that none of this was really happening and that they would change their minds by the time they got back. I was waiting, listening for the sound of Dick's station wagon coming up the road and into the driveway, but it just kept getting later. I listened for the engine for some time, but I was easily distracted by the ticking of the second hand on the plastic clock plugged in next to the bed. I had turned off the alarm earlier, knowing that in ten minutes, I wouldn't be asleep.

I felt like a statue that had once stood somewhere important but was taken down, crated up, and placed into storage in a nondescript warehouse. My whole body felt like marble or bronze or whatever they might've made statues of me out of. Feeling cold and fragile, it was probably wax. During a school trip, I'd seen a few of those wax figures that looked somewhat real but weren't. I remembered how impressed I was at first, until the tour guide started to explain how difficult they were to maintain, that they had to be rotated through the museum and an air-conditioned storage facility, and that they were very, very expensive. When we walked back into the large workshop, the guide showed us various parts of the wax figures being built, with several people assigned to each replicated person. I lost all interest and felt an awful sense of jealousy when the guide blurted out that the statues were like children to the people who worked at the museum. I had become light-headed and sick and threw up on the floor moments later. Nobody had cared how I was being maintained, or if the temperature of the room didn't agree with me, or if I didn't look just right. What I had in common with the wax figures was that we all moved around a lot and we didn't know where we'd be put next. On display or stuffed back into storage, either way it was out of my control. My mother had often said that "children should be seen and not heard," and being only eleven, I had heard that quite often. I got the impression that the creators of these things had probably felt the same way. I had felt an immense rush of sadness roll over me like a wave when we were ushered outside. I remembered going pale from being sick and somebody joking that I looked like one of the wax statues in the museum.

Stuck in a loop repeating the memory of the field trip in my head, Dick's station wagon had pulled up the drive. I was jolted from my reverie by the slamming of the heavy car doors. Without turning on a light, I got up, quickly made the bed, and stood next to my suitcases. I listened to my mother and Dick laughing outside. They both sounded drunk. I stood in one spot, perfectly still like a permanent resident from the museum, careful not to let the floor creak underfoot. Dick was laughing idiotically as he fumbled with the lock on the front door. I could hear it all from my isolated position. I resisted the temptation to walk over to the window and look down. I stayed locked in the frozen moment of waiting for what was next. They had been out celebrating, although I really couldn't say what there was to celebrate. It was two days until my twelfth birthday, so I knew that it must be too early for that. Before they had gone out, I had overheard my mother and Dick as she was getting ready in the bathroom. I'd already blocked out their conversation and couldn't remember what she had said, knowing it was probably best to forget. If they were celebrating my leaving, I just didn't want to think about that either.

After a few moments, my mother hurriedly began to climb the stairs. My throat tensed as she closed in on the bedroom door. The thought quickly crossed my mind that in about ten more minutes it would no longer be my bedroom door, and a few minutes after that it would no longer be my bedroom.

"Ohh ... you're already up," she announced, surprised.

"Yeah, I just ..." I mumbled softly, my words trailing off, unsure.

"Bring down your luggage and get a move on," she commanded. I zipped up my jacket as if I had just put it on. She flipped on the light, turned, and rushed off back down the stairs. The water pipes in the walls rattled as Dick flushed the toilet downstairs in the back of the house. I gagged inside as I pictured him doing his business, drunk and trying to handle his cigarette all at once. My mother's new would-be husband was another winner in a long line of aging thoroughbreds. One more suitor who had queued up for what he must've thought was something special. Dick worked as an Allstate insurance salesman near the freeway. The only thing important for me to understand about Dick was that he hated being within five feet of me. After he had moved in, I knew it was only a matter of time before I'd be shuttled off to live somewhere else or beaten half to death, which had happened before and probably wasn't yet out of the question.

Half asleep, I pulled the heavy suitcases behind me. They thumped down the stairwell as I took each step in a daze. I felt sluggish and tired and wobbled momentarily as I descended, believing that I was going to heave over and topple downward, hopefully killing myself and bringing an end to all of it. I fantasized that my mother would feel guilty about wanting to send me away if I died, but then again, who was I trying to fool?

"Put the cases in the back of the car," she chimed in, aloofly. "You don't want to be late." It was only then that I realized my mother was wearing yet another new dress, gaudy orange flowers with sprawling red leaves wrapping themselves around her nether regions like poison oak. I just couldn't bear to look. She stank of cheap perfume and damp cigarette butts. "Your bus leaves in forty minutes." Unable to speak, I saw Dick's eyes following me. He could've helped me with the cases, but he didn't.

"Don't scratch my bumper putting them cases in, kid," he announced slowly. His voice had that certain bounce to it, as if he was relieved that I was leaving.

Outside, the air was colder and it was pitch dark with no moon. The streetlights buzzed like mosquitoes as the night slowly closed in on three a.m. I carefully lifted each suitcase into the back of the station wagon and pushed the tail closed. I exhaled deeply, watching my breath explode outward into the night. Dick was eyeballing me from the porch as he lit my mother's cigarette.

"Ugh, it's so damn late. Let's just get this whole thing over with," she grunted. My mother seemed more annoyed than sad or concerned that I was leaving. She thought, as usual, that I didn't hear what she said, but I did. Dick was Dick. In truth, it was the same as it ever was. I was again an outsider on the edges of my mother's love life. I was always more like an unwanted roommate than her son.

Watching the house disappear behind us, I knew it was yet another one of my mother's rented places that I would never see again. We had moved more than anybody I knew. Every year it was a new school, new friends, and a new house. Nothing ever seemed permanent, not even her. Every man seemed to change her into another woman, and every time she changed, it became harder and harder to be around her. These days, it was just impossible. Her only concern was a new dress, possibly a drink, a cigarette, and a man, all in that order. I watched her nervously inhale her cigarette as if she were trying to pose for a magazine. I wondered if this was something that all kids my age had to go through. I shifted in my seat uncomfortably as Dick weaved the car around corners, speeding to our destination.

"Remember, when you get to Los Angeles, wait for your Aunt Sharon. She's supposed to meet you there and stay with you during the afternoon layover."

"Yes, Mother."

"She'll make sure that you eat, and she'll probably give you some money. Don't refuse it either. She has more than us and can afford to give you a few dollars to travel with." Her tone was bitter, as if her sister had somehow cheated her out of something and owed her.

Dick pulled into the Greyhound station, parked in an open space close to the front, and killed the engine. It seemed as if he'd suddenly come to life and was a whole lot happier. He was as smug as my mother, and it was then that I realized they probably deserved each other and whatever horrible fate awaited them.

"Hey kid, let me help you with your things," he piped in, as he quickly sprang from the car like a hotel valet and circled to the rear, opening the tail to grab the cases. My mother was already heading toward the ticket window; the clicking of her orange heels struck against the pavement with a rapid sense of desperation. Everything was happening so fast that I didn't know what to think. I wanted to crawl back into bed or bite down on a cyanide pill like trapped Nazis did in old movies.

"One-way ticket to Altoona, Pennsylvania, through Los Angeles and Mount Vernon, Missouri, please." I stood back as my mother barked her commands at the lady behind the ticket window. The way she spoke to people made me want to crawl in a hole.

"Okay, just a moment. It's going to take me a few minutes to check the schedules," the woman rejoined, bowing her head and pouring her fingers over schedules that looked like endless grids of multidigit numbers.

"That's fine," my mother answered the woman eagerly, her purse unzipped, bills on standby and in the ready position. The woman behind the counter looked back up at my mother, trying to get a fix on just whom she was dealing with. My mother turned away, annoyed, and dangled her cigarette precariously close to my face.

"Sebby, honey, listen to me now ... always sit up front on the bus. Don't talk to strange people and always make sure you get back on the bus before it leaves. Do you understand?"

"Yes, ma'am," I answered her. She looked at me as if she wanted to say more, but I saw her face crumple up as if she didn't really quite know what to say. She tensed up and tried to find relief by sucking hard on her filtered butt.

"Look, I know you probably don't understand why you have to go stay with your grandparents, but everything's different now." The tone of her voice rose as if she believed what she was saying was the absolute truth. "Dick and I really need our space right now to be able to work things out. I wanted you to be there for the wedding in San Francisco, but having a babysitter to take care of you would just be too expensive."

"We've n-n-never had a babysitter before," I answered.

"Don't talk back," she chided, incensed. "And don't stutter in front of me, either! It's childish." Her concern for me quickly vanished and returned to the frustrated annoyance that I was accustomed to. It was the same frustrated annoyance that had surfaced with the ticket lady.

"Look, I've tried to explain it to you, but I'm afraid you just don't understand what a fragile time it is for Dick and me." She looked over at him in the distance. He was fumbling with some loose change at the vending machines. "And I just don't want to debate it with you.

I have to do this if I expect anything between Dick and me to work out. I can't expect him to want to raise another man's child. It's just not fair to him. Can't you see?"

I just nodded. She was always like this. It seemed to me as if she cared more for momentary Dick than she did for her own son. It felt more natural to call her Charlotte than it ever did calling her mother. But I'd been through this before. If it were two years earlier, I probably would've buckled in half and broken out in tears. But I stopped crying when I kept finding myself crying alone. Anyhow, like all the others, it was doubtful he would last, marriage or no.

"And don't forget to call me from Missouri as well. I would've wanted you to stay with *my parents,* but they said that they're too busy this time of year, and it would be too difficult for them to look after you. The last place I wanted you to go was to your father's parents. But since he left us cold and in the wind, they might as well help us out. It's the least they could do." Each time she spoke about my father, her face contracted like she had just eaten something rotten. She pulled some money from her purse and slipped it into my front shirt pocket. I watched her silently going through her performance of abandoning me as gracefully as possible, in the dark of night and on a cold and windy bus platform.

"Thirty-five dollars. It's all I can spare. That should be more than enough to keep you fed for the next three and a half days. Don't spend money on junk food or lend anything out. Do you hear me?"

"Oh, I hear you," I answered, uninterested.

"Don't talk to me with that tone, and answer me when I ask you direct questions," she barked. "You're just too damn quiet and too much to deal with." All I could do was shrug and look away.

"Don't forget to tell your sister that I love her. Every time I call your grandmother's house, she's always out." I heard the words, but nothing sounded sincere. The last time she called was more than two months ago. Every one of her words registered flat and lifeless.

"I will," I replied.

"She's trying to keep Beanie away from me, and I don't like it,"

she scowled. She started checking her pockets for another cigarette. I could tell she was done talking. I had nothing to say to her
anyway.

I knew that this was the moment when my mother was once
again pawning me off to go live with relatives. It wasn't the first
time, and it probably wouldn't be the last. I saw Dick standing on the
curb smoking another quick cigarette and drinking a Coke. Maybe
he knew to give my mother and me a few moments together, maybe
he just didn't want to be anywhere near me, which was typical. He
didn't like children and had made that fact abundantly clear. When
I saw him approaching with my cases, he was beaming.

"Here ya go, kid. Better keep these things close," he advised.
"They're heavy as hell. What do you got in here?"

"Just my stuff and some books," I replied nervously.

"Well, you'll probably need a porter to wheel these things to the
bus," he rejoined.

"I can manage," I answered, reaching for the cases and dragging them next to where I was standing in line. The ticket lady had
created an itinerary for my route across the country.

"You'll take the 1443, which leaves here in five minutes on platform number 2 to Los Angeles. After an hour and a half layover
in downtown L.A., you'll transfer to the 1364 through Phoenix,
Flagstaff, and Amarillo. You'll have a stop in Mount Vernon,
Missouri, and you can reboard at any time if you just show your
ticket. Continuing on to Pittsburgh and into Altoona, Pennsylvania.
Three days, 2,575 miles. Please check all the schedules at the stops
for changes and have a good trip."

"How much is the total?" my mother hissed.

"Fifty-one dollars and forty-eight cents."

"Is that the rate for a child?" she clarified.

"No, that's the adult rate," the lady replied. My mother shot me
a look and just thumbed her nose at the woman in silence.

"An unaccompanied minor?" The ticket lady looked back at my
mother as if she were insane. It was a fact that she may have suspected but I had already known.

"Yes, that's right. Just the boy," she spat venomously.

"Uh ... forty-four dollars, please," she announced, as she raised up in her seat to see me standing quietly out of view at the counter's edge. When she saw me clutching at my two cases for dear life with an incredibly frightened look across my face, she smiled.

"Oh my God, darling ... you sure are adorable, aren't you? Driving across the United States?"

"Yes, ma'am," I answered.

"Honey, you are about as precious as they come." She smiled again and sat back down. As she did, the smile on her face vanished and crumpled back up into an irate glare. Judging from her reaction, I wondered for a brief moment if she already knew my mother. My mother shifted around nervously and averted her eyes, trying hard not to make eye contact. The sound of a loud machine under the counter seemed to vibrate the partition and the small glass window in front of her. The woman handed my mother the tickets and her change.

"Have a nice trip. Remember to tell the driver that you're traveling alone, okay?"

"Sure thing," I responded, smiling back. I thought she was nice, but my mother seemed upset and was grumbling under her breath all through the lobby of the terminal. Dick trailed just behind us carrying the one bag that didn't have wheels. It must've been his one and only kind gesture. It was far too early in the morning to worry about what was going to happen next, or what Dick would say, or leaving my friends again—which was lately something that I did frequently but never got used to.

The bus terminal was clean but small. The lobby was adorned with a few rows of plastic chairs and lots of incredibly bright lights that seemed well intent on keeping everybody wide awake. Loud music played through a speaker near the ceiling, but a woman's voice was constantly interrupting whatever song was playing.

"Now boarding 1602 for San Francisco on Platform 5. Final call."

I wasn't the only person traveling alone, but I was the only person who wasn't an adult. There were several soldiers carrying large green bags that looked more like tube sausages than luggage, and they were all traveling by themselves.

No one noticed me walking next to my mother in her gaudy orange dress with the strangling vines. And no one cared who I was, or why I was about to embark on a coast-to-coast journey by myself, possibly being swallowed whole in the midst of it. The thought of it made me tremble. Something inside of me was hoping that somebody would approach us, give my mother the third degree, and put a stop to it, but I knew that nothing like that was about to happen. I couldn't say anymore that I had any real family. I definitely didn't have any real friends, and I sure didn't believe in saviors. So far I hadn't seen even a glimmer of proof.

Standing next to the open doorway of the large, vibrating metallic bus on platform 2, I started to feel a little scared again. The air around me smelled of gasoline, oil, burnt rubber, and something else that I couldn't quite label.

"You going to take notes, kid?" Dick asked me, seemingly interested.

"Huh?" I replied, looking up at him blankly, curious but confused.

"The pencil and notepad in your shirt pocket, Douche!" His index finger was pointing straight at my heart like a gun.

"Ohh," I muttered, finally aware. "Maybe, I guess."

"Don't f-f-f-forget to st-st-st-stutter, I mean write!" Dick teased. He was working in his final jabs at me while he could. "Dou-Dou-Douche stain."

"Don't call him that, Dick," my mother interrupted, laughing as if it was a joke, guffawing at his boyish humor. It seemed to be his favorite word—he called me "douche" or "douche bag" every chance he got when my mother wasn't around. It was the first time he'd used the word in front of her. She was giggling as if it was something said by Johnny Carson, as a punch line on *The Tonight Show*. Making fun of my stuttering, though, was nothing new, and my mother never said anything to Dick about his mean streak toward me.

"Sorry, Charlotte, honey. I was just teasing the poor little stut-stut-stuttering runt. Maybe if I tease him enough he'll stop doing it," he suggested. I wanted to reach out and strangle the life out of him. Maybe I could make him stop. He didn't have any reservations about punching me in the face, and I had no desire to get on the bus with a bloodied lip or wake up in the morning with a black eye. It was just one of those things that I had to let go, like always.

I scratched my head to feel more comfortable, but I only felt more out of place. My mother bent down one more time, kissed me on the cheek, looked me over, and stood back up to light another cigarette.

"Okay, off you go. And don't forget to call." She was acting as if I were going to have dinner with a friend on the next block over, instead of traveling across the country, possibly leaving her for the last time. An elderly black man wearing a thick blue jacket and a cap with a Greyhound patch came over to us. He took my bags and gave my mother a ticket, which she immediately handed to me. The porter witnessed the whole exchange and was watching my mother with an extremely concerned look and a frown.

"Hold on to that ticket, son. You'll need it to get these bags back. How far ya goin'?" He was looking directly at me now.

"Pittsburgh, sir."

"Pittsburgh!" he parroted in exclamation. "That's one hell of a long trip, boy. All by yourself?"

My mother grunted.

"Yes, sir," I answered.

"Well ..." he smiled, looking at both my mother and Dick carefully as if getting a mental picture in case he had to later describe them to the police. "Just make sure that you tell the driver." It was the third time that I'd heard this instruction, and it began to sound more ominous. For the first time, I really began to question if this was a good idea and did so aloud, or rather, tried to.

"Maybe ..."

"Just get on the bus and get a seat up front," my mother growled at me, pushing me up the stairs. I went begrudgingly, but after I took the first three steps upward, I was face to face with an old, meaty-faced driver. It was then that I realized that I had crossed the point of no return. Everything had just begun.

When I turned around to take a last look at my mother and Dick, they had bolted off and were quick-stepping it off the plat-form. They were already on the precipice of crossing back inside the lobby. She didn't look back at all, and from the side of her face, it seemed as if she was laughing. Dick looked back, though. He glanced at me before slipping away with my mother through the sliding glass door. It suddenly felt as if it was all a part of some mas-ter plan of his that I was only just now being made aware of. The whole thing was over quickly and was meaningless.

"Ticket," the driver announced. I turned back to see the old man who was seated behind the wheel staring at me with his hand out. I made out his name from the plastic badge on his shirt: *Jim.*

"Los Angeles," I managed faintly, as I pulled out the ticket, handing it over.

"Have a seat, Bucko," he answered, returning my stub.

"I'm traveling alone," I announced.

"So is Jesus. Now stop advertising and find a seat, chief," he grunted, pulling the doors closed with a big handle that was right at eye level and closer to me than I first thought. I flinched, think-ing it was going to whack me.

"Take it easy, kid. Find a seat," he said, shooting me a concerned look. Now I was locked in with no escape and no way to change my mind. I realized that I never had a choice in the matter anyway. Several seats were vacant, but only toward the back. The very back seat was a row of three seats next to a toilet door with a small light near the handle. The whole rear end of the bus smelled like Pine-Sol or some type of cleaning product. Now, close up, I recognized it as the smell I had detected earlier out on the platform but couldn't identify. I thought to make a note of this as soon as I got settled.

I plopped myself down next to the window in the back row after walking past almost four rows of vacant seats. I relaxed and leaned into the wall of the back corner, which was made of an odd fake wood laminate. I felt as if I were at the end of the world now. It gave me a bad feeling to imagine why there would have to be wood on a bus. My imagination ran wild. The last thing I wanted was to get lost somewhere on this bus and have to end up pulling off the wood paneling for firewood or some type of improvised shelter. The wood only went up to my chest and shoulders and ended with a small metal grate just below the window.

What was supposed to be air-conditioning was being pumped upward through the vents at full blast. I began to wonder why every smell on the bus seemed to make my hair stand on end and make me feel like something horrible was about to happen. It smelled like a tube was connected into the air-con system directly from the engine compartment and was blowing noxious exhaust through the cabin. I began to feel a little sick but immediately became distracted as the bus started rolling backward with a soft beeping noise. Outside, the speaker in the terminal was still announcing departures. I could faintly hear the message over the engine.

"1443 leaving for Los Angeles on platform 2."

The thought crossed my mind that anybody in the terminal needing to hear that was already too late. The lights inside the bus dimmed, and we sat idling in the driveway for several moments, waiting for the driver to receive some unknown cue. I wondered if I would've been able to see Dick's station wagon hightailing it away, but the bus went nowhere near the front parking lot as we pulled out.

"Good evening, folks," came the driver's voice over the loud-speaker. *"I'm your driver. My name's Jim, and this is the 1443 to Los Angeles. We're looking at a total drive time of eight hours and twenty minutes, so we'll probably pull into the station in downtown Los Angeles around ten-thirty in the morning, just in time for lunch, or breakfast, if everything goes according to plan. So just sit back, relax, and leave the driving to us. I'll leave the overhead lights off, so those who want to sleep, can."*

The speaker made an odd clicking sound and then went quiet. Jim's message set me at ease by giving me a small preview of what was to come. The bus drove down several side streets, past all the shops I was familiar with. But at night, everything looked like a ghost town from another era. The small one-screen theater was still showing *Popeye*. I had seen it alone, a few days before. Every street was now deserted. Every window in every shop was dark and vacant. I stared out at the diminishing city as we idled at the different red lights before pulling out onto the highway. I was feeling lonely, but I was actually glad to be rid of my mom, away from Dick, and on the road heading toward my grandma's in Altoona. With thoughts of seeing her again and the driver's message reverberating in my head, I was able to close my eyes and drift off to sleep for the first time all night.

2.

FRESNO, CALIFORNIA

When I opened my eyes, the sun was up and shifting red across the face of the loose billowy clouds above. Only the gradual slowing of the bus seemed to break my slumber. For three hours I had managed to sleep soundly. I vaguely remembered waking at one point when the bus had stopped in the middle of nowhere, but I barely stirred long enough for it to even register. Sitting up and rubbing my eyes, I noticed that most of the passengers had disembarked during the night. My mouth was dry and tasted like Pine-Sol. I searched my pockets for the multicolored pamphlet I had picked up at the counter in the Stockton Terminal. It was a schedule of stops from Seattle to San Diego. Moving my finger down the page, I discovered that we had stopped in Modesto, Merced, and Madera for five minutes at each station.

The bus slowed gracefully as it merged from the freeway and onto the off-ramp. A sign designated the exit as *Fresno Street.* Turning left at the top of the off-ramp, the bus passed several vacant lots, a few industrial buildings, and a strip of rust-colored train tracks. The overhead speaker clicked on, and the driver tried to make the last of us feel at home once again.

"Good morning, folks. Welcome to Fresno. Pulling in, you can see it's a good-size stop, so if you need to get out and stretch your legs or eat, now is a good time to do so. We'll be laid over here for almost forty minutes, so enjoy yourselves, keep your tickets handy, and make sure you're back on the bus before we pull out. Also, please secure any valuables, and don't leave anything in the seats."

When he clicked off, we were slowing to a stop and parking between two other buses. Through the window, the terminal appeared busy with morning travelers. Suddenly my focus was broken by a tall, bald man in a suit coming out of the lavatory beside me. Casting me a quick glance, he smiled. The smell of the toilet threw me off. I recoiled in my spot, and I failed to respond. I now understood why most of the people riding were sitting toward the front. I could've sworn that the plastic fixtures started melting.

For a few moments, I actually contemplated not getting off the bus for fear of losing the backseat to another rider. The urge to try to catch a few more hours of sleep before getting to Los Angeles was tempting. Once the bald man made his way down the steps, Jim, the driver, stood up and looked at me with curiosity.

"You coming, chief?"

I got up and nodded, acquiescing immediately. "Okay."

"No sense stayin' cooped up in here for no reason, suckin' on toilet fumes. Here ..." He stuck his hand in his pocket and pulled out some loose change. When I got to the front, he grabbed a hold of my hand and thrust the coins at me.

"Get yourself a cuppa coffee, on me. It's not too bad here. Just don't get into any trouble—you got a long journey ahead from what I hear."

"Thank you," was about all I could manage. I slowly eased down the metal steps and made my way off the bus.

"Don't mention it, chief," he laughed, and locked the bus after we were both off. I wandered inside the terminal alone, as he stayed behind to walk around and inspect the vehicle. The building was larger than it appeared, and a lot busier. Groups of people were standing in small clusters, hugging family members who were getting ready to take a long journey. The ones getting ready to leave all had the same scared look on their faces that I had had a few hours earlier. It was one of the few things I could recognize. Their cases stood below them, well packed and prepared. Maybe there really was something insidious going on that I wasn't aware of. Maybe this was my chance to alert the authorities or tell somebody. I just didn't know what to say.

In the main terminal, rows of black vinyl and chrome seats expanded out across what seemed like the length of a church hall. Many of the seats had small televisions affixed to them by metal arms. Most were occupied by various Greyhound passengers who were fast asleep, surrounded by luggage, trash, and rolled-up newspapers. A large, middle-aged black man was snoring loudly with one foot resting on top of a cylinder-shaped ashtray. The intercom system now had a man's voice listing arrivals and departures and their corresponding platform numbers.

"1236 to Yosemite, Bridgeport, and Lake Tahoe, platform 7. Final boarding call."

As I made my way through the lobby toward the smell of food, I heard the loudspeaker issue the same final boarding call at least two more times. I scratched my head, wondering about Greyhound's meaning of the word *final*. A security guard and a janitor pushing a mop bucket that smelled of hot water and Pine-Sol passed me. The only portion of their conversation that I could catch seemed meaningless.

"I think he's pissed himself, and he's been passed out in the same ..." The janitor's voice was loud and agitated. I looked back and watched them turn a corner toward an endless bank of vending machines. I meandered through the terminal, feeling invisible and separated from everyone else by something unexplainable. Maybe it was just my age. The café was nestled past the ticket booths, near the front entrance of the building, which overlooked the parking lot. Trees encircled the building outside like Indians ominously getting ready to burn the place to the ground. The morning sky felt threatening through the glass windows. Rain clouds seemed to be standing guard with the trees, trying to keep whatever was trapped inside the terminal from escaping. The world outside the windows of the Grey Café might as well have been a battlefront. It was a dramatic change from being on the bus, but maybe that was the way they wanted you to feel. Maybe they wanted you to feel eager about getting back on the bus and not loiter around the terminal, "up to no good," as Jim put it.

I sat down at the counter to read what was on the lighted menu that was sponsored by Coke. I knew I had to spend my money wisely, having only thirty-five dollars and some loose change. A tall, slender redheaded woman wandered over toward me with a coffeepot in one hand and a glass of ice water in the other. She wore a gray uniform that looked similar to our driver's outfit, except for her white apron. When she put the water down in front of me, she stared back at me, transfixed.

"You lost, honey?"

"No, ma'am. Just hungry."

She laughed. "I bet you are. You sure are a cute one." She seemed mesmerized by me for some reason. I thought she was nice from the first moment I saw her. "Are you traveling alone, sweetheart?"

"Yes, ma'am."

"Polite, too. You want some bacon and eggs?"

I nodded.

"Don't worry then, I'll take care of you. Just sit right there and relax. Okay?" She was watching me from across the Formica countertop.

I smiled in agreement. "May I have a cup of coffee?" The name printed on her tag read *Jenny,* but I felt awkward using it. I had never had coffee before; my mother never allowed it.

"Coffee?" She laughed again, shaking her head. "You sure take the cake, sweet stuff. What's your name?" The inner panic inside my head began once more. It was the million-dollar question, and even though I had the answer, getting it out of my mouth clean was a gamble.

"Um … it's a … Sebastien Ranes."

She repeated my name back to me slowly. It sounded nicer coming from her mouth than it ever did from mine. I always felt awkward about my name and tripped across it as if it were a foreign phrase I barely recognized. She poured me a cup of coffee, put it in front of me, and placed a hand on the counter, watching me, stupefied. "Would you like some condensed milk with that?" she suggested.

"Yes, please," I responded quietly.

"How far are you going, Sebastien Ranes?"

"Just past Pittsburgh."

"Oh good Lord, child! Just past Pittsburgh? You make it sound like it's just down the street. Baby, that's on the other side of the planet!" she exclaimed, surprised.

"I'm going to go live with my grandma and my sister."

"You're going to go live with your grandma and your sister," she repeated. "Do your folks know about this?"

"Yes, ma'am. My mother put me on the bus last night in Stockton."

"Your mother put you on the bus last night in Stockton!" She did it again, but now slower. "Did she manage to give you any money?" It seemed like the obvious next question.

"Thirty-five dollars," I replied, without considering my own words.

Jenny's face glassed over and turned gray, which seemed to be the theme. She stared long at me as if she wanted to repeat what I had said one more time but couldn't. She scrambled around the counter and came directly toward me.

"Let me get a better look at you." She ran her hand through my hair and across my face, looking straight into my eyes. I had no clue as to why she was examining me in such a manner, but her hand was soft, and it felt nice against my cheek. She hugged me, which caught me by surprise.

"Good gracious, you are adorable. But you're a half-starved lit-tle scarecrow, aren't ya?" It was strange, but when she hugged me, I felt different. I couldn't recall the last time my own mother had hugged me, apart from quickly shuttling me onto the bus the night before. This was different, though. It felt as if she really cared about me, and it didn't make any sense. Five minutes before, she had never laid eyes on me. Now it was as if I was her only child coming home from a bad day at school. How could it be? My mind felt heavy and dry like cork or cardboard. Something wasn't right.

"I'll get you fixed up so you won't be hungry. Does that sound like a good idea?"

"Sure," I answered.

Jenny disappeared behind the counter to put in my order with the cook and tend to the other customers. At the end of the counter, the tall, bald man in the suit from the bus was eating breakfast and reading the newspaper. He looked at me, but only briefly. He ate his food, and I took care of putting the condensed milk into my coffee. The intercom system came on again, this time announcing my bus.

"1443 to Los Angeles and San Diego on platform 7, departing at 7:30."

I looked at the clock on the wall and noticed I still had another thirty minutes. I wasn't in any hurry. A few minutes later, Jenny approached with my food, which consisted of scrambled eggs, two strips of bacon, wheat toast, and hash browns.

"Coffee good?" she asked. "And don't say 'Yes, ma'am' either."

"The coffee's good. Thank you."

"That's better. Now eat up."

Music came on overhead, and I lost myself in my breakfast. I hadn't eaten since dinner the night before, which was only a box of macaroni and cheese in a kitchen that I was destined never to see again. I wondered what my mother was doing at that moment. I imagined she was probably asleep in her bedroom with Dick. It was still too early for either of them.

The coffee was hot, and I slowly began to feel a little more like myself. I heard Jenny repeating my name again off in the distance to no one, as if she was astounded by the sound of it, or possibly trying to memorize it for later reference. The darkness that had surrounded me earlier, regarding traveling the country alone, began to lift. I thought if everyone was going to be this nice to me, I wouldn't have that bad of a journey. After all, it was only three days and some change.

When I finished, Jenny brought me a piece of pumpkin pie with a scoop of ice cream. I didn't think I would've ever had room for that much food, but I might as well have inhaled the thing whole. I couldn't refuse.

"Thank you," I uttered.

"Don't you fret, sugar."

I looked her over as she walked away. Her whole body swayed

with an importance that I hadn't seen before. She reminded me of one of those models on the calendars that hung on the wall of the mechanic's garage and looked like artwork from the 1950s. I watched her serve plates of food, pour more coffee, and take orders. She was a striking figure, and everyone was glad when she came by and tended to them.

A few more young men filed into the café, soldiers again. These men were wearing well-pressed blue uniforms and appeared more refined, unlike the men in Stockton, who were rough, shabby, and constantly smoking. These men seemed smart, polite, and much more reserved. I figured they were probably officers. Several of them had a small set of wings, a few inches wide, pinned on their light blue shirts just above their hearts. Their uniforms seemed more complex. I was pulling money from my pocket when Jenny returned.

"Put that away, child," she commanded. I looked up at her, dumbstruck. I slowly went back to trying to fish out the smallest bills.

"Don't worry about that. I'll take care of it," she insisted, as she came around the side. She pulled me in close to her again, and my head sunk into her large breasts. She was soft and smelled nice, like flowers, butter, and makeup. Her hands were warm and gripped tightly onto my arms.

"You don't smell like cigarettes," I said. As soon as the words had left my lips, I felt stupid for saying it.

"What an odd thing to say," she replied, startled, as she rocked me from side to side. "Of course I don't, baby. I don't smoke. That's an awfully nasty habit."

"My mother smokes and smells like an ashtray. You smell really nice," I rejoined.

She laughed. "Why, you sure are a smooth talker, aren't you?"

I smiled again and thanked her for breakfast. She kissed me long on the cheek and rubbed my hair lovingly. I finally began to settle down and not feel so edgy from being out in the world alone. Without any warning, she handed me a brown paper sack.

"Here, sweetheart, you take this with you on the bus. We usually have these for the drivers, but they never want them, and we always throw away more than we give out."

"That's awful nice of you." I looked inside. It was a sandwich that smelled of peanut butter and jelly, a box of raisins, and an orange.

"Okay now, Sebastien Ranes. Make sure you sit up front, and you tell the driver you're traveling alone." I couldn't believe it; she gave me the same advice as everyone else. I was beside myself. But at least she was nice and she smelled good, and to me that was all that seemed to matter anymore. She hugged me a third time, pulling me close, before releasing me back into the wilderness of the world. It was almost painful when she let me go. I waved as I stepped across the threshold of the café back into the lobby. She was leaning against the counter, smiling and waving. My mind was taking snapshots of her. All I could think of was how pretty she was and how I wanted her to hug me one last time.

I straggled nervously around the terminal, trying to kill time, feeling weird and out of place, before I realized I needed to go to the bathroom, which was located at the far end. In front of the men's toilet, a man and a woman were arguing and shouting. The woman kept pointing her finger at the man and calling "asshole," "shithead," and "fucking retard." I had heard much worse at home many times before. I was no stranger to arguments or even knock-down, drag-out fights. The man just kept telling the woman to shut up and called her a "fat cow." I laughed as I walked by them and slipped into the restroom. I glanced behind me a moment later, concerned that they might've heard me.

I wandered into the low-lit, dark green–tiled bathroom and went pee. The bald man in the suit from the bus had come in right behind me. He saw me as he slowly walked past and closed himself into one of the stalls. After I finished, I shifted over to the sinks to wash my hands.

"Hey, boy ..." I heard him speaking softly. He was whispering from the other stall, but I didn't respond.

"Hey ... can you get me some paper from the stall? This one's out. It's all empty in here," he beckoned. I didn't know why he was whispering. Maybe he felt embarrassed. I wiped my hands on the towel roll on the wall after forwarding the cloth to a would-be clean spot. I wondered where all the dirty towel went, as it seemed to disappear back inside the plastic housing. I slowly walked back toward the stall to check out what he wanted.

"C'mon, kid. Help me out, would ya? I could use some paper," he pleaded. He was in the third stall down, the very last one in the row. I opened the door to the first empty stall and saw a full roll sitting on top of the holder. I grabbed it and turned to head back out of the stall, but he was immediately behind me at the stall door. I was surprised that he had moved so quickly. Another man came into the bathroom at that same moment; the door squeaked loudly on its hinge.

"Sorry, kid, I thought that you'd left me hanging. Thanks, though." The bald man smiled, took the roll, and headed back into the stall and locked the door. He started coughing nervously and clearing his throat. I shrugged the whole thing off and left.

"*1443 to Los Angeles platform 7, now boarding. Five-minute call.*" The music came back on after the announcement. I had heard the song before. It was "The Most Beautiful Girl in the World." The song reminded me of the waitress. Walking back to the bus, I began to notice a lot of people sleeping in the terminal. It made me think back to all of those nights at the YMCA, stuck sleeping on a cot next to my older sister, Beanie. I had too many of those nights to forget. My mother always called it "rock bottom," but I never knew why. The security guard was asking different people to show him their tickets.

"Can't you see I'm trying to watch TV? I've paid for it!" The obese black man from before was angry and yelling at the guard. I quickly walked back outside hoping to get a good seat on the bus and not miss my ride. I didn't want to end up getting stuck here. As nice as Jenny was, I thought it might be uncomfortable if I had to see her again and explain that I was stupid enough to miss the bus. Everything with her seemed perfect. I didn't want to mess it up. It was the beginning of a good memory, and it was something to take note of in my journal.

I stood at the back of the line of people who were reboarding the bus. It didn't seem as if we had picked up many more riders. When I climbed the stairs, I saw Jim staring down at me with a smile and a cigar in his mouth.

"Here he comes, the luckiest man alive, I swear!" he bellowed and guffawed. "I saw you over in the Grey Café all deep in that broad's jugs. Good God, son!" I was stunned by what he said. It was as if I had been hit by a wave of thick air hearing the driver's descriptions of Jenny. I was embarrassed and probably blushed.

"Good job, chief!" he exclaimed. "A woman in every port! That's my motto."

I didn't know exactly what to say, so I made my way toward the back of the bus. The back row was once again completely open. A man was sitting on the opposite side against the window reading a book. I thought maybe he wanted to be near the toilet. I sat back in my seat and looked out at Fresno in the afternoon. Fresno seemed, from where I was sitting, like a forgotten town in a sea of concrete at the far edge of the world. The sun was cooking everything within its reach. I felt the heat oozing through the aluminum bus and slipping through the air-conditioning. It was the only thing the old people on the bus seemed to be talking about. I listened to their comments, not really having an opinion.

I pulled the notepad and pencil from my shirt pocket and wrote down three sentences, soon to be a memory, of my thoughts on Fresno.

Paper bags with peanut butter sandwiches. A waitress with soft hands. She hugged me in a sea of concrete.

As we pulled away from the bus station and back out onto the main street heading toward the freeway, I struggled to say more, but realized that three sentences were enough. Then I wrote the name *Jenny* in the margin.

We pulled out onto the freeway again. The road signs said it was the 99. After the bus built up speed, Jim came on the overhead speaker one more time.

"Good afternoon, ladies and gentlemen. Just want to welcome you to the 1443 to Los Angeles. Our travel time is approximately four and a half hours, which should put us in Downtown just after noon. A little later than first expected, but close enough. This portion of the drive is pretty steady and mostly downhill, so we may pick up a few minutes. Please remember, no drinking alcoholic beverages on the bus, and thank you for choosing Greyhound."

When the speaker made the clicking sound again, I noticed it was louder than Jim's voice, which was jarring, as the speaker was just above my head. It was the hardest thing so far to get used to. In the first twenty minutes of driving, several people had made their way back to the rear of the bus to use the toilet, including the tall, bald man in the suit. He nodded at me with a smile as he disappeared inside and locked the door. The *occupied* light came on with the sound of the lock sliding into place. I quickly figured out that most of the people who were going into the bathroom were going in there to have a cigarette. With every person who went in, the air following them out smelled heavier and heavier. I told myself that I would never smoke when I was older, no matter how good they might be. Cigarettes made everything stink. People's clothes, their faces, their hair, and their hands. Their teeth were yellow, the whites of their eyes were yellow, and their collars sweated cigarettes when it got hot. The smell burned my nose and bothered me to no end. But maybe it was necessary, as every adult I knew always smoked or "needed one." My mother always said she was "fiending for one." I had heard her say that smoking was romantic, but I just couldn't see how. It seemed like a death ritual more than anything else. All the Catholic services that I had ever sat through always burned incense. At least that smelled better, but not by much. The thought of Jenny stayed with me. She was beautiful and kind, she smelled nice, and she didn't smoke at all. My mother had also said that "people who don't smoke are squares." I had now come to believe this wasn't true. I felt angry at her for lying to me again. But I was happy to finally be sure about something about which I used to believe otherwise.

The bus sped quickly, and the world passed by the windows. I was just an observer but very glad to be seeing it sweep by beside me. Endless farmland, sewn together like the massive bed quilts that my grandma would make, one piece after another. Jim turned music on over the loudspeaker at a low volume to help break the monotony. I read the road signs, trying to count the rare occurrences of the letters *x*, *y*, and *z*. Several large yellow signs alerted drivers not to pick up hitchhikers because there was a prison nearby, but I didn't see any signs of hitchhikers or prisons. Maybe that was the way it was supposed to be. Early-morning commuters started to crowd next to us on the freeway. People were driving with an intense focus, and most of them were still eating their breakfast and drinking coffee from Styrofoam McDonald's cups. Everybody else's life seemed so different from my own.

I put my attention back inside the bus. Someone else had just locked himself in the bathroom. Sitting quietly on the row of seats alone, I fully realized my boredom and wished I had brought something to read—a book, a magazine, or even a newspaper. Stuffed inside the seat pocket was yet another ad brochure like all the others conveniently placed in the Fresno Terminal.

Lifting the leaflet from the seat pocket, I surveyed a woman's smiling face printed across the front in full color. She had bushy brown hair and a laughing smile. It seemed over-the-top as an ad for Greyhound. The words *Go Greyhound* were printed in red across the front like an alert. I couldn't figure out the purpose of the small booklet, as everyone on the bus had already clearly chosen to *Go Greyhound*. Opening the multipage brochure, I scanned it for anything interesting but only saw multiple photos of American landmarks like the Grand Canyon, the Saint Louis Arch, and the White House. I only knew these names as they were printed below each one, and every photo was accompanied by a short statement about seeing the world from a bus.

I put it back in the seat, a little confused. I would've expected the people in charge of making the flyer to advertise the cafés inside the terminal in order to persuade anyone not wishing to disembark on a layover to break down, give in, and go have a cup of coffee, just as I had. I had a frightening thought that maybe the cafés were rare and there weren't going to be that many as we got farther from California. If that was going to be the case, I imagined I'd be stuck eating food from the vending machines.

I would have to pay for food at some point. I estimated that my breakfast would have cost me just over four dollars if I had paid. I slowly added the numbers up in my notepad.

$2.85 for the bacon and eggs
75¢ for the coffee
$1.25 for pie

It came to $4.85, which was a little more than I had thought. I realized I probably wouldn't eat pie with every meal and so could deduct it from the total amount. But with pie, eating twice a day would cost me $9.70 a day. With three and a half days worth of driving, I had just enough. If I had added it up properly, I would have almost six dollars left by the time I got to Altoona. I fretted about other problems coming up and it costing me more than I could afford. If that happened, there was nothing I could do.

My mother had told me that my Aunt Sharon would give me some money and I shouldn't refuse it if she did. I hadn't seen my aunt in almost three years, but I never thought of her as generous. My mother had taken my older sister and me to go live with her one summer when she lost her job in the city and couldn't continue paying the rent. At the time, my Uncle Gerald had a pig farm in Lodi, near Stockton, but now he was driving a truck, and they were living in Los Angeles. Aunt Sharon was a lot like my mother, smoking cigarettes constantly and angry anytime I spoke up or said absolutely anything around the adults. She was my mother's eldest sister, but not any nicer, and I wasn't looking forward to seeing her. I reckoned that she would probably just tell me what a bother I was to have to come downtown for and that there was something wrong with me. She always told me that I was slow and that I was a mistake. At the time, I didn't know what she meant. After I retold this to my grandma, she told me not to listen to any of that nonsense.

The two-hour bus ride to Bakersfield went by quickly, even though I was bored silly. I felt determined to grab something to read once we stopped again. Driving to the Bakersfield station from the freeway off-ramp took longer than I expected. I had to use the bathroom, but it seemed eternally occupied. I had already reconsidered going inside and closing the door on one occasion because the smell was so awful that it made me turn away. The smell was horrendous, and my body had instinctively curled away before my brain had caught up. I was just trying to hold it until we got to the terminal, but I didn't want to wet my pants either. The only change of clothing I had was packed away underneath the bus. After winding around numerous city streets and standing still at eternal red lights, we pulled into the Bakersfield Greyhound Station.

"Good afternoon, everyone. Welcome to Bakersfield. We'll be stopped here for approximately twenty minutes. For all those permanently disembarking, thank you for choosing Greyhound."

Jim slowly pulled the bus around the terminal and angled it into its spot on platform 1. Looking out the window, I noticed that instead of being called platforms, the word *aisle* was painted down the metal stanchions that supported the awning above. I was the last rider to disembark, and Jim and all the other passengers were already headed inside the terminal. A Mexican lady with a broom and a mop bucket was waiting for me to get off so she could clean the floors and lavatory.

Bakersfield was a lot hotter than Fresno, and it seemed that most of the people wanted to be inside. Heading through the sliding doors, I noticed the tall, bald man in the suit watching me. He was curled around a pay phone, talking in a very low voice. He waved, but I moved too quickly through the entryway to wave back. I found the men's restroom without delay and was shocked to see only one urinal affixed to the wall. All the others were either ripped out due to construction, vandalized, or leaking water from the pipes. Several large puddles had formed on the floor, making the place seem dangerous. A soggy copy of *Reader's Digest* floated around in the slop. The bathroom was in bad shape, but I was thankful that no one else wanted to use the toilet. I wouldn't have been able to hold it if I had to stand in line. I felt relieved as soon as I started to pee—it must've been all the coffee going through my system. I could smell it as it blasted against the porcelain bowl. The aroma of ammonia and burnt coffee rose up strongly from the urinal below me.

"This bathroom's closed!" a voice barked from behind me. I turned my head to see a large man in a gray uniform glaring at me. "Didn't you see the 'out of order' sign on the door?" he snapped, one hand holding the door open.

"No, sir, I did not."

"Hurry up and let's go then, I ain't got all damn day," he blustered, ushering me out of the toilet and locking the door behind me. I felt bad for anyone who would've been caught short and really had to go.

Everything inside the Bakersfield Terminal was closed. The Grey Café was shut tight, the lights were dark, and the place had a chain-link fence blocking the entryway. A sign affixed to the fence read: *Closed until further notice*. It looked as if a bomb had gone off.

The only thing to eat or drink was made possible through an endless row of vending machines. My nightmare had become a reality. I was confronted by a glowing bank of colorfully lit, well-stocked machines. They sat waiting for me, evenly spaced along one whole wall inside the main terminal. I counted six Coca-Cola machines, two that dispensed only coffee, three that vended sandwiches and fruit, and five machines that spat out candy bars, gum, and potato chips. It looked like a cafeteria from the not-so-distant future. There was a smell of something rotting, but I couldn't follow it home, as it seemed to fade behind the monstrous display in front of me. It was like knocking at the door of Oz.

Most of the chairs in the lobby were full of people who looked like permanent fixtures. For the first time, I got the feeling that most of these people were homeless and didn't have anywhere else to go.

I stuck a quarter in the soda machine and pushed the red button for a can of Coke. I heard the thing come to life and the metal can seemed to tumble around in its guts until it dumped into a small tray toward the bottom. The journey it took was a violent one. I thought twice about popping the top, as it might explode in my face after such an expedition. I decided to save it to have with the sandwich and the orange Jenny had given me.

I wandered around the lobby, hunting for something to read before being herded back on the bus. The sound of static coming from the pay-television sets was deafening. It was hard to imagine how the people in front of them could manage to stay asleep. The intercom came on numerous times, alerting passengers not to loiter, leave baggage unattended, or park personal vehicles in the bus aisles. Boarding calls repeated endlessly, one after another. The place was quickly getting to me. Intense white lights above flickered in despair or warning. I couldn't determine which. I gave up my search for a book and headed back toward the platform outside.

In front of my bus, a man was yelling at the Greyhound driver, but it wasn't Jim. I wasn't expecting this, but I probably should have. A shift change had occurred, and they had switched drivers. The new driver was younger, had black, oily hair and large, dark sunglasses. He looked like Frank Burns from the television show *M*A*S*H*, but real, in the flesh, and without the soft music and laughter. His face was snarling at a passenger below him on the platform. He stood on the steps, blocking the way with his arms crossed.

"You cannot get on this bus without a boarding ticket. I don't give a damn what your story is, pal!" he said, snarling at the man below him in utter disgust. I wondered what had happened to Jim as I watched this man in action. I searched my pockets for my ticket, hoping I hadn't left it in the seat compartment in the back. The man who was arguing with the driver had been on since I got on back in Stockton. Every time I saw him, he was either sleeping or reading his book. He was pale, in his early twenties, and had long red hair. He was wearing a green army jacket but didn't look like a soldier.

"All my stuff is on the bus, you asshole!" he yelled at the driver, who stood unmoved.

"How about your ticket? Is that on the bus, too?"

"I already told you, buddy. What the hell is your problem?"

"I don't like your attitude, Mister Man! You better settle down now before I eject you from this station!" He was pointing his index finger directly at the middle of the man's forehead, almost tapping at it. Frank Burns had a stern look on his face, but he seemed to be enjoying what he was doing. From behind his dark sunglasses it was hard to see how he really felt. I imagined he had a lazy eye or long girly lashes and was teased a lot for looking like a woman. Then I imagined that he had no eyes at all, just black sockets instead. The last thought creeped me out so bad, it made me shiver.

"If you let me get my book, man ... I can show you my ticket," the young man continued.

"Fine," Frank Burns from the netherworld snapped. He pointed his index finger at him again from the elevated steps. "But you can board last after everyone else gets on. Got it, buddy?"

"Jesus Christ, who the fuck are you? The Reverend Jim Jones?" The young man growled in frustration as he dejectedly turned away and headed for the back of the line.

"Keep it up, pal," Frank Burns shot back angrily, as he turned and got settled in his seat. Most of the passengers were a little shocked and hesitant now to get on.

"Let's go, folks. 1443 to the City of Angels." People started milling toward the door frantically, pulling out their boarding passes. A frenzy of bus riders searched their pockets in fear. I didn't have a good feeling about him at all. I was one of the last to board, and as I got to the top of the stairs, I held out my ticket. The driver just stared at me without noticing the stub.

"What the hell is this, kid?"

"It's my ticket, sir." The words stumbled out of my mouth.

"'It's my ticket, sir,'" he repeated mockingly. "You sound like Oliver Twist." He looked behind me, but only to check out the red-headed guy waiting at the bottom of the stairs with a cigarette hanging from his lips.

"Hey, no smoking on the bus, freak!" he shouted directly at me, but obviously meaning it for the man behind me. After a brief amount of grunting and fumbling in his seat, he focused his sunglasses at me.

"Are you traveling alone, Twist?"

"Yes, sir," I answered, hoping for my interaction with this man to end.

"Look, you're supposed to tell me immediately. Didn't they tell you that at the ticket counter?" He looked at my ticket stub quickly, but I doubted that he even read it. It seemed as if he was still watching the man behind me.

"Make sure you sit up front where I can keep my eye on you."

"All my stuff is in the back," I lied. "And it looks as if all the other seats are taken." He glanced in the long mirror, quickly surveying the seating situation.

"Fine, just go sit down. If I catch you vandalizing the bus, I'll throw you off," he grumbled. His name tag said *Frank*. Maybe it was a message.

A tall, wiry man with darkly tanned skin that looked like leather was watching me as I came up the aisle. He had sharp, beady eyes like a falcon's. His neatly pressed, dark olive green uniform looked like a businessman's suit. He grabbed my arm as I shuffled past.

"Son, if that shit-for-brains gives you anymore grief, I'll personally stick those sunglasses of his so far up his ass, he'll think I'm making room for the rest of his gay ensemble." His voice rolled like gravel across a cast-iron skillet. He smiled as he let go of my arm, all the time keeping part of his gaze on the driver.

"And if that son of a bitch tries to throw you off, I'll personally see to it that we leave his sorry ass on the side of the road to hitchhike home to his momma's basement." The old man smiled at me, unfazed by the evil Frank Burns, but he was the only one.

"Thanks," I responded. Everyone mumbled quietly among themselves, wondering what had become of Jim. Ironically, the new driver reminded me of the sort of man that my mother would've fallen in love with and brought home to try to be my new father.

I made my way toward the back of the bus, just hoping to get my seat. Several of the passengers talked quietly about the new driver.

They all had a different name for him, not one of which was Frank, Jim Jones being the most popular.

Once I took my seat, I popped the top on my soda and began to eat the lunch Jenny had given me. I decided to save the orange for later, just in case I got hungry in the next terminal during the layover. After the ruckus between the driver and the man in the green jacket subsided, the bus pulled out and away from the station, accompanied by the customary beep-beep-beep while in reverse.

"*1443 to Los Angeles.*" That was it, and nothing followed. I felt cheated for information. Jim's address was a soothing message, whereas this was nothing more than an extension of the reverse-beep signal. Everything with this guy was an instant travesty. Even though the air-conditioning was working perfectly, the air in the bus quickly began to smell like an ashtray. The driver, perched, elevated, and quiet behind his dark sunglasses, chain-smoked as he pushed the bus to breakneck speed down the highway, weaving in and out of traffic and smaller cars. He had already come over the intercom once to let everyone know that smoking on the bus was prohibited. The bus swayed dangerously several times. I hadn't stopped to question anyone about whether the driver was permitted to smoke, but it was clearly printed on the ticket that passengers were prohibited from smoking inside the bus and the restroom. Frank Burns wasn't playing by the rules at all, at least not the ones from all the pamphlets and overhead announcements. He was operating within some unseen loophole that was hard to distinguish. I doubted anyone wanted to challenge him.

Several people complained, some loudly. But he ignored them all and kept right on puffing. The old Marine looked back at me once as I watched another argument escalate between the driver and the hippie. It would've been nice if Frank Burns had turned on the radio through the overhead, but it just didn't seem like he was the type of person who was likely to do us any favors. His presence made me feel as if we were all somehow being punished for something. I immediately thought about my luggage under the bus. The thick, acrid air that was recirculating through the vents made me think of my mother. I'd been trapped in worse fogs in the backseat of the car, inhaling poisonous gas with the windows shut tight, on more occasions than I could ever forget. Every time I cracked the window for fresh air, I'd be scolded immediately with a barrage of absurd statements like: *"I'm not heating the outside. Close the damn window,"* or *"That sound is giving me a headache. Close the damn window,"* and the ever-popular *"Close the damn window, god-damnit!"* Sitting against the window in the fetal position, my eyes would burn, my throat would dry up, and my voice would become rough. I would count the seconds until I could just get out of the car and breathe again. The air on the bus was less severe, but the smell was the same.

A large woman in the front stood up and headed quickly toward the restroom. She was digging madly through her purse like an escaping prisoner looking for the key to the dungeon door. The thin lavatory door slammed hard and locked immediately behind her. Moments later, the intercom switched on.

"Please be advised that passengers are prohibited from smoking on the bus or in the lavatory. Any persons not cooperating with this policy will be ejected from the bus and have their tickets confiscated." I imagined the woman inside the bathroom being ejected through the roof like an aircraft fighter pilot while she was sitting on the toilet. I couldn't believe the driver had that much nerve. After the message, the clamor on the bus died down, and the steady humming of the tires on the freeway below was the only audible sound. The lock on the bathroom door tripped, and several people turned around in their seats to see the frustrated face of the obese woman emerge as she skulked back to her seat in tears.

"It's just not fair," she whimpered as she sat down.

"Oh, shut up!" Frank Burns gushed belligerently. Moments later, the hawk-faced man in the uniform who had grabbed my arm stood up, glanced back at me, and winked, then quickly walked up toward the front of the bus. The driver, without the aid of the intercom, craned his head around and yelled at the old man to sit back down in his seat. I shifted over toward the center of the aisle to get a better view. The level of intensity on the bus had risen and was at a breaking point. Something wasn't about to happen; something was happening.

"I said sit back down, old man!" The driver yelled angrily.

"I've had enough. You're being relieved!" the man answered, almost with a laugh in his voice. "Pull this goddamned bus over. You're taking your ass off this coach as of now!" The man in the olive green uniform spoke as if he was giving the driver an order. He stood erect, with his hands on his hips, towering over Frank Burns like a parent speaking to an unruly child.

"Last chance to move, dickhead. Otherwise, it'll be an early bedtime, and I promise you'll wake up with a headache." His voice boomed throughout the length of the bus. Every passenger was now fixated with rapt attention, watching the showdown in disbelief. The Greyhound driver moved in a spastic fashion, seemingly trying to pick up the mic for the radio.

"I didn't say pick that up, goddamn you!" The old Marine punched the driver hard several times across the face and reached for the wheel. The bus swerved in the lane as the Greyhound version of Frank Burns was shaken from the blows and became severely disoriented. Several people gasped, and a woman crossed herself and cried out to "sweet Jesus" a few seats in front of me. The man with the red hair laughed out loud. I was awestruck and froze. When I shook it off, I moved forward a few seats to get a better view. Everyone else seemed like department store mannequins. It was a singular moment of role reversal.

"I told you to pull this bus over now, and don't make me say it again!" he yelled. Something garbled came out of the driver's mouth like a vicious feminine yawlp.

"I said sit down, now!" The driver was screaming at the top of his lungs. It was completely off-putting and strange. The gravel-voiced man landed two more hard blows on the driver's head, which seemed to incapacitate him and make his entire body go limp. The man had one hand on the wheel, and with the other he was yanking Frank Burns from his oversize seat. The bus slowed dramatically, but the old Marine had control and forced the bus to the side of the road and onto the soft shoulder. Everything was happening faster than anyone on the bus could process. The driver was slumped over like a sack of potatoes and whimpering for him to let him go, as he started to come around. It looked as if the military man had him by the scruff of the neck like a dog. The evil Frank Burns's face was now beet red, and he was out of breath and exhausted.

"You ain't kicking anybody off this bus, but this is where you're going to find something new to do." He pulled the emergency brake as the bus crept along through the dust in the lane beside the freeway. Most of the passengers were standing up watching the whole affair now, but nobody was willing to help the Greyhound driver. This struck me hard as I thought about my own situation and how nice everyone had been. The fact that no one was interested in helping the driver made me realize that he had crossed some imaginary line with his behavior.

The old Marine pulled the driver into the aisle and began beating him furiously. People slowly sat down without saying a word. It must've been what everyone called an "ass-whipping," because the driver was getting one in spades. When the driver started crying loudly, the man picked him up, hurried him toward the back of the bus, and threw him in the small bathroom. Frank Burns's sunglasses were still hanging onto his face but were badly crushed and broken. The old soldier didn't even break a sweat.

"Don't you come out until I tell you to, sweetheart. You're lucky I don't leave you on the side of the road. Now, lock the goddamned door!" As soon as he said it, the *occupied* light came on without hesitation.

"Don't open it until I give you the command. Do you understand me?" he bellowed, shouting with his face millimeters from the flat surface of the door. Frank Burns was crying but didn't answer the question.

"Do you understand?" he repeated, gravelly and menacing all at once.

"Of course I do...." Frank Burns answered, sobbing uncontrollably.

When the old man turned and headed back down toward the driver's seat, something in the bus had changed. The uniformed man got behind the wheel and pulled slowly back out onto the freeway. He immediately came on over the intercom.

"Ladies and gentlemen, please excuse our interruption of service and the gross display of behavior. If you need to smoke, please do so, but try to keep it to a minimum out of respect for those that don't. I think we've all had enough cigarette smoke for a while anyway. As for the other driver ... he's indisposed in the bathroom and won't be joining the rest of the adults until he can learn some manners. We're still on time and should be at the Greyhound Terminal as scheduled. If you have any questions, my name's Master Sergeant Black. Thank you all for your patience, and enjoy the rest of your trip."

As soon as he clicked off, everybody started clapping. It was overwhelming. I had witnessed a fistfight between two men in a moving vehicle and a hostile takeover of public transportation. I felt like laughing out loud, but I could hear the driver in the lavatory crying and moaning like a small child. I could hear Frank Burns sobbing on the other side of the bathroom door, and it became uncomfortable sitting in the back next to him. I was just glad that for once it wasn't me.

Several people had begun conversations and were happily enjoying a cigarette. The old obese lady got up, walked over to the driver, and kissed him on the cheek. A few people laughed. Master Sergeant Black was a much better driver and handled the large coach with steadiness, unlike the faux Frank Burns in the sinister sunglasses. I moved to the very front seat, now empty as other riders shifted into different seats to talk with other passengers. Looking out the large front window, I felt the view of the world had become immense and much more impressive. I began to see why everyone suggested I sit up front with the driver. Almost an hour later, Master Sergeant Black came back on over the loudspeaker.

"Ladies and gentlemen, hopefully everyone's enjoying the drive. As we're approaching Pasadena, I need to take a head count to see who will be getting off either there or in Glendale. Please raise your hands."

I looked around and noticed that no one raised his hand or seemed interested in either of the two stops mentioned.

"It seems then as if we're going to be downtown about thirty minutes early," he concluded. *"Thank you again for your patience, and God bless America."* He clicked off.

The sequestered driver in the back yelled out, "You can't just skip stops!" but no one paid any attention to him or seemed to care. An elderly woman smiled at me as I looked back. She was humming what sounded like a church song and enjoying the ride. The red-haired man had returned to reading his book in the seat behind me, and some people had dozed off again to catch a few minutes of rest before getting into the station.

The tall buildings of Los Angeles appeared on the skyline as we slowly closed in on the city. The driver stuck in the bathroom started yelling obscenities as we got closer in to the station. Several people told him to be quiet, including the red-haired hippie. The bus seemed to cut through the heavy throngs of city traffic all by itself. It was the largest, most densely packed place I'd ever seen in my whole life. My heart raced as I tried to read all the names of the passing stores, businesses, and street signs. Master Sergeant Black knew exactly where we were going, but instead of pulling the bus around the back of the station and onto the platform, he just drove the bus up onto the curb and parked on the sidewalk in front of the station on Third Street. People quickly stepped out of the way of the oncoming motor coach as it inched forward up the sidewalk. I laughed out loud as I realized that most of the people didn't care too much or even pay any mind at all that someone was parking a Greyhound Bus on a busy sidewalk, midday, in downtown Los Angeles.

"Thanks, folks. It's been a pleasure," Master Sergeant Black announced, as he opened the door, disappeared down the steps, and folded into the crowd that was quickly gathering. Supervisors from inside the terminal were now sprinting toward the bus, but they all passed Master Sergeant Black, never noticing him at all. An older man climbed up the steps, confused and angry, looking as if he was having a heart attack. He began quickly scanning the bus for the driver. He looked confused as he stared at the vacant seat.

"Where the hell's the idiot responsible for this catastrophe?" he bellowed, mortified. Most of us just pointed back toward the restroom, where the driver was nervously standing in the doorway of the lavatory with a toilet paper wad sticking out of his right nostril.

"I demand a refund!" shouted one of the passengers. The supervisor's face changed immediately from anger to bewilderment. "I want my money back!" someone else belted. The next moment, everything became complete chaos.

3.

LOS ANGELES, CALIFORNIA

From where I sat on the bus, looking out through the window into the madness that awaited, I realized that Los Angeles was never a place *ever intended* for an eleven-year-old to be cut loose into on any day. It was the first time I felt afraid since I had left the night before. I couldn't remember the last time I wanted adult supervision, either. It was a first on many accounts.

After the police had taken everyone's names and found out the whole story behind the hijacking, the Greyhound personnel escorted us from the bus. We had all been told that a portion of our fare would be returned to us as compensation for the inconvenience. Several of the passengers immediately responded with laughter and angry shouts, and after several more exchanges, we were all told that our fares would be *fully refunded* to us at the ticket counter and we'd be given several free lunch vouchers redeemable inside the café. To me, it seemed like a godsend. Not only was I about to receive an extra forty-four dollars but I was also going to be fed for the entirety of the journey. Many of the riders were outraged by this. A few people made puking sounds, but nothing further changed, and we were all herded off the bus and into the terminal.

When I came down the steps, several porters busied themselves with unloading our luggage onto large metal carts. Seeing my bags once again brought me a strange sense of joy. The porter heaved the bags onto the cart and immediately noticed how heavy they were. Police officers in dark blue, well-pressed uniforms stood on the sidewalk surrounding the bus. Every one of them was well armed but appeared completely bored. They all huddled near the front of the bus smoking cigarettes and fell into conversation. They could have been planning a shoot-out, but I imagined they were just talking about their bowling scores and women.

I couldn't believe the throngs of people jammed on the sidewalk and bursting through the doors of the bus terminal. An old man, overdressed in a thick, ratty winter coat, slouched over, pushing a grocery cart full of plastic bags, slowly weaved in and out of the crowd, blending in with the Greyhound employees. I was surrounded by clear skies and tall buildings above me. The air smelled of fumes and food, wafting around me on all sides. The sun somehow emanated from below me. There was so much sunlight that every surface was caught in a permanent glare. I had to squint just to see where I was going. The large white bleached stone of the city expanded around me like hot blank paper. The bitter faces of the cops and people must've been the words, but I didn't want to wait around to see the punctuation.

Going through the doors of the terminal, I followed behind the man with the long red hair. I was momentarily stunned by the roar of the immense station, the stale air-conditioning, the back-to-back platform calls from the overhead speaker, and music that all went on uninterrupted.

Every lobby seat was occupied by what I could now easily identify as homeless people or permanent Greyhound travelers. The difference between the two seemed a fine line; unfortunately, the security guards had to deal with both. Walking past the rows of small televisions, I noticed every one was running and paid for, each one tuned to a different station. I became dizzy with the crashing sounds of what was apparently commonplace to everyone else. I followed close behind the other passengers as we walked to the ticket counter, escorted by the manager. Another man, older and distinguished with a trimmed mustache and wearing a hat, stood by authorizing the refunds and passing out café tickets. I began to worry that I wouldn't be in the right place to meet my Aunt Sharon. I started to look around nervously for her stern but manly gaze.

I could barely remember what she looked like as I waited, and after everything so far, I didn't want to hear a lecture, get in trouble, or be beaten senseless in a toilet stall for being an inconvenience. When I finally reached the front of the line, both the old man and the girl behind the ticket counter looked at me strangely.

"Were you on 1443, young man?" His name badge said A. *Hastings*.

"Yes, sir."

"Where did you get on?" he questioned me, shifting around in his spot, leaning against the counter.

"Stockton," I replied. I dug out my ticket stub and handed it over. He examined it carefully.

"Alone? You're traveling alone?" His words seem to stumble out of him one at a time.

"I am, sir. I'm supposed to meet my aunt on the platform."

"Is that right?" he asked, studying me behind his furrowed brow. "How far are you traveling?"

"Past Pittsburgh," I replied. Mr. Hastings's eyes became as large as bicentennial dollar coins. The girl's mouth also became slack and dropped open.

"Pittsburgh ..." he parroted, scarcely believing it. He examined the stack of café tickets in his hand and stared into the air as if he were calculating time and space all at once.

"Issue the boy forty-four dollars, Marie," he commanded, speaking to the girl firmly and counting out six café tickets. "Here, take these," he said. "What's your name?"

"Sebastien, Sebastien Ranes."

He smiled as he handed me the money and returned my bus ticket. He watched me stash everything away and then placed a hand on my shoulder and led me across the lobby. "Well, Sebastien, Sebastien Ranes, your bus leaves from platform eight at two-fifteen." He examined his watch and led me through the crowd. "Have you ridden the bus before?"

"Yes, I have, Mr. Hastings. Last year I rode from Altoona to Sacramento with my mother."

"Altoona, eh?" he asked.

"Yes, that's where I'm headed."

"I've been through Altoona. Very green," he said with a slight tone. "Almost like the place that time forgot. Your grandparents live there?"

"Yes, how did you know?"

"If I told you that it makes perfect sense, does that clear it up?"

"Not really," I answered. He laughed as we walked out onto the platform where our old bus was now parked.

"Seeing that your bus got here early, there shouldn't be any problem with your relatives. Do you see them?" he asked me, looking around. I scanned the almost empty platform without seeing any trace of my Aunt Sharon of Uncle Gerald.

"No, not yet, Mr. Hastings."

"Strange. Well, they should be here for you soon. I guess waiting is probably the best bet. Do you have all you need, son?"

"I do, Mr. Hastings, thank you."

"If you need anything else, just come to the ticket counter and ask for me by name, okay?"

"Thank you for the café tickets."

"No, no, don't worry about that. Your bus leaves over there, understood?" He was pointing several rows down at an empty spot under the awning. I nodded that I got it. He headed down the platform toward the sliding glass doors leading into the lobby. I sunk into myself and prepared to wait it out for my aunt and uncle.

"Mr. Ranes!" he called. I turned and acknowledged Mr. Hastings, who was standing in the doorway.

"Yes, sir?"

"Have a nice trip, son," he shouted. I waved as he slipped away inside. I took a seat below the painted sign that read *San Diego*. A large group of Marines were standing around in two small clusters, smoking cigarettes, telling jokes, and laughing. The older ones in the group had similar-looking uniforms to Master Sergeant Black. The younger ones were spitting into soda cans and waiting to get on the bus that I had just left behind. There was no sign at all of my

Aunt Sharon. I wondered if she knew where the Greyhound station was, or if she was confused about the arrival time.

Sitting on the bench, I calculated my money and figured that I had over seventy dollars in cash now and enough café tickets to see me well past Altoona. As the minutes passed, I watched the driver of the old bus reappear wearing a new pair of sunglasses. He saw me but apparently wasn't about to make eye contact. He shifted sheepishly across the platform and stood out by the open door smoking a cigarette as if nothing had ever taken place. His face looked a bit swollen but hadn't yet bruised. Maybe he was just hoping to make up the money for the shift. I watched him climb the stairs, start the engine, and usher all the passengers aboard. It was a steady but even and predictable process.

"Final boarding call, 1442 to San Diego. Platform 2. Final boarding call." I was directly under the speaker, and my head rang with the echo of each word. The giant door of the bus swung shut with loud "shooshing" hydraulics. My eyes fixed on the backward American flag painted just off to the side of the closed door. I had remembered reading that an upside-down flag meant *treason* and was a signal to others during the Civil War of trouble. I wondered what type of signal a backward flag could mean? It seemed like a bad omen, but I was now putting some good distance between myself and my mother, and it couldn't have all spelled doom.

Perhaps everything was now going in reverse, or that I had somehow entered a mirror universe of the world that I was originally supposed to be in but wasn't. In the other world, I speculated that if I were still on the bus, I was probably traveling with my mother and father. If it was to set everything right, I might as well set it all right. I was going back to live with them and my grandma in Altoona because everything was better and I didn't feel the way I had anymore. I didn't want things to end as badly as I longed for them to. I was confused about this line of thinking and decided to give it up. It was making me feel even more unhappy than I already was. What was the use of feeling this way? I had already been thrown to the wolves, and nobody cared in the slightest, except some perfect strangers. But maybe that was what made them perfect. I just couldn't tell anymore. I felt useless, my situation felt useless, and I wondered where my aunt was.

For almost two hours, I sat perfectly still, poised on that bench as if I were put there like a forgotten doll to be a dull witness watching buses, people, and homeless folks come and go. People boarded and got off, and their expressions were all the same. I knew I should've felt differently about it, but I didn't. Nobody seemed happy, and I was aware of it. The only people at the bus terminal who were smiling were the people who were living there, its permanent residents. The homeless parked in front of static-screen TVs, either half asleep or apparently drunk and laughing at everybody with a type of madness that no one wanted to get near. Most of the folks tried to ignore it and were just busy getting from one bus to the next or hurrying to get out to the front of the terminal.

I could've sat there all day, and no one would've noticed me. Every seat outside on the platform was taken; all the benches were filled except mine. I felt isolated, and it seemed like no one wanted anything to do with me. Something in the world wasn't right, but I didn't need to be sitting on a Greyhound bus all day to know that.

"Everything okay?" A voice called out above me like it was coming from the speaker. I turned and saw Mr. Hastings standing beside me.

I sat up. "Uhh, maybe they forgot," I said. He had two cups of hot liquid in his hands.

"You drink coffee, young man?" he asked, taking the open seat next to me on the bench. He handed me a red paper cup that was almost full of hot coffee. "Here. I came out earlier and saw you nodding off. Thought this might do you some good."

"I thought for sure they would've been here by now."

"Hmmph," he grunted, fully resigned.

I looked over at him. The whole thing finally came together for me. "They're not coming, are they?"

"They never do."

"I'm not the first eleven-year-old traveling alone, am I?"

"For someone so young, you sure do catch on pretty fast."

"I don't have any other choice, do I? I mean, I'm here and they're ... wherever they are." I petered out and sipped my coffee.

"Your mother included," he said softly, lighting a cigar. Mr. Hastings was laughing. "I just want to let you know that I called the information operator up in Stockton. I found a listing for a Charlotte Ranes."

"My mother."

"Mmm-huh. Anyway, I called the number." He looked over at me darkly.

"You probably thought I ran away or something."

He laughed again. "Or something ..." he admitted. "Nobody picked up." He showed me a piece of paper with my house number on it.

"You get a lot of this, don't you?"

"Well, Sebastien ... I've been the station manager for about eighteen years, and I've seen a lot of kids come through here. But not many come through here having been sent alone by their own parents. People are shocked to see you here, that's for sure. It's obvious that you're not a runaway. You don't *look* like a runaway." He glanced around, watching several people stepping down off an arrived bus. "You get a lot of this, don't you?" He repeated what I had said, putting it back at me.

"I never thought much about it. But I know my mother's not normal, Mr. Hastings."

"No, I wouldn't think she is."

"She's probably in San Francisco. She went with another new man to go get married again," I continued. He looked me over, shaking his head.

"Not the first time, eh?" he rejoined with laughter.

"No," I answered, sipping my coffee. Sitting there talking to him, I started to feel better. It was much better than being alone and being stuck in my head wondering about my aunt, who still hadn't surfaced.

"Well, look ... you hungry?"

"A little," I answered.

"Why don't we get something to snack on from the café. If they come looking for you, I'm sure they'll page us. Okay?"

I got up and left the platform with Mr. Hastings and headed for the Grey Café once more. He told me all about how he'd been driving Greyhound buses since just after the end of the 1950s. I figured that was a long time to be anything.

Inside the terminal, the loudspeaker was still going full tilt.

"Departure to San Francisco through Simi Valley, Ventura, Santa Barbara, and San Simeon. Aisle 4."

"1202 arriving on Aisle 1 from Palm Springs." I found it hard to hear everything Mr. Hastings was saying, so I leaned in close as we sat at the counter, trying to catch his words. He probably just thought I was interested.

"Maybe I should try to make a call from the pay phone," I interrupted.

"Go ahead, that's probably a good idea. I'll be here."

I wandered across the lobby, speeding up and slowing down, trying to get to the pay phone and around the thronging masses. I reached up, grabbed the receiver, pressed zero for the operator, and requested a collect call. It rang twenty times before the operator came back on and apologized. I imagined the phone in the front room sitting on the small table ringing off the hook. Listening to the sound of it began to bother me, and I felt incredibly let down. I could've been killed or wounded in a bus crash, and my mother wouldn't have known or thought to care. I made note for the second time that the only people who gave a damn about me were complete strangers—just like the mannequins. Only the people looking in the shop windows ever cared, even if it was only momentary. Maybe that's all real love was—just something that happened quickly and vanished, a kind gesture to a stranger or a fleeting moment of passion. One false move or embarrassing slipup, and I'd be pulled from the display and either put back up into the storeroom or thrown into the industrial-sized trash compactor out back. At least my department store counterparts seemed to have a destiny. I had no clue about mine.

When it was time to board the bus, Mr. Hastings made sure I was the first person on. I saw the porters wheeling my bags around from behind the counter where they were stored. I thanked Mr. Hastings for taking care of me and told him that I wouldn't forget him.

"Send me a postcard once you get to Altoona. Would you do that?" he asked. I nodded and shook his hand. He was very generous and kind.

"Have a safe ride, Sebastien Ranes. I'll call ahead and check in on you as you go through the major terminals." He handed me a few more café vouchers and his business card. "If you need to get in touch with me for any reason, call me collect. If you miss your bus, call me immediately. Okay?"

I nodded again.

"If anybody asks about all those vouchers, just show them my business card. But always make sure to get it back."

I boarded and looked back as he stood on the platform with the cigar in his mouth and his hands in his pockets. Once the bus was full, the driver climbed on and closed the door. The only open seats on the bus were the two next to me at the very back. I had opted, once more, to sit in the rear seats, and thankfully, I was alone. I either had the plague or everyone really hated sitting next to the toilet. I now knew that it was probably the latter. After Mr. Hastings went back inside, the driver came on over the intercom and did his business.

"Welcome aboard the 1364 to Columbus. My name's Bill. We'll be traveling through to Phoenix just before midnight and Gallup, New Mexico, tomorrow morning. All those continuing on toward Pittsburgh and New York, you'll transfer in Columbus. Please remember that there's no smoking inside the bus, no alcoholic beverages, and no swearing. Please alert me of any emergency immediately. Thank you for choosing Greyhound, and enjoy the ride."

It was then I realized that every driver's overhead announcement was different and probably originated from a well-practiced script that over time had slowly become their own. I decided, though, that there were several things they were obligated to say like "welcome," "no smoking," and "enjoy the trip." Just as Bill was closing the door, I saw a black man in a leather jacket running for the bus, carrying a small backpack slung across his shoulder.

"Wait for me!" the man yelled. Bill stopped the bus and reopened the door to let him in.

"Almost left ya behind, buddy!"

"Thank you," the man acknowledged, producing his boarding ticket. I saw him coming up the aisle looking for a seat, knowing that the only seats left open were next to me in the back row. He had a wide smile and just seemed relieved to have made it. I was watching him approach, and when he saw the open seats, he saw me. So far, I'd been lucky to have the backseat to myself. Now the thought of company didn't seem so bad. I was more relieved to be pulling out of Los Angeles than anything else. I was still reeling about my Aunt Sharon not showing up. Those feelings were floating off in the background, surely to confront me soon enough. I was tired, it was the middle of the day, and I figured that at some point I'd fall back asleep.

The man settled himself in his seat quickly, stashing his bag at his feet and breathing another sigh of relief. "How far you going?" the voice beside me asked. I hesitated, unsure how to answer.

"Ohh ... me?" I finally responded. He was now looking me over with a very curious expression. He looked on the verge of laughter.

"Yes, you!" he replied. "How far ya headed?"

"Pennsylvania," I mumbled feebly. I watched his face for the obvious response that I had received from everyone else, but he just watched me. Nothing in his expression gave away that telltale sign of shock. He lifted up in his seat and peered down the rows over the heads of the passengers. Pointing with his fingers, as if he was trying to select somebody from the crowd, he landed on an older couple who were oblivious to the world around them.

"Your parents? They keeping an eye on you?" I didn't know what to say, so I just stayed quiet. I shook my head no. Looking around, he was chewing gum slowly, but stopped when it suddenly hit him. He was overtaken in the next moment with nervous laughter. "Wait ... no?" Now he shook his head in disbelief. "You've got to be kidding me." Hearing the words coming out of his mouth made me feel for the first time that I wasn't alone in the way I felt.

"No, I guess not."

He stuck out his hand. "Marcus Franklin," he announced. I smiled, grabbed his hand, and shook it.

"Uh, I'm ... Sebastien ... Sebastien Ranes." I felt as if I had whispered my name, as if I was wholeheartedly ashamed. He smiled a second time and went back to chewing his gum. He dug in his pocket and produced a green pack of gum and pushed it toward me.

"Stick of gum?" he offered.

"Thanks, Marcus."

"No problem, Sebastien. Pittsburgh, huh?"

"Well, just past there actually. Altoona. I'm going to go live with my grandparents."

"Is that right? And your folks just put you on the bus, all by your lonesome, said 'Happy trails ... don't forget to write,' and away you went?"

I felt both nervous and stupid for being put in this position by my mother. All I could do was just look away. "I guess. Something like that. Just my mom and her boyfriend. I got on back in Stockton."

"How old are you?" His voice now had the same sound of concern the rest of them had. He was slipping into the emotional hole that had surrounded Jenny the waitress, Mr. Hastings, and the ticket lady.

"I'm eleven ... or rather twelve tomorrow. It's my birthday."

"Sebastien, forgive me," he said, taking a deep breath and leaning forward. "Traveling the country, eleven years old for one more day, and cruising solo?" There was a certain comic appeal about him that made me chortle.

"Yeah, I guess I never thought about it like that," I responded. The loudspeaker came on, and the driver's message interrupted our conversation.

"Stuck on a bus on your birthday? Damn, that's cold, man."

"1364 to Phoenix, Amarillo, and Columbus. No smoking on board, and enjoy the ride."

Another truncated greeting from the great Greyhound speaker

in the sky. I took out my notebook from my shirt pocket, clicked my pen a few times, and made note of what was said. "Short and sweet," I mumbled to myself.

"And we can count ourselves lucky for that, partner. I once heard a driver talk in that mic as if it was his own late-night radio show. The guy talked for five hours straight before people started yelling at him to stop." Marcus made a face of someone getting upset and yelling over the seats.

"You've traveled by Greyhound before?" I asked.

"Sure, many times actually. Not always by choice either, but I've spent a lot of time on buses. You look like a seasoned pro on the bus." He leaned in and gave me that look as if I was in on a secret with just him.

"Whaddya mean?"

"It's pretty easy to spot a pro. Someone who travels light—you ain't surrounded by a bunch of plastic bags or anything like that. Some people bring their whole damn house on the bus. Also, you chose to sit in the back, which is the most choice spot. You can stretch all the way out if need be, and you have direct access to the trash and toilet too."

I laughed again, looking out the window, watching the bus slowly make its way through a labyrinth of buildings, skyscrapers, gas stations, elevated parking garages, and kamikaze people making mad dashes on the street, trying to get to where they were going without a thought to traffic.

"Yeah, I saved all my lunch money for a year and skipped school just to be here," I joked back. Marcus gave me a strange look.

"I'm just kidding, Marcus. I don't even get lunch money."

He laughed heartily and made note of my mood.

"You doing any better now?"

"Yeah ... I guess. Thanks."

"You guess about a lot of things, huh? Well, don't worry too much about it." He grew quiet and watched the path of the bus out the window for a few blocks, as if he was seeing Los Angeles for either the first or last time.

"Are you from Los Angeles?" I asked, wondering if this was his home by the expression that had overtaken him. He pulled a paperback book from his jacket pocket and clapped it a few times against the palm of his hand, trying to decide how to answer. I looked at the title, trying to see what he was reading. Something called *The Panther and The Lash*. I'd never heard of it. He caught me looking at the cover of the book trying to read the title.

"Well, I guess there's no harm. Yes, I'm from L.A." He was leaning in close now. "A place most people call the ghetto." His voice had dropped to almost a whisper.

"Really?" I replied, wide-eyed. "I once lived in a place with my mom and one of her boyfriends called The Grotto."

"Say what?" Marcus responded, a little shocked and quite possibly annoyed.

"It was the name of our trailer park on Watt Avenue. 'The Grott' ..." Before I could finish, Marcus had burst out laughing. This time it was loud, and a few people even turned in their seats to look back at us.

"Ahhh! The Grotto!"

"Di-di-did I say something wrong?" I stuttered.

He was beside himself with laughter. A tear formed in his eye and rolled down his cheek, and he was now doubled over, gasping for breath.

"Wow ... I've really heard it all now. I thought I'd seen and done it all too," he answered, calming himself. His long arm reached out and grasped me by the shoulder, patting me thoughtfully.

"Nice to meet you, Sebastien Ranes from 'The Grotto.'"

"Nice to meet you too, Mr. Franklin from The Ghetto," I answered, a bit dumbstruck in my naïveté.

"Just call me Marcus," he responded, wiping the tear from his eye.

The bus drove slowly through the thick traffic, taking up its own space on the freeway, which made all the other passing cars steer clear. Los Angeles sprawled onward, as if it was the city with no end. Endless communities of houses with red tile roofs collected at the sides of the interstate like a fungus. They were all connected together with miles of thickly layered electrical wires, light poles, and off-ramps that all had Spanish sounding names: Arcadia, Duarte, Pomona, Rancho Cucamonga, Fontana, Temecula. Outside my window, mountains rose up in the distance, which were ever moving in and out of the obscurity of thick, acrid smog that covered the sky like a blanket.

I looked over at Marcus a few times while he was reading, wishing again that I had brought along a book. I couldn't read the brochures jammed in the seat pocket again, although I felt tempted to pull them out every few hours to look them over to make sure all the information was still the same.

"What are you reading?" I asked, feeling bad for finally cutting in on him.

"Poetry," he answered. It wasn't the answer I had expected. He looked at me from the top edge of his book. "Ever read any poetry?"

"Once in a while, in school," I replied. I had a vague recollection of having to read something aloud from a bulky textbook in front of the class, only to have embarrassed myself when I opened my mouth and spoke.

"*Only* once in school," he repeated. "Well, that's a damn shame. What do they teach kids in school anymore?" Marcus asked, being forward. I shrugged.

"You've never read anything by Langston Hughes, have you?" he asked.

"I've never even heard of Langston Hughes."

"Good God ... you've never even heard of Langston Hughes!"

"I've read *The Hobbit*," I remarked, trying to redeem myself somehow.

"You've read *The Hobbit*, huh? What else?"

"Uh ... um ..." I had to think about it. "I've read a lot of Sherlock Holmes. I finished reading all the stories last December."

"You mean you've read Arthur Conan Doyle?"

"Oh, yeah ... right," I replied, embarrassed. "What's that book about?" I asked, trying to get the focus off of me. Marcus stared hard at me but glanced once more at the cover and then took a long look at the world outside the window.

"Well, here, I'll read you some. How's that?"

"Okay. Sure," I rejoined.

"Take a deep breath first," he stated.

I blinked twice and tilted my head. "Why?"

"Don't ask. Just trust me and think about what I'm reading. Now take a deep breath." I did as he said and took the same kind of breath that I would take at the doctor's office every time they put one of those cold stethoscopes to my bare back.

"Do you know what the word *deferred* means, Sebastien?"

"No," I answered bluntly.

"*Deferred* means to postpone, or put on hold, like layaway, or waiting for Christmas in May. Got it?"

"Okay. Deferred is like layaway."

"Now listen to me.

What happens to a dream deferred?

Does it dry up
like a raisin in the sun?"

He hammered out the words with immediacy and I could almost see them with my own two eyes. Each one was sharp and flew at me like an object, sending my thoughts reeling. His voice changed just slightly as he read, like he was becoming someone else for a few moments.

When he was done, Marcus settled back into his seat, which he'd been leaning out of to speak to me, and watched me for a response. I could see it all: the raisin dry and crinkly on the hot, white sidewalk, and then a steak in the dirt. I had never heard anybody read poetry like that before, not even my teacher, who had forced us to read aloud from the oversize textbook.

"I never heard anything like that before," I stated.

"I know," Marcus responded. "What are you going to do about it?" he added.

"I'm sorry?" I asked.

"I said, What are you going to do about it?"

"Uh ... what can I do about it?" I answered. I felt confused and confronted all at once. I didn't know what he was talking about.

"The point of poetry is to make you feel something. When you do feel something, you should write it down on a piece of paper. I know you got a notepad."

I pulled out my notebook again and clicked my pen a few times. When Marcus saw me deep in thought, he disappeared back into his book. I made some notes, stared out the window, and then wrote some more. I thought about the two words that stuck out the most: *Dream Deferred*.

We passed smaller cities that were still a part of Los Angeles but paid them no mind. Suburbia ended once we crossed over the Riverside County Line. It was as if everyone living outside of Los Angeles County suddenly just became unimportant. All the development halted like it had hit a brick wall. The farmland that I had left behind in Stockton once again reared its head as if reminding us that none of us would outlast it.

Two and a half hours later, the driver announced that we were going to momentarily stop in a small town called Palm Springs, and then Indio. Marcus leaned over and asked me if I was going to get off to stretch my legs for the five minutes we were going to stop.

"Nah, think I'll just stay put this time."

"Cool. Hold our seats then. I'll get you something from the vending machines. You got any favorites?"

"Pretzels," I answered, without thinking about it.

"Pretzels it is then."

When we pulled off the interstate and headed down into Palm Springs, the sun had begun to finally set and was fire red. Tall mountains loomed up on the opposite side of the bus. A steep, jagged incline rose from the desert floor and disappeared into the thin stratus clouds above. I could see that the peak of the tallest mountain was still snowcapped. I watched lights going up a lonely road through the desert, toward something just above the base. Palm

Springs was as rural and absent of real life as Stockton was when I had left in the middle of the night, except here it was just going on seven-thirty. The drive from the freeway took quite a while before we got to civilization. The closer we got to the mountains, the more flat earth we traversed, until a few stoplights emerged out of the quickly darkening desert.

When we pulled into the station, I was surprised at the number of people waiting around. Most of the people on the platforms looked absolutely miserable. An old woman with a walker that was being held together with duct tape pushed herself slowly toward the bus going back into Los Angeles. A large crowd of men was clustered together on the platform, and all of them were smoking. Near the terminal, several Mexican men were sitting against the wall with their knees to their chests and their faces hidden beneath sweat-stained straw cowboy hats. I watched Marcus meander carefully up the platform, assessing all of them. It was as if he was weighing everybody for some kind of future judgment. A few of the men noticed him and made a gesture to him in acknowledgment. When Marcus got to the small row of public pay phones, he dropped in some change and made a call. I watched him as he stood there patiently letting it ring. He never moved his lips or said a word. When he hung up a few seconds later, he seemed a little distressed, looked up at the bus, and then headed inside the terminal.

Outside, just below my window, I watched the porter pull a man's bags out from under the storage compartment. Someone was getting off. Palm Springs must've been his home. When the man took his bag from the porter, I watched him slip away on foot, alone, across a dirt lot into God knows where. No one came to pick him up or give him a ride. Did God even keep tabs on all the people traveling by bus? Was there a patron saint of Greyhound riders that protected us?

The thought quickly crossed my mind to get off and try to call my Aunt Sharon to tell them that they had missed me. But I was being foolish, as I realized that they knew this and probably weren't concerned about me in the slightest. I also didn't have their phone number as my genius mother didn't see fit to supply me with it.

Maybe she knew and just didn't want to tell me, trying to give me some false hope and something to think about during the layover. I could've called her as well, but she was probably somewhere racing around San Francisco with Dick, wearing another new dress and fresh pumps. She was most likely furious with me, but I knew it would be pointless. The only phone number I knew by heart was my grandma's. It had never changed in all the years that I'd been alive, and for that I was thankful.

I looked up and saw Marcus coming up the aisle, holding several small bags of potato chips and a few bags of pretzels.

"Two bags of pretzels."

"Wow. Thanks, Marcus. What do I owe you?" I asked. He seemed surprised.

"Don't worry 'bout that. I've got you covered. Remember ... you're from The Grotto!"

"I'm from The Grotto, it's true," I laughed. I popped open one of the bags of pretzels and began chewing them down with fervor. I made short work of my snack, absentmindedly, as I couldn't help but stay fixated on the endless one-story buildings that made up the bulk of Palm Springs. The layover ended abruptly, with the sound of the large metallic monster moaning back to life. The engine compartment behind my head started making loud, squeaky noises, like a fan belt was getting ready to break loose or disintegrate at any given moment. Marcus paid the continuous noise no mind and sat back in the seat, next to the lavatory, from which he could look all the way down the aisle. I watched him rest himself easily against the wood laminate wall and close his eyes, as if he were casually leaning against a tree in an open field at midday. I was a little stunned at his ability to block out the offending noise, but the engine gradually quieted after a few blocks. The bus made its way along a wide and smoothly graded roadway that was lined with tall, thin palm trees that reached upward, awkwardly trying to escape the hot ground like it was too painful to touch. We moved along, traveling ever farther from the interstate.

Looking at the world through the safety of a four-foot window, I quickly lost count of the fast-food restaurants, 7-Elevens, liquor

stores, pawnshops, steakhouses, and all-night diners. My focus
shifted a few times from the world outside to the partial reflection
of my face on the glass. I kept looking myself over like an object on
display, as if I didn't recognize who I was. I stared unwavering, trying to study my face. My brown eyes failed to blink. My lips were
taut and sealed, absent of either a smile or a frown. My dark blond
hair looked heavy and matted against my head. Strangely perfect. I
couldn't read the emotion, but I knew from my own thoughts that
it was nothing drastic, nothing dangerous—or at least not yet. I told
myself that I wasn't Charlotte's son anymore. I knew from what I
heard over whispers that I was *that kid traveling across the country
alone.* I was the one who had been told numerous times to sit up
front next to the driver, but here I was in the very back row against
the window, freaking myself out with my own reflection.

I looked over, carefully at first, to see if Marcus was still doz-
ing. I could hear faint music coming from his headphones, but I
didn't recognize it. I glanced down at his hand, which was gripping the square metal box that had the word *Walkman* embossed
on the front. There was a small window that displayed two small
wheels, slowly turning in time, advancing the cassette tape. I
couldn't make out most of the writing. The only thing that was
clear was *Side A.*

"Miles Davis," he muttered low. I sat back and molded myself
once more into the corner. He smiled and closed his eyes.

"It's alright, I wasn't really sleeping," he said. I didn't respond.
I didn't want to disturb him, as he seemed at peace. I went back to
staring out the window. Low in the sky, just above the horizon, the
first bright star of the evening blinked. Mountains that looked like
crumbling chocolate melted into the reddening sky that was fading
into a darker shade of early twilight. We moved along the floor of
the desert at top speed, now past most of the urban development and
surrounded by fields of palm groves. Several billboards advertised
date plantations, date shakes, and even a *Date Palm Fairgrounds.*

The small towns along Highway 111 came and went quickly,
each marked by an oblong green sign with the name of each place
in reflective white lettering. *Cathedral City, Rancho Mirage, Palm*

Desert, Indian Wells, La Quinta, and finally, *Indio.* I slipped the note-pad from my shirt pocket, clicked the pen top a few times to warm up my brain, and took a few more notes about Palm Springs. Stuck for words, I drummed the pen against the window and chewed on the pen top. Marcus looked over at me, noticing that I was obviously bored out of my skull.

"You taking notes?"

"Yeah, I guess. It's interesting to read later. If I didn't write anything down, I'd probably just forget it, you know?"

"I do," he rejoined. "I've always done a lot of writing. It's a good habit." His eyes were cast outside the glass with mine, watching the world disintegrating slowly from the safety of our metal shell.

"It builds character," he added.

"What do you mean?"

"Do you read much?"

"Yeah, that's about all I do anymore. I spend a lot of time alone in my room."

He chuckled a little. "I guess you could say the two of us have a lot in common. I spent a lot of time alone in my room as well, doing absolutely nothing but getting lost in a book, for quite a long time, too."

I laughed.

"What's so funny?" he responded.

I shook my head and turned away. "I don't know."

"What? C'mon now, don't leave me like this ..." His expression was exuberant and pleading.

"I don't know. People just don't usually talk to me or ask me questions. Most people aren't really this nice either. I guess I was just expecting everything to be different."

"What did you expect to be different?"

"Being out here alone, by myself. I was really scared for the last few days about leaving my mom, but it's not what I thought."

"Well, Sebastien ..." he leaned in toward me, "... here's your first lesson. Don't wrap yourself up in all the bad stuff, and definitely don't expect everything to always go against you. Sometimes ..." he sat back, considering his words, "... you just don't know. Things usually have a way of working out for the best."

Listening to Marcus talk made me feel better. The world seemed to move a little closer to being in its proper place, and I felt at ease—less like a department store figurine and more like someone with a friend. I was starting to feel like more than just an unwanted accessory of my mother's. The thought occurred to me that he was probably going to be getting off and I'd be alone again.

"How far are you going?" I asked, now concerned.

"New York City. Just a few more days and I'll be there. Hard to imagine."

"Are you going back to see your family?"

Marcus looked me over again very carefully. He seemed to think about every question that I put to him, instead of how I just blurted out whatever came to mind.

"I'm going home to see my father," he answered quietly.

"Does he know you're coming?"

He smiled again. "I suppose he does, probably."

We both watched the bus turn off the highway and down a side street. After a few blocks, we pulled into one more terminal. The overhead speaker clicked on just after the air brakes sneezed as we parked.

"Indio. We'll be here for fifteen minutes only."

I yawned and stretched my arms in front of me. "You getting off, Marcus?" I asked.

"Nah, little man. I'm staying put. You want to get out and stretch?"

"Yeah, why not? You want a soda?"

"Dial it in. I'll watch your seat."

Marcus's words repeated over and over again in my head. I had never heard that expression before, "dial it in." I knew it must've been a good thing. I stepped over to the Coke machine on the platform, which was trapped behind a black steel cage, and paid for two cans of Coca-Cola. They came down, ice-cold, one at a time. A short distance away, I saw an empty pay phone connected to a brown pole. The thought of calling the house nagged at me. If my mother picked up, or was even home, I'd be yelled at. I knew the way I was feeling was more from habit and not from any real concern. I didn't want to call, and I knew it. It would just end up being a waste of change.

I looked away, distracted by several people moving across the platform who were leaving the bus behind with an exhausted look of frustrated thankfulness. It was confusing, but I understood it. I just wanted to get to Pennsylvania as soon as possible.

I left the blinking light of the empty phone kiosk untouched and climbed back up the stairs with my cold sodas.

"Alrighty, there he is..." the driver greeted me, as I made my way up the dangerous-looking metal steps.

"Another day, another soda." It was the only witty remark I could think to say. He laughed out loud as I disappeared inside and made my way back to my seat. Outside, Indio seemed to make absolutely no impression on the world at all. It looked like a ghost town or a studio set from an old Western movie that someone now thought to occupy. The Greyhound Terminal was surrounded by flat earth, wooden structures, and palm trees. A breeze pushed the treetops around high above us, as if they were screaming, waving for help, and hoping someone would notice them. If you didn't look up, you could've missed them completely. Maybe down here on earth I felt the same way.

Night started to close around us completely. The freeway was an endless stream of white headlights coming from well past the far horizon. The bus was the most comfortable for a few hours just after each layover, when they had filled the gas, emptied the toilet, and given the engine a rest. The air-conditioner was steady and cool and lacked the sooty gas-chamber odor that it normally forced from its tiny vents.

"You said your mother's getting married?" Marcus asked. He was drinking his soda as if it were the greatest drink on earth. He was fixated on the shape of the can or what was printed on it.

"Yeah, San Francisco."

"Any reason why you weren't invited? Seems odd you not being there, don't you think?"

"Yeah, but I've been to a few of her weddings already. They

never last," I answered. "She's only interested in the idea of being married."

Marcus chuckled. "What does your moms do for work? She got a job?"

"My moms? I've only got one?" I answered, confused.

"Moms ... it's your moms, the lady that you love. The only one. Got it?"

I stared back at him with a blank expression. It took a second for it to settle in. "Oh ... yeah. I got it."

"You got to learn to blend in, little man. It's important. No one ever told you 'bout all that, did they?"

I shook my head no. He just grunted "hmmph."

"So what does she do?" he asked, getting back to the main subject.

"She's a bank teller, handling money, opening checking accounts. Stuff like that. She works in a bar at night as well."

"Well, at least she's got a gig. That's something—and don't say 'I guess'!"

"She works in a bank, but we never have any money for school clothes, food, or the rent. She always has money from the bar though—single dollars."

"Singles, huh? That might be a conversation for later, but it sounds like you should be happy she's getting married. Who's the guy?" he asked.

"Dick," I grunted in disgust. "I really hate him. He's an obnoxious insurance salesman." I did my best to sum him up in as few words as possible.

"Damn." Marcus's face cringed as if he had just bit into a lemon. "That can't be good."

"Tell me about it," I answered, dejected. "It's not. He went to prison a few years ago. I overheard them talking. He doesn't think I know."

"Prison?" Marcus responded curiously. "Did you hear what he went in for?"

"Yeah." I lowered my head.

"Well, don't clam up and be ashamed about it. You ain't the one that went in," he smiled. "C'mon now, what was he in for?"

"I heard him say that he held up a liquor store and also set a house on fire when they tried to arrest him."

"Damn, that ain't right. Robbery is one thing, but arson is a whole other bag of problems. Maybe that's why he sells insurance."

"I don't understand," I responded.

"Don't worry. It'll be clear to you later on. People who set stuff on fire shouldn't be trusted. At all. Got it?"

"Okay," I answered.

"So, your moms doesn't see anything wrong with her working in a bank and marrying a man who has a taste for armed robbery and who will set himself on fire when backed into a corner?"

"I guess I never thought of it like that."

"I bet he did." Marcus finished his drink and put the empty can, along with mine, into a small paper bag and then stowed it under his seat. "Smells like real trouble, if you ask me," he rejoined.

"Why, because he went to jail?"

Marcus gave me a stern look. Maybe I'd said something wrong. I had a tone in my voice when I blurted out what I had said. It was difficult for me to swallow *all* of my anger.

"First, to answer your question, no—I don't have a problem with him going to prison. A lot of people go to prison. It's just a fact of life. Almost every man in my family has done a bid, or served time somewhere."

I was shocked. Dick was the only person I'd known who had been to prison. "Really?" I answered, my mouth agape.

"Second, jail is one thing and prison is another. Don't confuse them. Trust me when I tell you that there is a world of difference between the two."

"What's the difference?" I asked on cue.

Marcus just shook his head with a slight grin. "You really want me to tell you, huh?" he asked. He seemed reluctant.

"Sure, why not? I honestly don't know."

He looked around the bus quickly and then shifted in his seat a little, moving closer, as if he was about to tell me an important secret.

"Ever see someone get pulled over on the side of the road by the police?" he asked.

"Yeah, all the time."

"All the time?" he answered incredulously, with a broad smile. "Well, guess where he went." I knew better not to answer right away. "He went to jail. May have even stayed the night. But in the morning, he probably went home or someone came to post his bail. Someone paid hard cash for that man's freedom."

I nodded in understanding, following his logic.

"When you go to prison though, chances are you're never going to get to go home again. And no amount of money will break you free," he emphasized. His words were terrifying. It was a reality I'd never considered. He sat back in his seat again, looked away, and then stood up.

"If you do get to go home again, it's only by the grace of God. And they usually let all the wrong ones out, like your good friend Dick. Like I said, arson—don't trust 'em," he added, as he opened the lavatory door and quickly stepped inside.

The bus cruised through the empty desert, slipping through the black of night, vanishing without an argument. The only interruption was the headlights on the freeway, breaking the world apart like a knife wound across its invisible face. Stars dotted the sky above us like nails, pointing downward as if there just might be something to pierce and hold down. Low voices were barely audible over the sound of the tires roaring underneath us. The sound of a chuckle from the front was the only familiar thing, the only human thing. Trapped inside the large aluminum shell, we were not of the same world.

We traveled for an unknown period of time, sliding through a black vacuum at an easy speed with a continual low groan. Occasionally, my head would jerk and dislodge itself from the folded-up jacket that separated it from the window. As I watched the road beneath me, several cars swerved and were pushed left and right as they tried to whip around the bus, passing us at break-neck speed. The large bus weaved dangerously a few times into the next lane from the occasional blast of wind.

"You're pretty quiet, huh, Sebastien?"

"Yeah," I nodded. "It's a problem. Sometimes I want to say something, but I can't."

"You do alright in school?" Marcus queried.

"No ... not really. We move around so much, it's impossible. As soon as I start meeting new friends and getting comfortable, my mom either has a change of plans or I have to go stay with my grandma."

"You don't have any say in it, do you?"

"What do you think?" I scowled. "They never ask me. That's for sure."

"All you have to do is speak up. Hasn't anyone ever told you that?"

"Yeah ... and then I get smacked and told to 'shut up' or 'go to my room.'"

Marcus didn't take an eye off of me at all. "Yeah, so? You telling me that you're afraid to get hit a few times?"

"Wha ...?" I answered, confused.

"Lesson number one: everyone's going to—always—dish it out and do everything they can to beat you down. You better get with that, quick." His face was calm and relaxed. He blinked a few times and even cleared his throat. "But it doesn't mean that you have to take it. You gotta be ready to repeat yourself and make your case, and for you that's a problem."

"Are you insane or something, Marcus?" I was a little annoyed at him for pushing it. He just laughed it off without a care.

"I bet you get into a lot of fights in school, too, don't you?"

Now I was watching him. "And how would you know that?"

"Just a lucky guess, I guess," he rejoined with a grin. He was being funny at my expense. It was alright though. I wasn't bothered.

"Kids make fun of me all the time at school. Every time I start a new school and find myself surrounded in a classroom full of people staring at me, it starts without fail, and it's always the same. They tease me because I stutter."

"You stutter?" he asked, incredulously.

I opened my second bag of pretzels and slowly began chewing a few to give my brain a break. I didn't answer right away. I don't know why I told him that, but it was too late to take it back.

"I stutter a lot," I responded, almost in a whisper, as if I had only thought the words rather than vocalized them.

Marcus spoke with concern in his voice. "I couldn't tell, honestly," he confided. I shared my pretzels with him. He took a few from the bag and then handed it back.

"I have to be careful what I say. Sometimes the words just won't come out, no matter how hard I try. There's a lot of words I can't say, because if I do, well ..." I paused. "It turns into a mess. Sometimes I just have to think up other things to say, even though what I want to say is clear in my mind. That's when things go wrong, and I end up saying some really stupid stuff."

"And that's why they tease you, huh?"

"Yeah. I try to be cool, but it just makes things worse. My mother always gets mad if I stutter when I'm around her. She usually tells me to stop stuttering or stop talking, period. She said that I would probably stutter my whole life because of the way I was."

"And what way are you?" he asked.

"I don't know. It's ..." The tension approached, causing me to pause and re-route my mouth. "I'm just always alone."

He laughed. "You're a loner."

"A what?" I responded.

"A loner?" he grunted. "Someone who's by himself, alone, doesn't travel around in a pack or a large group of people. Like a lone gunman or a gravedigger."

"Yeah, that's me then. The Lone Gunman."

Marcus laughed, cracked his knuckles, and stretched his feet out into the aisle. "So, you're a loner. You travel around a lot without your parents. You get into fights at school, and you stutter. I bet you don't have many friends either."

"Most people don't like me. Even when they say they do, they're usually lying. I had a friend for about six months at one school, but when he found out that I was moving again, he didn't want to be friends anymore."

"I knew it. You got it rough, kiddo," he remarked.

I felt strange talking with Marcus. I wasn't hesitant to tell him what was on my mind. He was probably the only adult who had ever listened to me or asked me questions, or rather the only adult who asked me questions not related to some kind of trouble I was in.

"My cousin has a stutter," Marcus said after a few moments. I paid close attention as I ate my pretzels. "He used to get teased a lot in school too. It started a lot of fights, and he was always messed up in some kind of hassle with the school or the police. He wasn't too well liked either. Trouble always found him, no matter what. He was pretty smart though, but always being under the eye, he eventually got kicked out of school. After he was gone a while, everybody just forgot about him, even the boys who'd picked on him."

"What happened to him?"

"After he dropped out, he started working as a janitor for a clothes manufacturer where my moms worked. It was easy work, because he didn't ever have to talk. He just kept the floor clean, helped move the large bolts of fabric, and straightened up the dock on the ground floor. Pay wasn't bad. Probably the best he had."

Marcus looked away without saying anything. He was quiet and stared off into space. For a few moments I thought he might say something, but he didn't. When he looked down at his hands, I had the urge to speak.

"What's your cousin's name?" I thought it was the best thing to ask. He looked up at me again.

"His name was Elias." His response was cold. "The two of us used to spend a lot of time together, but it's been a long time since I've laid eyes on him. He's thirty-five now. I haven't seen him in seven years."

"What happened to him?"

"Take a guess, but let's see if you get it right." Marcus began folding up his jacket, getting ready to close his eyes for a while. I was starting to feel sleep catching up to me as well.

"He went to ja ... I mean prison."

Marcus nodded, made himself comfortable, and yawned. "Yep. You got it, chief."

"What did he go to prison for?"

"You really want to know?"

"I do," I said steadfastly.

"Well, Sebastien ... he killed a man. It wasn't his fault though." He shook his head. "The man had broken into my mom's house in the middle of the night. My cousin was there ..." Marcus seemed reluctant to tell the story. "He hit the man across the head with a lamp. He fell quick. They said the blow had killed him instantly."

"He went to prison for that?" I asked, surprised.

"The man he killed was white."

"What does that matter?" I answered.

Marcus grinned and eased back into his seat. "Well, unfortunately, life is a little more complicated than you may realize. But that's another story." He yawned and slowly began to disappear into the darkness of the bench seat, his clothes and the wood laminate wall behind him.

"Did your cousin ... stop stuttering?" I asked.

"Why do you want to know?" His eyes were still closed as he answered, and he shifted around a little, trying to find the sweet spot on the seat.

"I don't know," I answered absently. "I sometimes wonder if it will go away."

"How long have you stuttered? Since you could first talk?"

"No," I rejoined. "Just two years ago."

Marcus opened his eyes and glanced over at me sideways. "Two years ago?" He seemed surprised as he repeated my words. "Usually kids who stutter start young, pick it up early. You were, what, ten years old then? Something happened, didn't it?" His words seemed sharper, more direct. His tone was crisp and had an edge to it. I didn't know what to say to Marcus about that. Maybe he knew. I wanted to say something, but I realized I was having one of those moments where my mouth wouldn't function without falling to pieces.

"Stuttering is often the result of something really bad, something traumatic, that happens. Why don't you tell me what happened to you two years ago?" he continued. He spoke just above a whisper.

I turned my face away toward the window, feeling a little ashamed and a little upset. I didn't have any way to explain it to him, and my brain was telling me that my mouth wouldn't have a way to speak the words without fumbling all over them.

"Can ... we ..." I tried slowly.

"What? Can we what?" he asked, concerned.

"Nothing. Can we not talk about it?" I cut myself short, satisfied with what I was able to get out. I felt light-headed, and my throat went dry and began to constrict, as if someone was choking me. The grip felt unbearable. I closed my eyes and did my best to shut down. I was becoming convinced that I was slowly turning into one of those mannequins. I was absolutely useless. They probably wanted to speak but couldn't, their throats wooden and closed, unable to articulate the personal hell that they were trapped in. It was a life of constant manipulation, with no ability to respond. I feared for myself and what was up ahead. Slowly, I slipped away, letting go of it and everything else. Sleep was the only thing that I had any reasonable control over. Lately, I hadn't had much of it either. When it came, I didn't feel like struggling against it just to watch the constant river of headlights passing outside the window. For the moment, drifting into darkness was better.

* * *

I was barely able to open my eyes, as they were crusted shut and blasted dry from the air-conditioning vent. My lips were cracked, and the inside of my mouth tasted like the strange blue water that was now very evidently fuming from the bathroom toilet.

The overhead lights dimly shone down from above. The engine

was still. The bus had stopped. I got up and noticed that I was the only one still aboard. Everyone else had disembarked, including Marcus.

As I made my way down the center aisle, I couldn't hear any noise coming from the overhead intercom outside, but the exterior of the pale concrete and iron terminal was brightly lit up like an airport or a UFO landing site. It looked like the middle of the day outside, but it was closer to nine p.m. From the rafters of the overhang, I saw a sign that read *Blythe*.

Outside the bus, Marcus was having a cigarette with the driver. "Look who's awake," he announced, as I came down the metal steps. "I didn't think you were ever gonna wake up. You looked dead to the world back there."

I rubbed my eyes, assaulted by the intensity of the bright light. "Where are we?" I asked.

"California-Arizona border," the driver bellowed with a smile. It took me a second to realize it, but he wasn't the same driver that got on in Los Angeles. The man's name tag read *Monty*.

"Looks like the middle of nowhere," I said after glancing around at the alien structure, which was surrounded by a massive, flat parking lot and sat a long distance from the freeway. My eyes had a difficult time piercing the blackness that was being held off by the flaming white lamps.

They both laughed at me. "It is. Literally," Monty answered. Monty was older than all of the drivers so far. His hair was white and curly. He was darker than Marcus and had an easiness about him that made him look comfortable in his oversize Greyhound uniform. He might've been driving some type of transport his whole life just by the way he was standing close to the bus, smiling and palming his cigarette. He had deep lines around the edges of his mouth.

"You best go use the latrine now, youngun'. We'll be leaving directly." He spoke his words kindly, with just enough purpose.

"What time is it?" I asked, as I thrust my hands into my coat pockets, yawning.

"Just past eight-thirty. Be leavin' up outta here in 'proximately ten mics." Monty spoke to me in a type of elusive military/truck-driver code that seemed perfectly normal to him and Marcus. As I wandered into the terminal, I felt relieved that I had figured out some of what he had told me.

Inside, soft music was dropping down from the high ceiling above. The large center of the lobby was devoid of any of the riders and residents that I'd seen back in Los Angeles. Blythe was a stark contrast. Along the main wall stood a long row of old-fashioned enclosed telephone booths from another era. They had sliding glass doors for privacy, which were edged with dark wood, and the inside had a soft amber light shining down on a small wooden seat next to the dialing pad. Almost every one of the twenty or so phone booths had someone inside. Maybe this is what you're supposed to do when you come to Blythe. Call home. Maybe it had something to do with crossing a border. I turned away, having no desire to call anyone. It was three hours later at my grandma's in Pennsylvania, and they were most likely in bed. It was too late to call. My grandpa wasn't the type of person who appreciated late-night interruptions. I didn't blame him. I wouldn't want a phone call from me either in the middle of the night at the border of California and Arizona. It just wasn't worth it.

On one of the large walls hung a huge painting of a sprawling green forest with a winding stream and craggy mountains rising up in the background. The words *Welcome to California* were painted neatly within the upper portion of the canvas like it was a good thing. A very unconcerned and innocent-looking bear was frolicking in the stream, grabbing at a fish. I stared at the painting for a few minutes, locked in a trance. It wasn't the California I knew at all. Maybe this is what it was for the adults or everyone else. Maybe this is what it was for my mother on her honeymoon with Dick. In my mind I pictured the innocent bear fishing them both from that frothy stream. They were gasping for air, their mouths full of ice-cold water, trying to get away. That was possibly the only California that would've made sense to me.

The Blythe Terminal was something to see. It was large, well-built, and clean, which was quite the opposite from the overcrowded and dirty Los Angeles Terminal, which was too small, too cramped, and falling apart. It would've made some sense if they could've switched terminals, but that just wasn't possible.

I made my way across the charcoal gray marble to the far end. Two thin signs hung above two doorways and read *Mens* and *Womens,* amber-lit from inside. The bathroom was covered in white square tile from floor to ceiling. In the middle stood a large, round stainless-steel fountain with running water that was being used by one other man. It was the first time I'd ever seen anyone peeing in a water fountain. I surveyed the room for urinals. Once I realized that the fountain contraption *was* the urinal, I stepped up and did my business. Thankfully, the center portion of the fountain was raised, obscuring me from the other man directly across from where I stood.

A short row of stalls that was made of the same wood as the phone booths was set back opposite the sinks. The bathroom was bigger than a lot of apartments I had lived in with my mother. The sound of someone flushing cut through the calm sound of my pee mixing into the running water below me.

I noticed that even though I was in a bathroom, the air smelled fresh and clean, and the place was considerably relaxing. A tile mural of horses running across a desert plain was embedded into one of the walls just left of where I was standing. The homeless people in Los Angeles would've loved this place.

I washed up quickly and left. I was starting to feel the vise grip of sleep closing in and twisting around me. My eyes were heavy, the joints of my hands hurt, and I couldn't stop yawning. I thought I was going to swallow a bug the third time my mouth stretched open to vacuum in the night air and fill my body with the dark poison of the middle-of-nowhere. As I stepped outside, I could see that the bus was running again and people were filtering forward in a hazy state. I saw a lot of the same riders from Los Angeles and Palm Springs, but only a few other people had been on the bus ride longer than I had: an old woman with her not-so-pretty daughter, the creepy guy in the suit, and the man with the red hair and green army jacket who had gotten hassled by the evil Frank Burns in Bakersfield.

We rumbled back out into the night, away from the Blythe Terminal with all of its clean and well-lit surfaces. A man with a janitor's cart and a hose was spraying down one of the bus platforms. After we left, the place looked vacant. It was easy for me to huddle back into the corner of my window seat and fade away. Marcus said it was okay for me to take two seats, as he was stretched out on the third and into the aisle, slowly drifting away.

When Monty had merged us all back onto the freeway, I looked across the bus and out one of the windows on the opposite side to see if the Blythe Terminal was still visible. With the glare from the passing cars, the strong glow wasn't all that impressive now and could've been easily missed if you weren't paying attention.

I had hoped that they had a gift shop, as the thought occurred to me earlier to see if I had enough money to buy a Walkman, a music tape, and some batteries. The gift store was closed, and I couldn't get a good look inside as everything was dark. Listening to music was a good way to pass the time and take my mind off the endless monotony, especially at night, when I either couldn't sleep or wasn't talking with Marcus. I could faintly hear Marcus listening to something. The light wisps of a man's voice drifted my way. "Mercy Mercy Me" was the only part I caught. The rest of it was too quiet and too far away for me to hear it.

Suddenly, after a few moments of driving, the intercom gently clicked on. It didn't crack at my ears like all the other times.

"Good evening, folks. Welcome back on the 1364 to Phoenix, Saint Louis, Pittsburgh, and New York. We'll be pulling into Phoenix in just about three and a half hours. It's a safe and gentle drive when the wind is still, and it's looking pretty calm. I'll leave the floor lights on. Other than that, get some rest, be courteous to the other riders, and please refrain from smoking after nine p.m. My name is Monty, and I'll be your driver for the next twelve hours. Thank you."

So far, we hadn't had a driver for that long. All the other drivers were only on for four hours at most. It made sense if they had to turn around and drive back home after their shift. I was just glad that we didn't have to deal with Frank Burns anymore.

When my eyes closed, I was thankful. It was the end of the first whole day on the bus, and I was a lot closer to being home. One of the last things that went through my head before I fell asleep was the luggage. I knew at some point, I'd have to get rid of it.

4.

Several times during the night I had opened my eyes and stared out into the blackness, counting the stars and letting my mind completely separate from my tired body. Reclined in the rear of a moving bus wasn't necessarily the most comfortable place on earth to find sleep, but it would have to do. My only consolation was that I wasn't wedged between a pay television, the homeless, and surrounded on all sides by other travelers stuck in the same predicament. The backseat of the bus was notoriously bumpy. While the suspension absorbed a lot of the repetitive bumps and dips, the majority had to be endured. This was another good reason for the sane of mind to not sit in the back row. After a while, it became something else to ignore, but every so often the metallic behemoth would hit an unusually large dip, sending me bouncing off the seat.

In one of those moments of deep sleep, I completely detached from the reality of being on the bus and believed myself to be somewhere else. I had my face buried in the seat cushion, drooling, when the bus hit an abnormally large pothole in the road and then swayed. I was completely knocked off the bench and sent directly to the floor. When I picked myself up, Marcus just sort of chuckled. "Are you alright down there?" he asked.

"Yeah, fine," I mumbled, shaken and dazed. I climbed back up onto the seat. I knew after I hit the floor that trying to sleep would be a lost cause, but at least I had a window seat. Marcus drifted back into slumber as we drove on, getting closer to our destination.

I was hoping that the café in Phoenix would be open, as I was feeling hungry again. Eating was just another way to pass the time and fight off boredom. I also had a good supply of café vouchers and wanted to use them.

When the bus climbed up the off-ramp, I rubbed my eyes, yawned, and prepared myself to step down. We slowed at a light for a moment and then made a few turns into downtown Phoenix. Streetlights now, no stars. Sidewalks, neon signs, parked cars, newspaper machines, and rows of parking meters. It was everything I expected to see as we drifted deeper into the heart of urban civilization. But every time I thought we were going to stop and pull into the station, we just kept on driving. It was a roundabout route that slowly took us away from normalcy and once again into an industrial wasteland. Maybe that kind of *out-of-the-way* Toiletburg, U.S.A., was a prerequisite for building the bulk of the terminals back in Greyhound's good-ol'-days.

When the familiar oblong, blue-and-white Greyhound sign came into view, we cut into the station and were met by the flashing lights of three squad cars. The spinning red-and-blue orbs bounced around the walls and ceiling of our coach, casting all of our faces in a more serious hue. Monty slowly and very carefully pulled the bus through the terminal. All of the passengers on the right side of the bus had stood up and moved closer into the middle aisle to get a better look. As we drifted by the entrance into the terminal, a group of police officers was escorting a man in handcuffs with his head bowed to the cars outside. He had a shaved head and a fierce look. Blood covered the front of his white T-shirt. We were just a few minutes too late to have seen the fight.

"Looks like the locals have been brawlin'," Marcus spoke, assessing the situation. He had one raised eyebrow and seemed to be shaking his head.

"That guy's bleeding," I replied, stating the obvious.

"Hate to see what happened to the other guy."

The bus pulled into its spot along the terminal wall. A painted sign in front of our space read *Los Angeles–Flagstaff.* When the bus came to a complete stop, the intercom switched on.

"I know everyone's itching to get off, but I need to make sure that it's safe for us to disembark and get the go-ahead. It will only take a moment."

Nobody protested, but everyone fidgeted anxiously to get a better look, despite being fast asleep only moments ago. Monty switched channels on his radio and called inside for instructions. The response came back pretty quickly, and Monty swung the doors open.

"Alrighty, folks ..." Monty had stood up and was addressing us without the aid of his intercom.

"Everything's fine inside, but apparently a little busier in the lobby than we thought. If this is the end of the line for you here in Phoenix, then just wait outside on the platform for your bags before headin' out. Be safe."

"Short, sweet, and to the point," Marcus commented. Everyone was now steadily getting off.

"He didn't say how long the layover was," I responded. I slowly paraded behind Marcus, following the crowd outside. When we were finally off, I asked Monty how long we were stopping for.

"Fifty minutes," he answered, never looking up from unlocking the baggage doors on the side of the bus. "Save me a seat in the café, boys," he shot back.

"You got it," Marcus replied.

We made our way inside. Unlike Blythe, Phoenix was crawling with people, like another version of Los Angeles. An old homeless man, wrapped in clothes made entirely from American flags, was jiggling a small Styrofoam cup in the entryway.

"Spare some change, spare some change, spare some change," he repeated. Another man in all black, with a black cowboy hat and a long black beard, stood frozen just inside the terminal doors with a very unpleasant look on his face. I could see him from a distance as the doors slid open. He was a stark contrast to his companion outside. As I passed the old man dressed like Uncle Sam, he put a hand on my shoulder and asked me for some money.

"Spare some change, little man?" he asked with a toothy smile. He smelled of booze.

"Okay ... 'nuff a that," Marcus interjected, ushering me away.

The man in black said nothing at all. He just flicked, or rather bounced, a stack of quarters in his palm, slowly and rhythmically, as we passed, never breaking cadence. He didn't smell of alcohol like the old man, but he stank like sweat, rotten milk, and poop. The smell made both Marcus and me recoil unexpectedly. It was unbearable.

Inside the lobby, a few policemen were standing erect and on guard, sipping coffee and conversing next to a cluster of Greyhound employees who were scrubbing blood from the floor and wiping down the seats of the vinyl chairs. Everyone's eyes kept darting quickly in that direction, wondering if they were going to see anything else, but it was clear that whatever had happened was over long ago.

Above, the radio played "I've got a peaceful, easy feeling," but the atmosphere was rigid and tense. The mood was anything but peaceful or easy. Up ahead, the main gift store was still open. It was connected to the Grey Café. I was eager to get inside and see if I was going to get lucky.

"I need to go inside the gift store and get something, okay?"

"Cool," Marcus replied. "Don't get lost. I'll go grab us a seat inside. You want something to drink?" he asked. I realized he was just being polite.

"Cup of coffee, please," I rejoined. Again, he looked at me in complete shock, as if I had just caught him off guard.

"Cup of coffee?" he repeated quizzically. "C'mon, man."

"I'm being straight," I pleaded. Marcus grinned as he vanished inside to get a table.

As I slipped through the doorway of the gift store, the teenage girl behind the counter was watching me intently. The shop space was small, but it was filled with magazines, books, candy, cold soft drinks, gum, and travel-size amenities. When I looked back, the girl was staring into a mirror and applying makeup. She pushed the black eyeliner pencil slowly under her lower eyelid. When she was done, she capped the pencil and put it into a small makeup bag next to the cash register. As I approached the counter, she looked me over one more time. What I wanted was locked inside a glass case under the counter.

"What do you need?" she questioned me abruptly. The music that was playing behind her on a small silver radio was loud, but her voice was louder and more immediate.

"Can I se-se-se-see one of those tape players?" I asked. My voice cracked, exposing my nervousness. She just looked me over without moving from her seat and started smacking her gum at me. I was looking at her now for a response.

"What do you need?" She repeated the same question as if the last few seconds hadn't existed, but spoke louder and sounded more annoyed. I scratched my temple, intimidated.

"I want to see ..."

"Yeah, I heard you the first time, kid. You can see the merchandise through the glass." She spoke at me as if she didn't give a damn.

"Well, I ... I ..."

"Look, you little fucking shoplifter, I ain't got all night. You want something, pay for it. Otherwise, beat it. I'm not your mm-mm-mm-mommy, and this ain't in-in-information." She was openly taunting me. I took a deep breath. I was used to it.

"How much is it?" I blurted out, a little upset now.

"How much is what, retard?" She flicked her feathered blond hair from her round face and blinked at me several times.

"The black Walkman," I answered her steadily.

Completely annoyed, she finally got up from her stool and bent over to unlock the case. "If you're jerking me around, kid, I'm going to beat the living hell hell hell out of you." When the small door slid open, I pointed at the box near the front. An unboxed Walkman was standing front and center as a display.

"This one?" she asked.

"Yes, please."

"Forty-nine ninety-nine, plus tax," she bellowed triumphantly.

My face fell. She must not have thought I had it, because she laughed and started closing the case.

"You filthy little brat, I knew it. Beat it."

"I'll take it," I answered.

I caught her by surprise. "Excuse me?" she responded.

"I'll take it, please." I reached into my jacket pocket and quickly produced the money. I gave her three twenties. When the cash hit the counter and I pulled my hand away, she knew I was serious and changed her tune.

"You gave me too much," she shot, after she picked up the money and counted it.

"I need some batteries for it as well." I was excited but trying to stay calm. When she bagged it all up, before she gave me my change, she put one hand on her hip and pointed the other to a small display at the end of the counter.

"You're also going to need a cassette tape if you're planning on using that thing. They're two ninety-nine. Go pick one, quick." She had softened a bit, but her face still had a sour look on it as she ran her tongue across the front of her teeth in between gum smacks. I stepped over to the small revolving rack and examined all the titles. I'd never heard of any of them. Toward the bottom, I saw a tape that said *Daryl Hall and John Oates*. That was a name I knew from a song that had been playing on the radio in Dick's station wagon.

"I got this," I said, as I set the Hall and Oates tape on the counter. The girl looked me over again and finally smiled.

"Not bad. You ever listen to headphones before?"

"Headphones?" I said. "I didn't see that tape on the rack."

"No, headphones ... what you just bought, silly child."

"Oh ... no. This is my first cassette tape." The words sounded odd coming out of my mouth.

"Well ..." she spoke, as she leaned under the counter beside her and quickly came back up with another cassette. "Take this. You can have it. We have multiples." I looked at it carefully. *"Simon and Garfunkel Greatest Hits,"* I read aloud.

"Don't worry, you'll like it."

"Thanks," I said.

"Sorry I was so mean to you," she remarked. Her expression had changed quite a bit.

"It's okay. I get worse at home."

"I bet," she replied, as I turned away and headed for the café. The smell of food hit me as I crossed over the threshold of merchandise and into the world of perishable foods.

When I got to the table, Marcus and Monty already had their coffee. Monty had just sat down from the looks of things, as he was blowing off steam and stacking his wallet, keys, and a radio next to him on the table.

"You get yourself a bad back sittin' on wallets like that. The secret of long careers behind the wheel: never sit on your wallet." Monty was running his finger across his teeth and gums and getting ready to stir his coffee.

"What did you buy?" Marcus asked, curious as to what was in the bag.

"Let me show you." I pulled out the box to show him.

"Woo-hooo, lookey look," Monty exclaimed. "Looks like somebody's havin' a summertime Christmas."

"Looks like you bought yourself a Walkman." Marcus looked it and me over with that all too familiar gleam. It was the same Walkman that he had. Model WM-7.

"Did you get batteries for it?" he asked. The waitress set down a cup of coffee in front of me.

"I did. Music, too."

"You boys eating today, or is it just coffee?" she checked. Monty was lighting a cigarette. "Slice a pie tonight, Dee. That's 'bout all I need."

"I know what you're getting, old man. How 'bout you boys?" she queried us with a thick Southern accent.

"I'll have the same, please," Marcus rejoined politely.

"Same, please. À la mode," I stated. Monty laughed and slapped his hand on the table.

"À la mode ..." Monty laughed between a little hacking and coughing on his cigarette. Marcus and I did our best to ignore it, but we were both smiling.

"Hall and Oates? Mmm mmm," Marcus noted. "That 'Sara Smile,' now that's *the cut*," Marcus remarked, as he looked carefully at the back of the tape.

"I'm tellin' ya," Monty began, "I heard that white boy on the radio. Swear to God I thought he was blacker than my mama's iron skillet. He's the whitest brother I ever heard in soul music."

"Fo' sho'," Marcus laughed. I listened to the two of them talking about Daryl Hall. Marcus even sang a few lines of the song that I had heard on the radio.

"Every time you go away ... you take a piece of me with you ..."

"That song sends a *chill* up my spine every time I hear it," Monty began. "Gets me thinkin' 'bout my ol' lady, y'know?"

"All I'm saying," Marcus interrupted, "is that Daryl Hall, boy ... he's as cold as ice." Marcus sipped his coffee; Monty pulled at his pie with his fork. I'd heard the song only once and could vaguely remember it, but looking down at the tape, I could see it was listed as the third song on the second side.

"Cold as ice, boy," Monty punctuated. "Probably see that white boy earn a spot in Ripley's Believe It or Not with a voice like that."

"You better believe *that*," Marcus rejoined.

It was the best time I could remember, laughing and listening to them both joke around and argue about different singers. Marvin Gaye was the only other singer they could both agree on.

"Now, you know that brother is smooth."

"Okay, straight!"

Listening to the two of them was like listening to another language. When I finished eating, I had to get up to pee. I wanted to use the *latrine* before I got back on the bus. I reached into my pocket and absently pulled out my dwindling wad of bills, but I was really looking for the café tickets.

"Whoa, whoa, whoa now, youngun'. Best put that right back in your pannie pockets where you found it," Monty urged. I wanted to pay for my food but was thwarted.

"But ..." I tried.

"C'mon, now. Better listen to your ol' grandpa. You know how they get when they're old and crotchety," Marcus joked at Monty's expense.

"Who you callin' old and crotchety, boy? I could take you in a minute." Marcus tried hard not to laugh and just stared at him with a disbelieving grin. "Well ..." Monty hesitated, "if I didn't have to drive you two all over God's green earth, and I got my hip too."

"Go on, now. I'll take your gear on up to the bus," Marcus instructed. I left him the bag with my Walkman and Hall and Oates tape and made a run for the bathroom. I had to piss something fierce. Monty and Marcus were both headed outside for a final cigarette before the first boarding calls began.

On my way to the bathroom, I heard more Eagles coming out of the loudspeaker in the ceiling. For once, the boarding calls were almost nonexistent and weren't constantly interrupting the music, like back in Los Angeles.

When I got into the bathroom, I saw the man in the suit standing at the urinal. He glanced up at me like a falcon sizing up a field mouse. I stepped into the urinal beside him. It was too late to try to hold it now. The urgency to go was pressing and needed immediate attention.

"You better be careful hanging around with that Negro. He'll get you in trouble before it's over. Understand me?"

I didn't respond. I was dumbfounded as to what he was trying to say.

"This is my stop, and I'm getting off here. I'm just waiting for my ride now. But you better be careful." I kept quiet as he walked slowly around me to the sinks and began washing his face and hands. His suitcase sat behind us against the wall, unattended. I saw tags dangling from the handle that read *SFO*. He'd been on the bus a day longer than I had.

Standing next to him at the sinks, I realized now how much he stank of body odor. The back of his suit was wrinkled badly from being stuck against a sweaty seat for several days. As he dried his face with a paper towel, I looked at him quickly in the mirror, hoping not to be seen. I got an incredibly bad feeling standing beside him. I now completely understood what a "bad vibration" was. I'd heard my mother say it about other women all the time, but that was probably different. I tried to hurry and make my exit through the door, but as I reached for the handle, he stepped in front of me and grabbed for his case, brushing past me at the waist. My brain made a mental note that this was the second time he had made a quick and startling movement toward me. I slipped outside and walked quickly, unsure if it was prudent to run.

"Remember what I said, kid." I heard his creepy voice behind me, trying to reach me now across the distance. I knew I wanted nothing to do with him and that his advice wasn't good either. Everything about him struck me as wrong. In my mind, I noted what he looked like in the mirror just in case. His face was beet red and covered in acne. He had beady eyes and a thin mustache that looked like a black line under his nose. The bottoms of his tan suit pants were wrinkled and blackened at the backs, where they had been caught under his shoes while he walked.

Before I made it outside, the overhead announcement came on. "1364 to Flagstaff, Amarillo, Saint Louis, Pittsburgh. Platform 4. Boarding now. First call."

The same folks were all lining up to get back on. The porter was helping a few new riders with their luggage. My eyes settled on an attractive young girl who was by herself. She had long black hair that hung straight down around her face. She was wearing a pink plastic jacket with little zippers all over it and tight blue jeans. As I got closer to the end of the line, I caught a glimpse of her face. Her skin was pale and looked as pearlescent as the crisp white porcelain of the bathroom sinks. I'd never seen anyone with skin that pale. She was beautiful, and doing her best to keep to herself. Even though it was midnight, she was wearing dark sunglasses. The terminal was bright—not as bright as Blythe had been, but definitely well lit. She was among the first group of people to get on. After Monty had examined her ticket absently and returned her stub, she quickly stepped up and disappeared inside. I was hoping that she would sit somewhere near us so I could get another look at her face. I hoped she was going to Pittsburgh. My brain fired thoughts off one after another about how all of us would hit it off.

I waited patiently to board, being the last person in line. I was feeling sleepy again and knew that after a short while I'd probably be dead asleep again. I was excited to open up my Walkman, but I had the feeling Marcus was going to tell me to wait till morning to mess with it.

"Alrighty, alrighty, alright. There's my boy. What's the word, traveler?" Monty greeted me in his typical jovial tone, hoping for me to have a good comeback. My brain scrambled for something that I wouldn't stutter over.

"Daryl Hall," I replied.

"Oh yeah ... now ya know!" he shot back, nodding his head yes. He cackled like a madman as I hopped up and stepped carefully down the aisle toward the back. My eyes quickly scanned the seats for the pale-faced girl, wondering where she'd sat. I was surprised and happy to see that she'd taken the two empty seats directly in front of us. The majority of the riders were still congregating toward the front, and the bus was still far from full capacity.

As I passed her, she caught me stealing a glance with a goofy grin plastered across my face. She returned a smile and went back to putting her purse in order. Her overhead light shone above her, making her appear strange and heavenly. I wondered what her name was, but I knew that I wouldn't ask. If I had to guess, I would've said "Amber." She looked like an "Amber," especially in the gold light faintly beaming across her face from the overhead console. I took my seat again, edging past Marcus. When I plunked myself down, he handed me my bag with the Walkman, tape, and batteries. I looked at him quizzically as I took it.

"Go on, then. I know you want to check it out and fire it up. If you hand me the tape, I'll help you unwrap it."

"Okay. But you're not going to be mad that I'm making too much noise or listening to music, are you?" I replied.

"Ha ha, you sure are funny," he quipped, taking the Hall and

Oates tape. "Just make sure you don't listen to it too loud or too long, or fall asleep with it on. You'll kill the batteries."

"Alright," I agreed, as I slowly began prying open the cardboard and plastic box that held the Walkman's contents. It was the first purchase in my entire life of something that had any real monetary value. I didn't usually have the luxury of so much money and the freedom to spend it all at once. As I pulled everything out, I quickly realized that there was a lot more packed inside the small box than I had first thought. A black cloth lanyard was wound up and tied close to the top. The next item out was the Walkman itself. It was just as heavy as I'd remembered from holding Marcus's. Also inside was a leather carrying case that fit the cassette player like a well-made glove. A small folded piece of paper with minuscule writing was tucked inside the back edge of the packaging, neatly out of the way. Examining the manual briefly, I noted that the nice people in Japan had seen fit to print the instructions in an endless collection of languages, all of which, save one, I couldn't decipher.

Marcus showed me how to put the batteries in, plugged in the headphones, and then explained what the buttons did. He told me about ASF, Dolby, the Hot-Line button, and Auto-Reverse.

"If you're listening to music and someone says something to you, you don't need to hit stop," he said, looking at me for recognition. "Just hit the hot button right there," his long black finger was pointing out a square metal button on the top of the player, "and their voices will be amplified in your headphones, and the music volume will dim, allowing you to catch what's being said. Got it?"

"Wow, that's pretty cool," I blurted.

"Sure is."

I pressed play and sat back to absorb my new Hall and Oates tape. When the second song came on, I listened to it intently. "Sara Smile" was one of the songs that Marcus and Monty had mentioned. When it finished, I rewound the tape and listened to it again. It took a while to find the beginning of the song, but it sounded incredible and worth listening to more than just twice. I didn't know much about singers, but they were both right: Daryl Hall could sing. I'd never heard anything like it. The music reverberated softly in my head and quickly put me at ease. The music was so close, it felt almost alive. Listening to the song over and over made me think of being at my grandma's, listening to her clock radio at the kitchen table. There was really a world of difference, and I was trying to wrap my head around it.

The bus pulled away, leaving behind another station and letting off even more people in the process. The man in the suit was gone now, as was the old lady who had kept herself busy with her knitting. It was hard to see in the dark who had taken their seats, as no one had his overhead light on and only the dim, yellow marker lights on the floor were illuminated. I wanted to take some notes about the Walkman, "Sara Smile," Phoenix, and what the man in the suit had told me in the bathroom, but I didn't want to disturb anyone, especially Marcus or "Amber."

Through the space in between the seat and the window, I could see the top of her head resting against a small pillow that she had put between herself and the large piece of cold glass.

The lights, streets, buildings, and traffic of Phoenix slowly began to evaporate behind us as we wound around on the dimly lit roads and back out onto the interstate. Maybe Charlotte and Dick were now married and somewhere in San Francisco, out getting drunk and smoking cigarettes instead of face down in that stream as I had imagined earlier. Any thought of Dick angered me. Maybe it was because I knew that my mother had successfully transmitted the message that he was more important, and probably always would be, by shuffling me out of the picture. She had stopped talking about my sister, Beanie, or even mentioning her name after Beanie refused to live with her last year and stayed firmly put at Grandma's. It had been just over a year since I had left for California, and it was the longest time that Beanie and I had been separated. Beanie didn't trust Charlotte's intentions or her sincerity, as all of my mother's promises usually meant nothing after a few days back together or after she'd got her way. Beanie and I both knew that our mother only wanted her around to watch me when she left for work, for the bar, for the next man, or whatever else was more important at the time. I had the impression that the only reason she wanted us around in the first place was to hold up appearances with everyone who knew her. A single woman is one thing, but a single mother with no kids in sight is another, and exactly what it looks like—suspicious. A single mother with children could at least claim welfare, but a single woman with no children probably went hungry and had to do "other things" to get by and eat. New dresses had to be bought. New shoes were always needed. How else could she trap a man?

I didn't blame my sister at all for not wanting to be anywhere near her, but it only made me focus on the "why" more often than I should have. It was bad enough never knowing my father, but dealing with a flaky mother too was tiring. I was getting a headache thinking about them. Hopefully my mother and Dick would be happy together, and Beanie and I would never hear from either one of them again.

Marcus tapped me lightly on the shoulder to get my attention. I hit the Hot-Line button as I looked over.

"You still awake?" he whispered.

"Yeah, I guess I was just daydreaming or something." I got the feeling that he wanted to talk for a bit, so I shut the Hall and Oates down and took off my headphones.

"Soon, this bus ride will be all over. I'll be back in New York, you'll be at your grandma's house, and all this will be just a vague memory."

"Two days away," I said.

"Almost three for me, but not much longer for sure."

"Did you talk to your dad on the phone yet?" I asked. What possessed me to ask that question, I had no answer, but Marcus seemed to be thinking hard about his reply.

"Y'know, Sebastien ... I didn't tell you before, because I really didn't know you, and it's not just something a man goes around advertising, if you follow." I didn't, but I nodded regardless. I didn't know much about talking openly with an adult and had never had any experience, but I had been told enough times not to interrupt my mother while she was talking.

He cleared his throat. "I haven't seen my father in almost eight years," he began again. "We were always pretty tight, but y'know ... things happen. Sometimes ..." Marcus stumbled, searching for the right words. "Sometimes, the choices you make may not seem important at the time when you're making them, but too often they are. My pops died five years ago. I wasn't able to go to the funeral. Something came up, got in the way. Understand?"

"What came up?" I asked with a blank expression. "Were you stuck in L.A. or something?"

"Stuck in Los Angeles?" He pondered my words. "I guess you could say that. A lot of people I know are stuck out in L.A. at the moment. It's a pretty messed-up place," he added, pausing on his thoughts.

"Prison," I stated. "Not jail."

Marcus looked at me and patted me on the shoulder. "Don't ever let anyone tell you that you ain't got no smarts, understand? Prison it was."

He told me the whole story—how he had been in the room with his cousin when the white man had tried to burglarize their house. He had called the cops, but they were both arrested. His cousin received a thirty-year sentence for manslaughter. He had received ten years as an accomplice but was released after eight years for good behavior. His cousin wasn't so lucky. They went to separate facilities, and he had a harder time adjusting to being locked up. Mostly because they thought he was mute as he never spoke. One day, in a fight during a meal, Elias killed another inmate in self-defense. That was now two people he'd killed that way, and the state didn't look too favorably upon him at all. He was given a life sentence without the possibility of parole. He had written Marcus a few times over the years, but eventually the letters stopped coming because, as Marcus explained, prison shaped Elias into something else.

"He became bitter, angry ... he wasn't the same. He slowly became a monster in there." Marcus was clearly bothered by what he was telling me. "But that's how it is if you're a brother," he admitted. "You get caught up in the system, and they own you. Believe me when I tell you this: they don't ever have to let you go if they don't want to. So do whatever you have to do, but don't *ever* get caught up and get sent."

"How did you get out then?" I wondered aloud.

He contemplated what I said for a moment before answering. "They released me on good behavior. I never did drugs. I never got into no fights or brutalized another inmate in any way. I worked in the mess hall morning, noon, and night, and I never missed a day. I guess they thought I'd be alright back in the real world."

"What's the mess hall? Sounds dangerous."

He shook his head and rubbed his eyes, shocked at the depths of my naïveté. "You can make a person laugh, that's for sure. The mess hall is the kitchen. I was a cook. After five years, I was promoted to the head chef, and I made breakfast, lunch, and dinner for the warden and the top screws."

"I'm not going to ask," I replied sheepishly.

"A few of the head prison guards and sheriff's deputies."

"You missed your father's funeral?"

He sighed. "I did. They wouldn't let me take an escorted furlough to go see it, which can sometimes happen if you got some juice, some pull. But it was out of state and out of the question. The toughest day of my life in prison was the day I heard he died. I always knew I'd broken his heart by going in, but he knew how it was."

"When that man broke into your house ..." I began.

"Where was my pops? You were gonna ask that, weren't ya? It's okay, it's a fair question."

I shrugged. "Mmm-hmm."

"He was down at the bar where he usually was, with his friends playing pool. My old man loved playing pool. He was like a duck in water on the table. Couldn't be beat. He was just late that night. It wasn't his fault, y'know. It's just another one of those choices that I was talking about earlier. Got me?"

"He must've felt bad about it."

Marcus gave his answer very slowly. "Yeah ... he felt real bad about it for a long time. He didn't forgive himself for what happened. My guess is that it ate at him until it finally consumed him. He loved me more than anything. Me going to prison was tough on him."

I looked away, rubbed my eyes, and crossed my arms. I guess having a messed-up life like Marcus's or my own must've been a part of something bigger, or rather something smaller. Something I didn't quite understand. I kept thinking about the word *choices* over and over, as if it was being whispered in my ear.

"You gonna see your pops back in Altoona?" Marcus asked, somewhat changing the subject, but in other ways furthering it.

"I never really met my father," I answered. "I mean ..." I struggled for what I was trying to say again. My head was in a maze of words.

"It's cool. I understand," he replied, trying to diffuse some of the pressure.

"No, it's not like that," I spoke, trying to move my brain into place. "I've seen him once, but I can't say that I ever really met him, because I don't know him at all. Does that make any sense?"

"It makes perfect sense," Marcus answered.

"One time, my grandma and my aunt took me to go see him where he lived in Pittsburgh with his new wife. She had three sons, and when I got there he didn't seem very happy to see me. He acted like I was intruding and the other boys were more his sons than I was. At least that's what I saw." I looked over at Marcus, who was now listening intently but with a concerned expression and a raised eyebrow.

"So what happened?" he interjected.

"Well ... that night ..." I coughed nervously.

"It's cool. Just between us and the bus."

I breathed out a sigh of frustration and lowered the volume of my voice. "That night, I peed the bed. In the morning, I didn't know what to say about it because I definitely couldn't hide it. He acted insulted and embarrassed about it, even though I felt really bad. I'd wet the bed before, and it was just something I was going through at the time. When the other boys teased me, he didn't say anything or try to stop them. He had a hard time even making eye contact with me at breakfast."

"That's pretty damn cold, man," Marcus uttered bluntly. "That ain't right by a long shot."

"My grandma and my aunt took me back to Altoona after we ate. I thought that I was going to stay, because we had brought along two suitcases with my stuff. But it didn't work out that way, and he didn't even say goodbye when we left. I haven't seen or heard from him since that day."

"How long has it been?"

"Almost two years now," I replied without thinking.

"There it is again ... that magic two years."

"What do you mean?" I started to ask, but stopped myself short. I knew exactly what he was driving at.

"Damn, Sebastien, that story you just told me?"

"Yeah ..."

"Damn, it was so cold, it's 'Ghetto Cold.'"

"It's probably 'Grotto Cold' too," I replied, trying to shake the heaviness and make light of it.

"Probably is," Marcus admitted with a chuckle.

"Let me tell you a quick story about a friend of mine. You'll laugh."

"Is it funny?" I asked.

"C'mon now," he quipped. "My old friend Big John, he didn't know his pops either. The man left when he was a baby, see? Well, Big John was a really nice guy all the way around, never started any trouble with anyone. One day, his momma said that his old man was coming to see him. Big John was really bothered by this for quite some time. He didn't know what he was going to say to the coward that up and ran off on his momma and his sisters like that. He wasn't happy about it any way you cut it."

"What did he do?"

"What do you think he did? He whipped up on the man and beat his ass within an inch of his life. He realized that there wasn't much needed to be said between them at that point. His dad was 'bout twenty years too late. Big John laid into that stranger until he couldn't pick himself up."

"Did he kill him?" I was taken aback by Marcus's violent story. It definitely wasn't as funny as I had originally been led to believe.

"No, he didn't kill him. But let's just say that he didn't live much longer either." I felt flushed and wondered in the darkness if I was turning pale.

"So that's the story?" I was stumped.

"Let me get to the end," he rebutted. "So Big John's momma went to that man's grave every Sunday for a year. At first, Big John thought maybe she went because he'd been gone so long and she missed him. Women can be like that, see. But after about six months, he got really curious about her going to the gravesite. And every Sunday, right after church, off she went. One Sunday, he followed her to see what was going on."

"She was putting flowers down."

He smiled. "Well, that's one way to look at it, but not quite," he remarked. "When Big John's momma got up to the grave, she looked around, got directly over top of it, and grabbed hold of the headstone. Unexpectedly, she lifted her dress, squatted down, and defecated without warning."

"Defecated? What, she puked?"

"She took a shit. She crapped on that man's grave," he answered in a burst of laughter. "Then she rubbed her butt up on the stone, straightened herself, and went on home."

I burst out laughing at the thought of the old woman pooping. Just then, Monty's voice came on over the loudspeaker.

"*Okay now, boys. Take it easy back there.*" Even though Monty hadn't heard the story, I could hear the humor in his voice too.

"Some people are gonna get theirs, that's fo' sho'. You can count on it." Marcus spoke in a whisper now.

"I guess I have something to look forward to," I replied. Marcus covered his mouth to stop from laughing out loud.

"Did Big John ever find out?" I asked.

"Of course he did. He told that story to me in prison, the day after I heard about my pops dying." Marcus sighed again, this time in some kind of relief.

"Look ... just remember this, Sebastien. There will always be cowards everywhere you go. That's why it's important for you to be a man and know the difference. Big John may have taken his anger out on his absentee father for abandoning him, but I believe his mother was the one who experienced the *real* satisfaction. That's what I think the lesson was. It's just a matter of patience."

"I guess."

"There you go again, 'I guess,' hmmph." Marcus laughed a little as he fished out his Walkman. It was blacker outside now than it had been before. Clouds had rolled in and blotted the thin edge of the moon that had previously lit the night in a blue-gray tint. It was late, and I felt like closing my eyes. I pulled my jacket over me and moved around in the seat until I was finally comfortable. I only lay there a moment or so before I drifted off, but the last thought I had was of Big John's mother squatting over that grave.

* * *

"*Flagstaff,*" Monty announced, as the bus swayed and he rounded a sharp turn off the boulevard and into the terminal.

"Hey, I'm getting off for a few minutes. Got some business to see to." Marcus was already out of his seat and ready to step off the bus. Most of the passengers were either asleep or staying put.

"Phone call?" I asked.

"No, gotta see a man about a grave," he joked. I knew what he meant though. Someone had plugged the commode shortly after we'd left Phoenix, and it was *mostly* unusable. People still filed inside. Some came out pretty unhappy, but Marcus told me that they were peeing in the sink and that they were animals.

"I'm getting off too," I said. My mouth was parched and tasted like dryer lint and ammonia. "I'm going to see if I can get some ice water if the café's open."

"Cool."

Marcus must've really had to go, as he disappeared inside before I even stepped down.

I was met by chilly air and a light sprinkling of rain. Small dark dots were collecting on the ground around my feet and tapping me slowly on the shoulder. I stopped for a brief moment to stretch and listen to the sound of rumbling thunder colliding far off in the distance. No lightning yet—just wind gusts and skittering debris across the flat tarmac.

After I stepped into the lobby, I had only taken a few steps when surprisingly I was approached by a police officer. But when I looked up at his face, I realized it was the man in the suit from Phoenix. I was shocked to see him again. He stood directly in front of me with his hands on his hips. I couldn't help but look at his gun holstered at his waist.

"Sebastien Rain?"

"Ranes," I answered, slightly blank and frozen. I was in trouble.

"You better come with me," he said. His voice was harsh and commanding. I felt as if I was being pulled away by a string without any will of my own.

"Why? What's happened?" I asked instinctively.

"We got a call from your mother, and she asked us to hold you here until she comes, but you have to come with me now," he replied. His voice had a sense of urgency to it as he ushered me away from the door and across the terminal to the front exit. A Greyhound employee brushed past us as we neared the door, but she didn't want to make any eye contact. The woman probably assumed that I was a runaway.

"What about my luggage? Let me get my bags," I said, slowing. I hesitated and tried to turn back. The man in the suit, now the man in the policeman's uniform, grabbed me by the shoulder and kept me moving in one direction.

"Don't worry about that, you can get it later. They'll take care of it," he replied bitterly.

When we stepped through the front doors and back outside into the dark morning air, I immediately got a strange sense of something being wrong. I was expecting to see a police car parked by the entryway, but there were only a few cars in a small parking lot that was attached to the front of the terminal, none of which were a black-and-white cruiser.

"Uh, where's yu-your p-p-police car?" I asked.

"Shut up, kid. Hurry up, and don't talk." He gripped my shoulder tighter, sensing that I might try to break free. The thought of escape hadn't crossed my mind at all, as I still felt powerless to react. He was now pulling me across the parking lot and had quickened his pace. A brown van was the only vehicle in our vicinity, and we were closing in on it fast. "Wait a minute," I said, trying to protest. I looked up at him, finally making eye contact and trying to gain control of myself again. His face was locked in a fierce and angry grimace, and he was grinding his teeth.

"Stop talking," he barked, as he grabbed me by the front of my jacket and then slapped me hard across the face. "And don't look at me either!"

He reached out, slid the side door of the van open, and threw me inside. I landed on the carpet and rolled. The man quickly slammed the door shut on its rails, enclosing me in total darkness. For a brief moment, I couldn't see or feel anything else around me but the musty carpet beneath me. My stomach felt heavy, and my chest quickly became constricted, making it hard to breathe. I wanted to scream or yell for help, but something was smothering me from the inside out. My hand extended and felt the metal wall confining me. I heard the man outside jingling his keys and opening the driver's side door. I looked up and saw his face at the opening. But then there was something else. The rain was spitting on the top of the van like thumbtacks, but I heard something else—like footsteps on asphalt, but running. And then someone spoke.

"I don't think so," a voice spoke very calmly just on the other side of the metal wall from me. It was Marcus. The man's face turned away quickly, then I heard a cracking sound. Marcus had punched the guy, and he buckled into the door and out of view.

"Get the fu ..." he protested, unable to finish. Marcus hit the man hard again, but I couldn't see it. Something inside of my head told me to get up and move. When I stood up and tried to escape through the front seat opening, I hit face first into a large piece of chain-link fencing that I hadn't been able to see in the darkness. I scrambled to the sliding door, trying to get out, but I couldn't find the handle or anything to open the door, as I fumbled around in the darkness. The windows in the back of the van had been boarded up and wouldn't open.

"Marcus!" I screamed in sheer terror. "I'm here!" He was still scuffling out of view with the man in the suit, punching him repeatedly. I was quickly becoming hysterical inside the van, trying to find a way out.

"Hang on, I'm coming!" he finally answered. A moment later, the door slid open, and I jumped out as if I had been spring-loaded. "Holy shit!" I swore, terrified, immediately clutching onto Marcus. He quickly grabbed a hold of me and maneuvered me around the van and back to the driver's side door, where the man who had tried to kidnap me was still lying on the ground, groaning.

"Wait a hot minute, Sebastien. You need to see this," Marcus spoke. I felt no desire to approach him, even in his current state of being beaten down and prostrate.

"Get a good look at his face, and don't ever forget it." Marcus was talking in almost a whisper. When the man rolled slightly on the ground, I finally saw his face again, but he didn't look near the same as he did when I saw him at the bathroom sink or even a moment ago. Marcus had crushed his nose, and he was bleeding badly. A large area on the left side of his neck was starting to swell as well.

"Help me," he pleaded. Marcus lurched down and grabbed a hold of the man and pulled him headfirst onto the bench seat of his van. What he did next surprised me. He yanked the man's wallet from his back pocket, opened it, and quickly dug out his driver's license.

"I got your goddamned license now. Ya understand that?" he yelled at him angrily, only inches away from his face.

"Here, keep this and don't ever lose it." Marcus quickly thrust it into the palm of my hand. I was still in shock, but Marcus was in complete control. He shoved the rest of the man's body inside the van, slamming the door twice on his foot before he got his whole body inside.

"C'mon," he spoke with great urgency, "we got a bus to catch." Marcus grabbed me by my opposite arm and broke into a sprint across the parking lot at top speed and rounded the side of the terminal, not bothering to go through it. As we came around the corner, I saw Monty standing at the bottom of the steps, looking nervously at his wristwatch. We were both sprinting for the bus, and there was no way we were going to stay in Flagstaff, Arizona, to explain everything that had happened. Even I knew it wouldn't be good for either of us.

"Where the hell y'all been?" Monty looked at us both, obviously concerned. "You two got some explainin' to do."

Marcus pushed me up the steps, getting me safely back on the bus. I turned back to see Marcus give Monty a very serious look. "We need to go, pops."

"That's all you had to say," he responded, without any questions or formalities.

My head was swimming as I headed for the back toward my seat. Several people looked up at me, annoyed that I had held everyone up. My face was without expression, and I had little thought for any of them considering what I had just been through. Usually, I would've been ashamed, but I didn't know how to feel.

The pale-faced girl was sitting in the aisle seat now and looking directly at me. She wasn't upset at all, judging from her expression, just finally awake. She pointed with her finger and touched the corner of her mouth. I raised my hand up and felt warm blood where I had been slapped across the face, slightly cutting my lower lip. She handed me a Kleenex. I took it and sat down, lightly dabbing at the corner of my lip a few times. I leaned forward a moment later.

"Thank you," I said.

"It's okay," she replied softly.

As the bus very quickly pulled away and rotated around the

terminal and back out onto the main street, Marcus and I both got a long, last look at the brown van still parked in the front lot of the terminal, unmoved. I exhaled and sat back as we drove farther away and deeper into Flagstaff.

"You alright?" Marcus asked. Maybe it hadn't fully sunk in yet, but I was already trying not to think about it.

"Yeah ... I'm fine," I responded mechanically.

"No, Sebastien, you're not fine. You're safe, but you're definitely not fine. Don't confuse the two." I looked down at my hand. I was still clutching the driver's license that Marcus had made sure I kept a hold of. I took a closer look at it, not thinking to just put it away.

The title *California Driver License* was written across the top of the card in capital letters. His picture was below, and his name and address were listed beside it. *"Leigh Allen."* Marcus was glancing over my shoulder.

"Vallejo. Long way from home, don'tcha think?"

"What does it mean?" I wondered.

Marcus exhaled a long breath. "Well, if I had to take a guess ... he gets on the bus and looks for easy targets."

"Like me."

"Yeah, like you," he admitted. "He seemed to know exactly what he was doing."

"Should we tell someone?" I asked.

"What exactly are you going to tell them? He'd just deny the whole thing. They'd think you were making the whole thing up, and they'd put me back in prison for giving him a beating, even though he deserved it." Marcus had a way of telling the truth that made sense even to me. He was right about the whole thing too. If it hadn't been for him, I'd be somewhere else right now, probably traveling in the opposite direction.

"I want to tell you thanks," I said. Marcus looked at me thoughtfully and nodded.

"It's cool. You didn't do anything wrong back there, so don't go inside your head over it. Okay?"

I nodded yes. "Thanks ... I mean it," I repeated.

He put a hand on my shoulder. "Cowards and men, Sebastien. Cowards and men."

"I felt like a coward back there," I admitted.

"Don't go into your head," Marcus chided. "Look, when you're older ... you may have to do the same for someone else. You'll have to see if you're a coward or a man. You'll get your moment."

"I hope I'm a man," I whispered contemplatively.

"You will be, don't worry."

Flagstaff was very quickly behind us. I put Leigh Allen's driver's license away in my inside jacket pocket in case I needed it later. The bus followed the freeway as it twisted in different directions through the desert and past a multitude of road signs. One sign in particular read *Welcome to the Navajo Nation*. The engine whined as we climbed several times but went quiet as we crested over high edges and slipped through the downgrades. The traffic on the roads became more spare the earlier it got. It was desolate for near three a.m. There were moments when it looked as though we were the only Greyhound bus left on earth. Semi trucks traveling in small groups in the opposite direction would pass us periodically, out of nowhere, and vanish again moments later as if they were passing into the afterlife.

Marcus was listening to his Walkman, but wide awake. Having to beat off the man in the suit made him more alert and more quiet than I had seen him. He had to use the restroom several times to wash the backs of his hands, as he'd skinned his knuckles and was bleeding. We didn't have any bandages, and he probably had no desire to ask for any, so he just got by using the brown paper towels that were stacked on the side of the sink.

After we'd traveled far enough away and had completely settled into our seats for the next few hours of driving, Marcus lit a cigarette and relaxed. The pale-faced girl had turned around and quietly asked him for one as well, which he very politely produced for her. She thanked him after he lit it for her. She turned back around in her seat and remained quiet. Marcus had the same look of satisfaction about him that my mother had after smoking. She seemed to need one every hour though. Marcus was more controlled about it and rationed his smoking to after meals and just before sleeping.

The smell of the cigarette made me wonder about Charlotte and Dick one more time. I considered if they would've actually sent someone as dangerous as Leigh Allen to come kidnap me, getting me out of her life for good and securing sympathy from everyone in the process. Then I would be just one less thing to worry about, if that was really the case.

I squirmed around a bit, trying to get adjusted again on the two bench seats at my disposal. I stopped thinking about Charlotte and Dick, as it only upset me to picture her in a wedding dress for the third time. As much as I despised them both, lying there I made up my mind to never live with her again. Living with Dick would be dangerous. I knew there was something definitely wrong with him and that I'd never be able to turn my back on him. He didn't seem that different from Leigh Allen, and after the run-in in the parking lot, I felt as though my eyes were all the way open and my senses on fire.

In front of me, I heard the pale-faced girl, "Amber," shift in her seat, cough, and stand up. After she finished her cigarette, she quietly disappeared into the lavatory with her handbag. My gaze was perfectly centered on the doorway, so I would be able to get a really good look at her in the light when she came out. I struggled to stay awake waiting for her but nodded off exhausted.

5.

GALLUP, NEW MEXICO

When I opened my eyes again, it was light out. Only a few hours had passed, but the sun had risen, and I felt as if I'd finally gotten a full night's sleep. I didn't want to budge yet from my spot, as I was feeling comfortable and snug zipped up in my puffy brown windbreaker. Marcus was still asleep but stirring and leaning against the lavatory wall beside him. When I saw his face as he awoke, I suddenly blinked several times, realizing that it wasn't the sun that had awoken me but something else. Marcus's expression was alert and signaling that something was definitely wrong and out of place. It was the smell that had awoken us.

"What's that smell? Do you smell that?" he quickly asked me, as he sat up, catching his bearings.

"I do. What is that? It doesn't smell like the toilet."

Just then, Marcus looked down at his feet in shock. He was trying to avoid stepping in something, but it was everywhere and all over the bottoms of his shoes. A large sticky mess had pooled in front of our seats in the back row. I thought maybe it was soda, but Marcus looked terrified. He slowly got up from his seat and began scanning the area in front of us.

"What is it, Marcus?"

"It's blood," he answered. His gaze shifted and settled on the seat in front of us, and he seemed not to know what to say. I started to sit up and lean over the seat without touching the floor, but just as I could see over the seat, Marcus told me no.

"Sit down, Sebastien," he said very calmly.

"What happened?" I asked, confused.

All I could see was that "Amber" wasn't moving, and she didn't look as if she was going to. She looked stiff and reminded me of one of the store mannequins as she lay across the seat with her arm hanging awkwardly down to the floor.

"Pull the emergency cord," Marcus ordered me.

"Wha ..."

"Sebastien. Please pull the emergency cord above you! We need to stop the bus."

"Okay!" I replied, startled.

As soon as I pulled on the red emergency cord, a bell went *ding* and was then followed by a long, uninterrupted buzzer. I caught Monty's gaze looking back at us in his large mirror.

He quickly came on over the intercom. *"You boys okay back there?"* he asked, intermixed with static. Several people were now awake, twisting in their seats and wondering what was going on.

"You need to stop the bus." Marcus spoke loud enough to be heard but didn't shout. Monty seemed to understand his tone.

"You want me to pull over?" Monty asked. *"We're only about ten minutes from the Gallup terminal, but I'll stop. Hang on."* The intercom clicked off and Monty slowed the bus and veered it off onto the shoulder. When we had come completely to a halt, he unclipped his seat belt, grabbed his handheld radio, and quick-stepped it to the back toward us.

"Stay seated, everyone."

Marcus was standing at the opening of "Amber"'s seat in front of the latrine. Monty only glanced at her for a quick second before his face sank. He reached down with one hand and placed it on her exposed neck and rested it there. I looked down at the floor and stared at the blood, trying to think what might've happened to her. I didn't have a clue.

"Dear Lord," Monty exhaled after examining her. He rose up and put his hands on his hips, looking as if he didn't know what came next. Then, as he caught me watching him, he turned on his small radio and called out to the terminal.

"Hello, 1364 to Gallup Terminal."

A brief moment passed while he waited for a response.

"Terminal. Go ahead, 1364."

"I have an emergency situation on the bus and require medical assistance." The bus had gone quiet. I could hear Monty talking over the radio. His voice remained calm as he reported the details.

"What's your twenty?" the disembodied voice replied.

"About ten minutes out."

"Can you drive? Is the coach functional?" the voice responded again.

"Yeah, I'm fine. The bus is still operational."

"Bring it in then, we'll have an emergency crew meet you here. Is anybody hurt?"

"One female passenger, deceased," Monty announced. A sound traveled around the bus. The other passengers seemed to be shocked by this, but everyone kept quiet, trying to listen in on the conversation. There was a long pause over the radio.

"Okay, 1364, drive to the station."

"Roger," Monty replied, and then turned a knob on the hand-held device. Marcus and Monty both shared a look, and Monty headed back to the front of the bus. When he got buckled back in, he grabbed the intercom and addressed us.

"Just hold it together, folks. We'll be pullin' into Gallup in just under ten minutes. I'd advise everyone to be prepared to take all your belongings with you when you get off, as they're most likely going to bring in another coach. If ya gotta pray, now's the time." His voice was soft and had a respectful manner to it that conveyed more calm and understanding than any words ever could've.

In the few moments being pulled over, I was able to get a better look at "Amber." All I could see of her was her two hands, which were now a very pale gray. One was resting on her stomach, and the other was sticking out over the edge of her seat and onto the floor. She was being held in place by her awkward position alone. I could see that her jeans and her lower torso were covered in blood, and the seat that she had been sitting in was also soaking wet. Her face was obscured by her hair. Before, I had really wanted to look at her, but now, seeing her like this, I had no desire. I knew she wouldn't be smiling. Her eyes wouldn't see me, they'd see past me, just like everyone else. And whatever I would say to her, she just wouldn't respond. It was overwhelming knowing that wherever she was going, she wouldn't make it. Her family didn't know yet that she had died in her sleep, and everyone else, not on this bus, was still waiting for her. I didn't know how she had died. I turned to the only person who knew me and where I was going.

"Marcus," I asked. "How did she die?" I kept my voice to a whisper, as the bus was silent and had remained so ever since Monty had pulled back out onto the freeway.

"All I can do is guess, but it's a bit complicated," he answered, slowly enunciating his words and speaking in a soft whisper.

"I'm sure you know," I asserted. After asking, I felt bad for pushing it. I would've been yelled at by this point if Marcus had been my mother.

"Ask me later. We'll talk about it when everything's squared away." He wasn't mad, nor did he raise his voice.

The ten-minute drive felt like twenty. The cabin of the bus was so quiet, you could've heard a pin drop in the bathroom. Listening to the engine was the only escape. I kept my feet elevated, and every few moments I glanced down to see that the blood on the floor had become like a thin syrup and was drying up. The smell now overtook everything and seemed to get stronger with every inhalation. Marcus had used one of the few blankets that Greyhound provided and had very gently covered her with it.

When we got closer to the Gallup station, a police car pulled in front of us to block traffic, which there wasn't much of. His red-and-blue lights blazed, sounding us out with the siren. We parked on the main street in front of the terminal and were met head-on with the squealing whine of an approaching ambulance. Monty gave a short message about disembarking and collecting all personal belongings. For the second time during the trip, we had unloaded on the street in front of a group of onlookers and been met by police and

Greyhound personnel. I couldn't help but begin to feel important because of it.

I stood on the sidewalk next to Marcus in the morning air, and we waited while Monty unlocked the luggage compartments to start unloading. The emergency crew disappeared into the bus, followed by a few firefighters and a police officer.

"Is there a fire on the bus? Why do they need firefighters?" I questioned, staring at the unfolding spectacle.

"It's just the way it's done, that's all," Marcus replied. "They'll probably be the ones to carry her off."

A few people stood by on the sidewalks, gawking. Most of them looked older than my grandparents.

An old lady in a crisp Greyhound uniform with long, white, neatly braided hair was ushering us inside single file. "Can everyone from 1364 please step into the depot?" she asked. She was darkly tanned and had an angelic tone in her voice that made her sound trustworthy. Monty was off to the side talking with a few other Greyhound people and a police officer who was clutching "Amber"'s purse. Every few words, they would glance in our direction. As we moved to go inside, it looked as if they were talking about us. The officer walked toward us and then pointed at us menacingly.

"You two, come with me." The police officer wasn't really asking as much as he was telling. After the incident in Flagstaff, I felt compelled to comply. I started to worry as we stepped into the terminal behind him. He marched us through a door that said *Employees Only,* which opened onto a long, narrow hallway where square offices were positioned on both sides.

The bulky policeman corralled me into a small room that was someone's office. "I need you to sit there for a few moments. Can you do that without getting into anything?"

"Yes, sir," I responded.

He lightened up a bit toward me after noting my response. "Okay, then. I'll leave the door open just in case. Don't budge from that seat."

"Yes, sir," I repeated. He turned and slipped away into another office next door with Marcus. I could hear the door close on the other side of the wall and muffled voices, but nothing more. All I heard before the officer shut the door was: *What's your name?*

I sat perfectly still for over ten minutes as I waited for my turn. The office usually belonged to a "Muriel Rodriguez." Her name was engraved on a silver plaque that was affixed to the door. The room had no windows anywhere, and every wall was covered by book-cases. The shelves were filled with both blue and gray three-ring binders. I was sitting off to the side near the doorway, along the wall. The chair was comfortable and swiveled, but it was small.

"Can I help you?" A large woman with black hair and deep brown skin addressed me. She was now wondering what I was doing in her office.

"The police officer asked me to wait here," I replied.

"Did you just get off the 1364 from Los Angeles?"

"Yes, ma'am." I looked at the name tag on her shirt; it read *Muriel.*

"Okay. Don't get into anything," she responded. She turned to leave but hesitated and spun on her heel.

"You want something to drink while you wait?"

Inwardly, I sighed in relief. "Thanks ... I'm fine for now," I replied. She turned and swished away farther down the hallway into another office.

After a few more moments, the office door where Marcus was being questioned opened, and he and the officer both emerged. When Marcus saw me, he was smiling. It was exactly the opposite of what I expected.

"I'll grab a table for us in the café, okay?"

"Uh ... sure," I replied unevenly. The police officer was staring at me. After Marcus slipped away, the officer closed the door and leaned against Muriel's desk, moving a few things on the surface out of the way. He was clutching a notepad and a pen, but they weren't open, and his arms were crossed.

"Sebastien Ranes, right?" he asked. I mechanically responded yes.

"Ten years old and traveling across the country all by yourself. Where are your parents?"

"I'm twelve, actually, officer," I spoke.

"Ohh ... you're twelve. Well, that makes all the difference."

"Today's my birthday," I blurted out, nervous. I thought it must've fallen on deaf ears. But he laughed.

"Today's your birthday, too, huh? One helluva present, don't ya think?"

"I'd rather not think about it, actually."

"I bet," he replied, looking me over. He opened his leather-bound tablet.

"So, one more time ... where are your parents?"

"My mom is getting married in San Francisco right now."

"Today? Why aren't you there at the wedding?" he asked.

"I dunno. Marcus asked me the same question."

"Don't you know that it's dangerous to be on the bus by yourself?" he quizzed.

"Marcus is watching out for me. As long as I'm with an adult, I'm fine."

He grunted. "Hmmph. Marcus is watching out for you, eh? Did you know he just got out of jail?" the officer asked.

"Prison," I corrected him for the second time. "He just got out of prison."

The police officer put his book away and stopped taking notes.

"Does your family know that you're on the bus, Mr. Ranes?"

"Yes, sir. My mother put me on the bus the other night."

"So you've been on the bus how long now?" he followed up.

"Almost a day and a half, I think. I got on in Stockton at three in the morning," I answered. I was beginning to feel pressured.

"Who's picking you up?"

"I have grandparents who are going to meet me in Mount Vernon, Missouri, and I'm getting off in Altoona, Pennsylvania, to go live with my grandma."

The police officer now looked horrified. "Let me get this straight: you've been on the bus for almost two days, and you're going all the way out to Pennsylvania alone?" He shook his head in disbelief. It may have been concern that registered across his face, but I couldn't read it very well.

"I'm telling the truth, sir," I rejoined.

"I guess you are," he answered, not knowing what else to do with me. "Did you say anything at all to the girl on the bus?" he asked.

"Amber? No, I didn't."

He looked at me with a raised eyebrow and made a quick note in his book. "She told you that her name was Amber?"

"No. I just thought she looked like an 'Amber.' That's what I called her. The only thing she said to me was 'You're welcome.'"

"Well, her name was Luanne," he corrected.

I needed to ask, as it seemed like my only opportunity. "How did she die?" I wanted to know. He looked at me hard and hesitated.

"Well, I guess you're man enough to travel across the country alone ..." he rationalized. "Do you know what an abortion is, Sebastien?"

"My sister's called me that a few times."

He buckled in shock at my words. "I hope not. She was pregnant and went and saw a doctor, probably in Phoenix. They cut her baby out of her, and she bled to death from the complications. I found the paperwork from her visit in her purse." A grimace was cut across the bottom of his face, speaking his true feelings loudly. He obviously disapproved. That much I could tell.

"Why did she have an ... abortion?"

He just shrugged and didn't respond. He stepped toward the door and turned the knob. I thought he was going to say something, but he only hesitated. He opened the door and ushered me back outside and into the hallway. Muriel Rodriguez was waiting for us to finish. She smiled at the officer.

"Finished?" she asked.

"All yours. Thank you," he replied. He was more interested in the woman than he was in me. I quickly made my way down the hall, happy that my interrogation was over and that he didn't ask anything about Flagstaff. I had sent myself into a panic for nothing. They were only concerned about the pale-faced girl, Luanne.

As I crossed over the threshold from the strange world of *Employees Only* and back into the land of listless travelers, I felt an immediate wave of relief pass over me. So much was going on around me that it seemed like the world was closing in on me. First, Leigh Allen in Flagstaff, and now Luanne in Gallup, dying slowly in front of us during the dark of night, not but three feet away. The moment had built into something both heavy and immediate and made me think of all the times that I'd wished I had died.

The Gallup Terminal was one large room and didn't have a gift shop. A small counter with six stools bolted into the ground was all the place could cobble together for a dining facility. Marcus was sitting quietly in front of a cup of coffee all by himself, reading the paper. No one else was at the counter, and the cook didn't look very friendly.

I edged in beside him, set my bag down on the ground below me, and just waited for him to say something. The cook looked surprised that I sat next to Marcus but oozed over slowly with a spatula in hand.

"You with him?" the cook asked. I didn't know for sure if he was addressing Marcus or me. One of his eyes seemed not to focus anywhere in particular but took a continuous direction all on its own. When I finally caught the one good eye, it was burning a glare at me, waiting for a response.

"Yeah, we're together," I replied. "May I have a glass of orange juice, please."

The cook didn't move a muscle, excepting his one crazy eye. I looked away, feeling embarrassed for a moment. Marcus was staring back at him, equally frozen in place. The world seemed to have momentarily stopped, and the only people within view were locked in a frozen showdown. For a second, my brain was telling me that life was now a shop display, but I knew it wasn't so. No one looked real anymore. Slowly, after a long delay, the cook reached under the counter, pulled out a small glass, opened another door to a small

fridge below, produced the orange juice, and poured me the smallest portion I'd ever seen. I wondered if that was a kid's size. He
slammed it down on the counter, spilling most of it in the process.

"You going to eat?" he asked. Marcus finally came back to life
and moved on his stool.

"I'm going to have two eggs over medium, two strips of bacon,
toast, and hash browns." Marcus spoke his words directly. His
words sounded more like a challenge than an order for food.

"I was talking to the kid, not you," the cook growled.

"I'm going to have the same, actually," I replied, maneuvering myself in between the two of them and the bewildering tension. Now several other people were watching us, and as I glanced
behind us, it seemed as if they were frozen too and that only the
three of us were moving. But I could tell that what was going on at
the counter wasn't exactly wholesome. I had the feeling that the
cook didn't like Marcus because he was black. I never thought I'd
be in this kind of situation.

"Do you see that sign, boy?" The cook was now slightly turned
and pointing up at a small sign on the wall behind him that read
The Management reserves the right to refuse service to anyone.

"Yeah, I see it," Marcus responded. "You're refusing service to
me or what?"

"No, I'm refusing service to the both of you." He grabbed Marcus's
coffee cup, dumped the coffee on the ground beside him, and threw
the cup in the trash. I thought Marcus was going to say something
back, but he kept cool, grabbed his newspaper, and got up.

"Let's go, kiddo." We both got up and walked out the front of
the terminal in disgust. As we stepped out into the morning air, our
footsteps hit the sidewalk simultaneously as thunder cracked above
us. The sky had clouded over, but the sunlight was still escaping
through the gaps and briefly making it down to earth.

Gallup was made up of one long street, which hugged the roadway with flat-faced buildings on both sides. A small sign jutting
up from the sidewalk designated the main boulevard as *Historic
Route 66.*

Off to the far right, wrapping a corner at the end of the block, was a Woolworth's Department Store. Marcus spotted it first.

"Woolworth's! Maybe we'll be able to get something to eat there, or ... we might just be surrounded by a bunch of redneck cracker asses!" His voice warbled, and he sounded a bit upset.

We walked across the wide street together, both with our hands thrust in our pockets, heading for the diner. I thought about what I had said to the police officer about it being my birthday. Of all the birthdays I'd had so far and could remember, this one was much more than I had bargained for. It didn't feel like it was my birthday, but birthdays with my mom were never that much fun either. Half the time, she'd forget or confuse it with my sister's. There were never any parties, no presents or cake or anything else that usually went along with the occasion. I'd never been to anyone else's birthday party either, so I knew I had low expectations. Since we moved so much, it was a given that I just wouldn't be invited to anyone's birthday.

As we passed by one of the shops, I happened to catch a glance at the window display. I wanted to turn away and ignore it, but it was too late. Four dummies were perched close to one another in a group. They were all decked out in hunting attire. It was supposed to be a family. The fake family was all dressed in red plaid button-down shirts and orange safety vests and hats. It was a mother, a father, and two children. The mother looked ecstatic, like she had just won the lottery, and had her hands at her sides as if she was going to fly away in delight. The kids could've easily been Beanie and me. The male child was the youngest figure on display and was staring directly at me. They all looked happy. The father had a shot-gun leaning over his shoulder and a devil-may-care attitude. He looked on the verge of lighting a cigarette. It was too much. I just wanted to block it out.

"What are you thinking about?" Marcus asked. "You're awfully quiet."

I glanced over at him, breaking my gaze from the window. "Nothing. Nothing, really," I answered.

"Don't say nothing. Give me a better answer than that," he smiled, putting his hand on my shoulder.

I hesitated for a second. I looked back at the window again, wondering if I should tell Marcus. Telling him about the fake family would be weird. "Today is my birthday, but it doesn't feel like my birthday. I'm traveling across the country on a bus. I woke up in a pool of blood next to a dead girl, was interrogated by the police, and discriminated against by a 'redneck cracker ass' with a lazy eye. I just don't think it can get any worse than that," I said, shaking my head. "You know what I mean?" I added, in frustration.

"Ahh, well, I'd say that's a whole lot more than nothing. Wouldn't you?"

"I just didn't think I'd be having my twelfth birthday in Gallup, New Mexico," I said, as we quickly skirted the flat sidewalk past evenly spaced parking meters and a variety of different shops. Some of the stores had large mural paintings on the outside walls. The most elaborate was an Indian Jewelry Trading Post that had a scenic vision of a wagon train crossing the desert under a red-and-purple sky. It looked impressive, larger than life, and covered the entire face of the building.

Marcus took note of the giant painting, laughed, and patted me on the back. "Check it out ... that's you," he began.

"Huh ..." I replied.

"Early American settlers, pioneers, travelers, nomads with no home. Loners. Living life against the odds," he said with a bright tone, smiling.

"I don't feel like a pioneer, though."

"Well, look at it this way," he suggested. "Neither did they. In fact, I bet they were all downright miserable, hungry, and panic-stricken."

"Well, that sounds about right," I joked. "Do you think that cook back there was a pioneer?"

Marcus grunted disapprovingly at the man's mention. "Hmph. He was probably an outlaw or a drifter. They probably shot his ancestors in a town square somewhere. People like that are miserable and want to make everyone around them miserable, that's all." His words trailed off as he stopped talking about the cook and probably began thinking about him.

Just as we got to the front of the Woolworth's, I grabbed at the metal door handle and questioned him jokingly. "You're awfully quiet. What are you thinking about?"

"Nomads ... loners. They're like the twisted roots of a dead tree," he laughed. His words had more meaning than I first realized. My mind skipped like a record as his words registered in my subconscious.

Woolworth's was busy for almost eight in the morning. Several people were already in the small restaurant area eating breakfast. Frying bacon, eggs, and coffee pungently assaulted us invisibly. The smell of food was pleasing. The sounds of talking and soft shopping music had a welcoming pitch to them.

Marcus had a concerned look on his face as he quickly scanned both the store and restaurant. He looked relieved when he saw a middle-aged black woman working the cash register, waitressing, and Monty sitting alone at a table eating breakfast, holding the newspaper.

"There y'all are. I was wondering what the 'heyll' happened to the two of you," he called out to us from where he was seated.

"We got turned around a bit and found ourselves south of the Mason-Dixon, if you know what I mean," Marcus replied, as we joined him. Monty was swabbing up his egg yolk with his toast, which sure looked good.

"Lemme guess ..." he began. "You two went over and copped a squat at Roger's in the terminal?"

"How did you know?" I replied.

"Hmph," Monty responded, finishing his mouthful of food. "Guess I should've warned you 'bout that. With all the grief on the bus earlier, I didn't have a quick minute. Somebody needs to tell that fool that the South surrendered long ago."

A young, skinny black waitress with long, puffy hair that hung down past her shoulders like a curly triangle approached with coffee cups and a full, fresh pot. She looked me over and hesitated giving me a coffee cup. "Well, well ... look who's travelin' in style. Good morning, sweet stuff."

"Good morning," I responded, beaming.

"Can I take you home? You sure are cute," she added.

Monty laughed and said something that I couldn't make out. She ignored both of their snickers and sighed. "Men is all the same."

"You never that nice to me, Jeannie!" Monty answered.

She addressed me again. "You want some breakfast, baby?"

"Please." I couldn't stop staring at her. I thought for a second that she must've been the most beautiful woman in the world. Maybe it was the constant assault of ugliness on the bus, or maybe she was that beautiful. Whatever it was, I couldn't stop staring at her.

"Bacon and eggs?" she asked. Her long, thin fingers touched down on my shoulder. I was thankful that I had taken off my brown puffy jacket. I just nodded yes endlessly, like a fool.

"Same for you, I suppose," she added, noting Marcus.

"Over medium."

She scribbled some notes on her pad and walked away. I watched her slip away behind the counter. All of us were fixated on her. She was better to look at than what we had been staring at for the past few days.

"Now, that's a woman," Marcus whispered, winking at me.

I sat in silence, drinking my coffee, watching the waitress in her red-and-white uniform quickly moving around the tables. She didn't have a name tag on either.

"Mmmm. Someone's in love," Monty pointed out to Marcus, who smiled and laughed at me.

"Did we get a new bus?" Marcus asked Monty.

"They's gassin' it up right now ... as we speak."

"You two got the rundown, huh?" It was more code that I didn't understand.

"What's the rundown?" I blustered.

Marcus debriefed me. "When you get the twenty-question routine from John Law."

"Ohh ... he only asked me how I knew her name," I replied.

"How did you get to know her name? Y'all get to socializin' back there? I thought she was sleeping the whole damn time," Monty questioned me.

"No. I actually didn't know her name." Monty looked at me, confused, but Marcus was leaning back in the booth, smiling. "Is that what you told the cop?"

"Uh-huh," I nodded affirmatively.

"Heh!" Monty spat. "You did good then, kid. Never tell the man nuthin'. Let them find it out on their own. They's getting paid to find out, and they don't cut no check for squawkers."

I sipped my coffee, not having any answer, soaking in Monty's logic. Monty and Marcus continued talking. I pulled out my notepad and started taking notes. I wrote down several words and phrases that I'd heard come out of Monty's mouth. I tried to recollect what I wanted to say about Phoenix and maybe even a few words about Leigh Allen and Flagstaff. The food came quickly but hung in my throat and sunk into my stomach like a rock. So far, it was some of the worst food I had eaten on the entire trip. I did my best to eat and not let on.

"Well, boys ... this is our last meal together. I'll be steppin' off up here and someone else'll be taking y'all onward."

"You're the best driver I've had so far, Mr. Monty."

"This boy does got that ol' silva tongue!" Monty remarked to Marcus. "I appreciate that, youngun'. Fo' sho'. Just remember, I don't eat with all the passengers on the bus. You just get on up to Pittsburgh with Marcus safely, hear?"

"I do," I replied. I finally understood everything he said. I guess it was just a matter of time. With that, Monty stood up and started putting all of his stuff back in his pockets, just like the last time I had watched him. He dug into his wallet, pulled out some money for the entire breakfast, and put it on the table.

"C'mon now. You don't need to do that," Marcus urged.

"No, no, no. It's alright. I spend my money my way, hear me?" He laughed as he stuck his wallet in his back pocket.

"Thank you for breakfast, Monty," I said.

"I'll see y'all up at the bus. I gotta go punch out," he replied, as he stuck a toothpick in his mouth and headed for the door. He waved at the young waitress on the way out, giving her a long look.

Marcus and I sat in Woolworth's restaurant for another ten minutes and finished the last of our coffee.

"Sebastien, I want to tell you something."

"Yeah?"

"That girl dying like that bothered you a bit, huh?" Marcus sipped his coffee and was watching out the window of the diner. The rain had intensified and was beating against the glass like it was target practice and the glass was just in the way.

"A bit," I answered. "I've never seen that much blood before."

"You ever see a dead person before?"

"No. I haven't. Have you?"

"Yeah, seen plenty. Saw a lot more in prison, but I was 'bout your age when I saw my aunt sleepin' on the couch. I just thought she was resting. She looked so peaceful. She looked the same at the funeral."

"I've never been to a funeral either."

"That's a shock. I've been to more funerals than I have weddings," he admitted.

"I've been to a lot of weddings though," I supplied.

"Well, that's the way it probably should be." He considered his words carefully.

"Marcus, why did that woman, Amber ... I mean Luanne, have surgery to take her baby out?"

"Who told you about that? The cop?"

"Yeah, he said that was how she bled to death." The waitress passed us one more time with the coffeepot, offering a refill. We both were done and said "No thanks."

"Well, you can rarely believe the word of a cop, but he was probably telling the truth."

"But why did she do it?" I repeated the question, hoping he had some kind of answer.

"Here you are in Gallup, New Mexico, on your birthday, half-way across the country with no family of any kind, travelin' with an ex-convict and the driver's license of a pedophile in your jacket pocket, and you're asking why some woman doesn't want her kid? I should be the one asking you. You're the one with the insight, not me." Marcus had a funny tone in his voice that softened what he was saying, but I felt the sting of it regardless.

"Well, it looks different the way you put it ... like that, I mean," I stumbled, more mumbling my thoughts than speaking them.

"My momma's waiting for me in New York. Where's your momma at? She waiting anywhere for you?" He put it straight at me.

"You know that she's not waiting for me."

He turned his coffee cup on the table with his fingers for a second. "Trust me when I tell you this, because it's true. I've told you a few things now that I hope you keep in the front of your mind. This is one more, understand?"

"What is it?" The words left my lips in a bare and cold whisper.

"You may love your momma, that's surely a natural thing, but nowhere is it written that she has to love you back. That's something most people don't want to know but I figure it's time for you to get with."

I didn't respond.

"Sounds harsh, huh? There's no guarantees on something like that, buddy. They either will or they won't. A woman who just off-handedly throws her child on a bus with thirty-five dollars just ain't right. Got that?"

I must've looked like a wilting flower because Marcus was right, but he eased up on me, watching me fade right in front of him.

"It's alright, though. It may be hard to hear it, but it will be a lot easier livin' with it. This is the kind of thing that knowing it makes a man out of ya. No one ever told me any of this, had to be learned."

I cleared my throat. "I hope I never see her again, or Dick."

"Well, buddy, I hate to say this, but you probably will."

"What am I supposed to do then?"

He shook his head, stood up, and left the tip for the waitress. Putting a hand back on my shoulder, he finished his thought. "Ain't much you can do, is there? Just don't be too bitter about it, and always treat women with proper respect, got that?" Hearing Marcus telling me about Charlotte made me feel a lot better and less angry inside.

"I'm cool," I said. He laughed.

"Cool, huh? You just might be from the ghetto after all."

"Have a nice trip, boys." The waitress hailed us as we left. I caught a last brief glimpse of her from the other side of the window. She was leaning over, wiping a table, and smiling at us. I couldn't help but look down the cut of her shirt. I knew I'd never see her again, but I hoped I'd never forget how pretty she was. I must've had a thing for waitresses now.

The rain was unrelenting as Marcus and I waited with the rest of the passengers under the building's overhang for the replacement motor coach to pull into place. We had passed a few porters who were standing inside the terminal with all of our luggage blocking the entryway. I didn't see my bag, though I grabbed only a quick glance, but if it got lost, rerouted, or stolen, I wouldn't be upset in the slightest. A light breeze pushed some of the falling rain against us, touching my cheeks in the cold morning air.

"Why is it taking them so long?" I wondered.

"Well, these dirt farmers ain't in any hurry out here like the two of us. There ain't a damn thing going on out here but the rent," he answered sarcastically.

We both glanced over at the automatic doors of the terminal as they slid open and Monty appeared. He saw us, smiled, and came right for us.

"Well, boys," he began. "This is it for the old man."

"Far as you go, huh?" Marcus asked. They shook hands quickly and then hugged.

"Thirteen hours behind the wheel is long enough for me. I'll be headin' back after my mandatory eight hours off."

"It was nice meeting you, Monty. I don't think all the Greyhound drivers are like you," I told him warmly. I meant it too. It was pretty easy to surpass Frank Burns, but it would be difficult to meet someone like Monty again.

"Either of you two want to tell me what y'all were up to in Flagstaff?" he asked. Something told me that it was bound to come up. I looked at Marcus, hoping he would explain it. He gave me the same look and then settled back on Monty. He pulled his pack of cigarettes from his pocket, lit one, and then offered one up to the old man.

"You remember the man in the tan suit? White guy, kind of tall, red face, bad acne?"

Monty gave us both a thoughtful look as he lit his smoke, trying to recall the passenger. "Yep. I 'member 'im. He had a funk like he didn't bathe and had a real dirty asshole."

"Mmm-hmm. That's the one," Marcus rejoined. "Let's just say that some of his interests weren't altogether wholesome," he replied, motioning at me. "After he got off in Phoenix, he showed up in a fake cop's outfit in Flagstaff. I had to sort him out as he thought the youngun' here was his luggage."

Monty's face hardened and grew grim. "He was like that then, huh? Kiddie fiddla. Folks like him showin' up on the bus more an' more," he responded bitterly.

"I'd appreciate it if this just stayed between us," Marcus asked of him.

"You got nothin' to fuss 'bout, young man." I was unsure of who, exactly, he was talking to, as he could've just as easily been addressing Marcus as myself.

"If I hear anything 'bout it at all, I'll send you a message, see. Best check when you get up to Saint Louis or Pittsburgh."

"You don't need to get involved," Marcus suggested. "It will just complicate things for you."

"I wouldn't want to get anyone in trouble," I said. My voice came out meekly, and I was unsure if they heard me.

"Best I leave y'all some kind of message that only the three of us will understand, else if it ever came back, people might ask."

Marcus and Monty contemplated the message over their cigarettes.

"You could just leave us the message with the information booth if people were looking for the two of us," Marcus uttered, more to himself though.

"But like code or somethin'," Monty spoke back. My brain spun upon the suggestion.

"How about 'Daryl Hall'? The message could just be 'Daryl Hall' if everything's fine and no problems," I spoke up bluntly, blurting it out just as the idea formulated in my mind.

They both laughed at my suggestion. I felt embarrassed and looked away, shaking my head for not thinking before I spoke.

"That's not a bad idea," Monty agreed.

"And what if people are asking questions?" Marcus joined in.

"'John Oates,' " I replied simply, somewhat relieved.

The two of them thought it over and agreed on the message, as it was simple and no one else would get it.

"I'll leave the message for Sebastien Ranes, alright?" he queried.

"Okay, we'll check in Saint Louis and Pittsburgh."

Monty laughed about the whole thing. It was humorous any way you looked at it.

"One thing though," Marcus interjected, gravely. "What if there's heat?"

"C'mon now, you shouldn't be havin' any of that kind of trouble. You sent that dirty white boy home to his momma, din't ya?" Monty was checking the severity of the beating Marcus gave to Leigh Allen.

"He was still in one piece when we left him crumpled up in his van," he replied.

"Sara Smile," I mumbled.

"Pardon?" shot Marcus.

"Just say: 'John Oates and Sara' if there's heat. Whatever that is."

"What do you think 'heat' is, youngun'?" Monty put it to me directly, shaking his head.

"Uhhh ... police?"

"Hmm. I reckon, huh?" he finished.

The three of us stood there for a few more minutes watching the clouds tumbling across the sky and slowly beginning to black out the last fragments of blue. When the bus finally pulled up, the porters slipped through the automatic doors and parked the carts on the platform alongside the huge, aging metal monster. The replacement bus was much different looking and noticeably older than our previous transportation.

"Damn, a forty-foot Buffalo! They must've had this thing in a garage somewhere. Sure glad I ain't drivin' that." He was fighting to conceal his laughter but couldn't help but let it slip out.

"Something funny, old man?" Marcus smiled at him.

"Oh no. Enjoy that ride, boys. Enjoy that ride."

When all the bags were aboard and the compartment doors were shut and locked, our new driver stood by the doorway welcoming everyone up and checking their tickets. Monty's replacement was a woman. I was only surprised for a moment, as I remembered that the majority of my school bus drivers were women too. After that, it didn't seem so out of place, even if she was the only female Greyhound driver that we'd seen so far. After Monty finally said his goodbyes to us, he meandered over to the lady and shared a few words with her. Marcus and I made our way toward the bus, hoping we'd be able to get the backseat again.

From the looks of things, it probably wasn't going to be a problem, as a few more passengers had disembarked, and on first glance I couldn't see anyone new. The thought crossed my mind that maybe at some point Marcus and I might be the only people on the bus, even though it was highly unlikely.

The thunder above us was loud and sounded like a bowling alley in heaven. As flat as the earth was in this part of New Mexico, there was probably plenty of room for bowling. As I stepped up onto the bus, it became clear what Monty must've been finding so funny. The seats didn't look as comfortable, and the coach wasn't as big and spacious as the one before. There were still overhead compartments, a toilet, and a backseat, but no overhead lights, no floor lighting, and the chairs looked worn-out and hard. The windows actually had red curtains on them too. I couldn't figure out why, but everything was red instead of the traditional gray-and-blue Greyhound color scheme. All those thoughts faded as I saw that no one, again, had wanted anything to do with the backseat.

6.

ALBUQUERQUE, NEW MEXICO

After we pulled out of Gallup, I started taking notes about what had happened with Leigh Allen in Flagstaff and Luanne's death. So much had actually occurred on the bus that I started feeling drowsy and experiencing a sense of complete overload. Most days I stayed glued inside my bedroom, protected from the world and avoiding as much as possible. But out here, alone, I was opened up to everything and didn't have the ability to hide if I needed to. I began thinking about all the conversations I'd had with Marcus, and it slowly began to dawn on me that for whatever reason, he had in twenty-four hours been able to give me more advice and guidance than either of my parents had in twelve years. I knew that feeling this isolated for so long wasn't something that only I was going through, but so far, Marcus was the only person who seemed to understand it. And he at least gave me the benefit of the doubt of being somebody worthy of his time and consideration, which again was more than I could say for Charlotte, Dick, and her endless string of useless men.

Flat earth whipped underneath us in various shades of tan, red, and rust. Road signs welcomed us to *The Petrified Forest National Park*. Several other signs also pointed out that we were crossing the Navajo Desert. When the bus stopped momentarily in Grants, New Mexico, two Native American men boarded the bus. The old man was wearing a wide-brimmed black cowboy hat with lots of light blue jewelry. His son, who was taller and hulked up, looked serious, with a stern gaze. They had taken the seats that would've been occupied by Luanne had she continued. Marcus said hello to the old man as he came up the aisle toward the back and was within earshot.

"Aho!" he replied. When the old man saw me in the back corner, he didn't smile or say hello but just sat down in the window seat in front of me. From what I could see between the crack in the seat, he was holding some type of bushy green plant in his hand and waving it in the air, singing something quietly, almost under his breath. No one else was talking, the driver didn't have the radio on, and no one protested or seemed bothered by it. Listening to the old man singing started to lull me and made my eyelids feel as heavy as lead. I listened to the sound of his voice as long as possible before I slipped off into unconsciousness.

The experience of sleeping on a Greyhound bus is unlike any other. Something about rattling around in the back of a large, badly vibrating metal coffin and crossing endless miles of uninhabited earth has a way of heightening not just a few of your senses, but all of them. Typically, a person would benefit from such unfiltered and pure input, but being surrounded by nameless, faceless, unwashed, and unhappy strangers who are all going through different levels of muscular discomfort and joint pain shuts down the possibility of experiencing anything meaningful. Even in moments of complete bodily failure and heavy drooling, I was still acutely aware of the groaning engine, Marcus's Walkman, and the smell of whatever the old man was waving around in the seat in front of me.

Lying curled up on the seat, I began to notice that my body was really starting to feel the pain from the constant assault of my surroundings. My shoulders felt as if they were slowly turning into knotty wood, and my hands ached from being constantly clenched into tight fists, and my fingers felt like a collection of steel rods. The bus was transforming me into something else, from the inside out, and I was powerless to stop it. My brain was telling me that one day I would achieve an even greater status by becoming a lobby fixture with a pay television and a plastic seat permanently attached to me in some type of hideous and grotesque fashion. It was another stage in my eventual development from a boy into a full-fledged mannequin that was evidently under way.

The few times I opened my eyes, I saw the quick flashing of more road signs and colorful billboards whiz past. New Mexico had apparently decided to turn its barren and unused open landscape into revenue-generating real estate. Many of the signs, in the absolute middle of nowhere, warned of hitchhikers and instructed drivers not to pick them up. I knew that if I was on my own on the side of the road, waiting for someone to come pick me up, the last thing I would want to see would be one of those signs.

One sign read *White Elephant,* designating a town, but as far as I could see, there was absolutely nothing in sight except a semi-truck rest area and a weigh station. There was another large sign, brown and wooden and unlike all the other signs, that told the reader he was now crossing the Continental Divide. But even though the visibility was dramatically shortened from the thick and pelting rainfall, either side of the divide looked equally monotonous. Each one was as flat and sandy as the other. Small bushes littered the shoulder and the ground below us. Tumbleweeds were getting carried away on the wind and floating off the opposite side with the rushing sheet of excess rainwater.

Although I was aboard a bus of twenty-plus people, and even with Marcus sitting two seats over, feelings of isolation were playing with me, making me thankful for even a single breath of fresh oxygen. A heavy chemical odor floated from the restroom like a frantic jailbreak every time the door swung on its hinges. Cigarette smoke did little to disguise it either. But when boredom strikes, especially in the middle of the desert, it can be depressing.

Marcus was reading his poetry book again. Several times I had been able to see the back cover of the paperback; the photograph of the author had been captured in the middle of his taking a drag from an ashy butt. The large, round-faced black man stared out at me, squinting with a half smile. His hand was perpetually waiting to take the cigarette out of his mouth. Marcus glanced over at me and hit the hot-line button.

"What's going on over there? You gettin' eaten by boredom?"

"A little," I answered. "What would Langston Hughes say?"

Marcus shifted in his seat, piqued by my interest in poetry.

"Did you have any thoughts about the last piece I read you? What did you think of it?"

I squirmed, unsure of what to say. I'd thought about the poem a few times and had borrowed his book once to read it myself.

"Getting left behind," I answered.

"Really?" He looked at me questioningly. I felt as if he was challenging what I said. "That's what you thought of?"

"I did. Is it wrong?"

"There's no right answer, but you're definitely not on the wrong track, that's for sure. It's more than what I thought you'd say though."

"Will you read it again?" I asked.

"How about I read you something else? You down with that?" he asked, leafing through his book now.

"Okay, *I'm down*," I replied. He laughed as he flipped a few pages, never looking up at me.

"Here we go." He cleared his throat. "This should go along nicely with your 'getting left behind' feeling.

Now dreams
Are not available
To the dreamers."

I was again grabbed by Marcus's reading. I noticed one of the other passengers glancing back at us, listening in. The boredom was enough to make anything worthwhile. I thought Marcus was easily the most interesting person on the bus, without doubt. I was just glad to be sitting next to him.

"But the dream
Will come back,
And the song
Break
Its jail."

He closed the book after he finished reading the passage and watched me for a few moments without saying anything further. He handed me the book turned to the page of the poem that he had recited, and I read it carefully.

"That's cool," I said. " 'And the song break its jail,' " I pondered aloud. "Does it?"

"Every time," he answered peacefully. We both lapsed back into silence and daydreaming.

I started taking more notes on the toll that riding across endless vistas of vast nothingness was taking, and the increasing fidgetiness of my fellow passengers. It seemed that people were now making more-frequent trips to the bathroom just to get out of their seats and move around. A couple of the same offenders were returning habitually to smoke cigarettes, which was beginning to cause noticeable tension for the riders who were getting stuck outside the lavatory, waiting for them to finish getting their fix, only to find the bathroom turned into a smoky and acrid choke box.

A large green road sign slipped by, pointing out mileage: sixty-five more miles to Albuquerque. The distance wasn't far, comparatively. The miles began to fade like they were falling faster the longer I kept my eyes closed. I had hoped, curled up on the seat, that it was all a dream, and I would soon wake up in my bed tucked away in the attic of my grandma's house, in front of the arched window that looked down onto the quiet street outside. But if I opened my eyes and discovered that I was in Gallup, or worse still, Flagstaff, I'd probably get off the bus and just wander away into the rain-soaked Painted Desert around me. But I knew better, and I knew that I could've never dreamed what I'd seen in the past two days. If I did, I probably would've jarred myself awake long ago. There was most likely many a great number of things that a person could dream about vividly, but driving across country on a Greyhound bus for three days surely wasn't one of them.

The hours of the early afternoon passed by us quickly and quietly. Marcus and I both reclined almost motionless and speechless, listening to our Walkmans and only breaking to use the "head," as he kept calling it. After I had successfully exhausted every song on my Hall and Oates tape, I gave a listen to the Simon and Garfunkel tape that the girl from the gift shop in Phoenix had given me. It only took a few songs to realize that Simon and Garfunkel was very different, and that each song told a story. One song that captured my attention was about traveling across America on a Greyhound bus. As I pieced the lyrics of the song together, it sounded as if the singer was going in the opposite direction. Another adult trying to make it out to California.

Around noon, Marcus and I briefly exchanged cassettes. He passed me two tapes and told me the order in which to listen to them. The first tape was *Chet Baker in Paris*. There were no lyrics at all and no photo on the front. My brain was far away, and I was startled when the machine clicked and grinded in my hand, going through its motions of auto-reverse. After listening to that strange voice singing "My Funny Valentine" once more, I switched over to the second cassette. *Oxygène* by Jean Michel Jarre. I made quiet guesses as to the proper pronunciation of the words in my head and wondered if the performer was a man or a woman. No words at all, but it was much livelier, more upbeat, and it sent my imagination into overdrive. The music seemed other-worldly and extra-terrestrial. Sound effects, synthesizers, and laser battles fired off in my head.

By midafternoon, the coach began to go through its usual set of operations as we slipped off the freeway and mounted the off-ramp heading into downtown Albuquerque. I was now two and a half days from Stockton and a day and a half from Altoona. As I checked out the schedule and my map, it felt like the halfway point, even though we most likely had already passed it. The rain was still angrily attacking the flat desert earth; brown water gushed through the gutters below us. In several places, the rainwater was already over the tops of the curbs and flooding the sidewalks. Mist and thick clouds rolled across the angular surfaces of nearby mountains that shot straight up. The tops were obscured and could've continued up into outer space. They could have gone higher than any peaks I'd seen before.

The bus slowed, the driver spoke a few words over the intercom, and the air-conditioning shut off, as it seemed mostly unnecessary now. The rainy May weather chilled the air outside and again
made me thankful for my brown Salvation Army windbreaker. My
mother called it "monkey shit brown" when she bought it, which
didn't make me very happy to receive it, or to have to wear it to
school every day.

I started to believe that all the terminals would look the same
after a few more miles, but when I stepped through the single glass
door, which wasn't automatic, I was shocked at how small the terminal was. There were only three double rows of padded black vinyl
chairs and absolutely no pay televisions, no vending machines, and
no homeless people loitering around in the lobby or in the hallways.
Large red tiles that covered the floors had the look of being recently
mopped. The trash cans stood empty, and the sand-filled ashtrays
were void of any *vachas,* which is what I had heard one passenger
refer to them as in Phoenix as he made the rounds collecting anything worth smoking. I had taken notes and committed the sight to
memory. I'd never seen anyone collecting used butts before. A few
stands holding brochures stood against the wall next to the ticket
counter, where an elderly man in a well-pressed and very neat
Greyhound uniform was standing guard and at the ready.

"Wow, this place is a real throwback," Marcus whispered in my
ear.

"What do you mean?"

"Smells like bingo balls, *Reader's Digest,* and hot coffee up in
here," Marcus said. I couldn't smell any of it. My nose was still
recovering from the vents that had been blasting poisons at me for
the last eight hours.

"Smells like old folks," I muttered, evaluating the mustiness of
the place.

"That's exactly what I'm saying," Marcus remarked.

We wandered over to the gift shop, which was also very different from all the other gift shops. Most of the merchandise for
sale was Greyhound-related: small die-cast metal replica buses,

Greyhound T-shirts and sweatshirts, Greyhound hats, Greyhound maps, and even Greyhound uniforms.

"Damn, this place looks like the Greyhound Command Center," Marcus joked.

My eyes continued along the shelves past the Greyhound shot glasses, bumper stickers, and dinnerware. A small book rack stood near the cash register but was filled with only one book, *The History of Greyhound*. I wanted something to read during the trip, but I just wasn't ready for that. I would have to take a rain check on Harley Earl's brief history of bus riding, as it seemed like the last thing that anyone in a Greyhound Terminal would want to do research on.

Along the back wall of the gift shop were plain white T-shirts, plain white socks, plain white underwear, and shower kits. Marcus was looking through the clean clothes for something in his size.

"They have pay showers here, and we got about an hour and a half. I think it's about time I got myself straightened up," he admitted. "How 'bout you? You got another two days almost?" he asked me.

"How much are they?"

The man from behind the ticket counter had now crossed over into the gift shop and was watching us both. We were his only customers.

"Showers are a dollar fifty in quarters. Fifty cents if you purchase a shower kit. T-shirts and shorts are all a dollar a pair. The socks are fifty cents."

"Water hot?" Marcus asked.

The man beside the counter smiled, leaning very casually with one hand on the register and another gripping a white Styrofoam cup. "That water will burn the road-weary right off ya faster than bird shit through a butthole!" When he was done speaking, he lifted his small white cup up to his chin and spat in it.

Marcus held up a shower kit and some clothes, indicating that he was going to take him up on his offer. "Fresh drawers. Should feel good to have a shower."

"I know it would. How long you boys been travelin'?" he asked.

His name badge on his shirt pocket read *Harley*. I wondered if it was Harley Earl himself. He was looking right at me for a response.

"Stockton," I replied.

"California, huh? Y'all come in on that forty-foot Buffalo?"

"Yes, sir," Marcus replied. "Got on in Los Angeles. They switched out our last bus back in Gallup after ..." he hesitated. Harley's eyes squinted a little in recognition.

"I done heard about that over the radio earlier today. Damn shame."

"Yes, sir," Marcus replied.

I walked over to the wall and grabbed a shower kit, which consisted of a small Greyhound towel, a plain white washcloth, and an individual bar of soap. I also grabbed up clean socks, underwear, and a Greyhound sweatshirt. I did the math in my head and tallied up another eight dollars and change that I would have to part with. I was running out of money, but I still had plenty of café vouchers.

The old man laughed when I set my shower kit down near the register. "Lemme guess," he started. "Young man travelin' alone, deer in the headlights look about ya. You must be Sebastien Ranes."

I just stood there, shocked, remembering that Leigh Allen had approached me in much the same way.

"Take 'er easy, young fella," he spat again, never letting up on his grin. "I got a call from Bob Hastings in Lows Angle-eeze 'boutcha. Told me to keep an eye out fer ya."

"Yes, sir," I answered accordingly. "I'm Sebastien Ranes."

"I betchyu are. You French or sumethin', boy? Got a name like that, must be."

"No, sir, I'm not French," I answered.

"He didn't say you'd be travelin' with this here Neegra fella," he said, motioning to Marcus, who didn't seem to take any offense to the old man at all. The old man's tone seemed calm and genuine. I couldn't feel any tension. He looked at me squarely for a second time.

"He's alright? Been keepin' an eye out for ya?"

"Yes, sir, he's my friend," I confirmed.

"Well then, seems like everything's shipshape." The old man laughed a little, spat in his cup, and began to ring us up.

"Back when I was in Italy, during the war, a young Neegra fella, 'bout your age," he motioned again toward Marcus, "pulled my bacon out of the fire. 1942. Anzio front. Saved my life." Harley spat into his cup one more time. "I'd still be over there pushin' up the daisies and those pretty *I-talian* girls as well if it weren't for that fella holdin' off them Gerries with that old Chicago Typewriter."

"Chicago typewriter?" I asked, confused.

"Heh, heh," he laughed under his breath. "Thompson automatic machine gun, son. Mow 'em down like yatta county fay-re. Marines always called it a 'Trench Broom,' but that's another story."

"You were in the army?" Marcus asked.

"Served twenty years in the United States Army. Retired out there in White Sands a few years back. Hard not to put on a uniform in the morning, if ya catch my meanin'." He talked to us as if everything he said had a happy ending. It was hard to know if he had an unhappy day in his life by the way he carried on. "Some things are 'bout as natural as buckshot into the back end of a turkey."

Marcus held out his hand to the old man.

"Marcus Franklin. Nice to meet you, Harley." Harley quickly gripped his hand, which was darkly tanned, spotted, and thick.

"Harley Earl. Always a pleasure to meet nice young boys like yourselves. Where y'all headed?" he asked.

"Going out to New York. Got some family to see," Marcus responded. Harley acknowledged it with a sort of faraway look.

"Been there once. Was in love with a woman, but she just didn't feel the same," he said, reminiscing. "I always thought she felt just fine though!" he hee-hawed.

"Pittsburgh," I answered, when he turned his gaze my way.

"That's right. Gon' out to see yaw grams. She's got a French name too," he said with a devilish smile.

"Don't worry. She called here askin' 'bout ya earlier this

morning. Checking to see if you were fine and if you were in on time. What was that last name again? Beau ..."

"Beauregard."

"That's right. That's what it was. Beauregard," he rejoined, motioning his Styrofoam cup at me.

"Well, y'all bess get unda that hawt whata instead a standin' 'round jaw-jackin' it with me all dang day."

"Did my grandma say anything else?"

"She did. She said to call her later on when y'all get up to Amarilla'. She'll be waiting 'side the landline for ya."

"Thanks, Mr. Earl."

"Just call me Harley. Everyone else does," he smiled.

The restrooms and showers were located down the hallway from the gift shop. Several men were coming and going from the toilet section, which was connected, but no one else was taking a shower. The shower room consisted of a long tiled wall of shower-heads and knobs on one side, a long wooden bench in the middle, which was bolted to the floor, and lockers against the opposite wall. An open area between the lockers had pegs hanging from the wall to hold towels or clothes and whatnot.

I was more than slightly apprehensive about stripping down and getting buck naked in public. I'd showered many times at school, in gym class, with all the other boys, and I eventually got past whatever shyness and the awkwardness of it, but this was different. After Flagstaff, stripping down to my birthday suit wasn't high on my priority list, but at the same time, I was filthy and I needed to bathe. I maneuvered myself to the benches and examined a large sign that hung on one wall: *Please return all towels into the linen basket when done.*

I sat down on the bench, nervous, and set my shower kit beside me. My clothes felt as if they were stuck to me with the sweat and grime that had been blowing through the vents. I knew having a shower was a necessity and had to be done.

"Yo, I'm gonna go sit over there and see a man 'bout a grave, got me?" Marcus joked, stepping away back into the adjoining bathrooms through the connecting doorway.

"Alright," I answered.

"Don't use up all the hot water, now!" he announced, as he vanished around the corner. Nervous about the whole situation, I saw it as my opportunity and quickly got undressed, leaving my dirty clothes in a crumpled pile that should've been burned instead of ever being put back on.

Naked and clutching my hand towel, the individual-size bar of soap, and two dollars in quarters, I hurried over and quickly dropped the coins into the car-wash-style apparatus that was affixed to the wall.

By the time Marcus came back, I was already dressed and running a comb through my hair in the mirror. I had thrown away my old socks, underwear, and T-shirt. The Greyhound sweatshirt fit me nicely. I examined the red-and-blue logo behind the sprinting canine mascot that was printed across the front.

"All you need is a name badge now and you can get on the payroll," Marcus remarked, getting undressed.

"All the café vouchers you can handle," I joked. "I'll wait for you in the lobby," I announced, as I made my exit, leaving him in peace to shower. It probably looked like I was rushing out of there. Anyway it got sliced, I was.

I waved at Harley Earl as I passed by the ticket counter. He was still gripping onto his Styrofoam cup and spitting into it.

"Got all straightened up there, I see," he said, examining me carefully, with eyes squinting in the lights, spying my Greyhound sweatshirt. "Your jacket's done run ya a bit small in the arm, huh?" he asked, taking a closer look at my brown windbreaker.

"It's in pretty bad shape," I admitted, raising my arms a few inches, showing how tight the coat was in the underarm and how short it was in the sleeve. It looked threadbare and well worn.

"Well, let's see if we can outfit ya in something from the lost and found, now. Couldn't hurt." Harley walked down to the end of the counter and pulled out a midsize cardboard box and slid it with his pointed cowboy boot into the lobby. We both looked through it and quickly surmised that there wasn't much to be had. Harley scratched his head a second and thought to himself.

"Let me see ... wait right here." He kicked the box back under the long shelf and disappeared through a door behind the ticket counter. I stood near the vinyl seats waiting for him to come back. He reemerged a few moments later holding a dark-blue Greyhound uniform jacket, like the kind that I'd seen the porters wearing outside on the platforms. The jacket looked almost new.

"Since you've already got that sweatshirt, might as well go full bore and sport a crew coat as well. How 'bout that?"

I was surprised, as it was a really nice jacket. The name patch on the front said *Hank*.

"Won't 'Hank' be looking for his coat?" I asked.

"That ol' thing's been hangin' by a hook for a couple months now. Some fella that just stopped showin' up one day must've left it behind."

"It's really nice," I admitted, as I tried it on over my sweatshirt.

"A damn sight better than that road-worn garment you came in with, if you don't mind me sayin'."

"No, I guess not. Thank you," I said. Looking up, I saw that he was smiling. He could see that I liked the coat a lot. It was a bit big in the sleeves, but it made it all the more comfortable.

"I guess this nasty thing should find its proper place," he said, holding my old jacket out in front of him with two fingers, like it was a rotting carcass. "Normally, I'd burn somethin' like this, but I think the trash will just have to do." He was already behind the counter with it and getting ready to drop it down into a larger trash can.

"Wait a minute!" I shot. I forgot about the license. "I left something in my pocket," I admitted. Innocently, Harley quickly went through the empty pockets of the jacket until he pulled out Leigh Allen's driver's license.

"Well, what's this?" he asked, with piqued curiosity. I was reluctant to answer. He was reading the information slowly and rubbing his chin. I felt that I was on the verge of blowing the whole thing and would have to come clean.

"Leigh Allen," he read off, concerned. Then it hit me.

"It's my father's. My mother gave it to me before she put me on the bus. It's the only picture we had of him. She told me to keep it." I was lying through my teeth, trying hard to be convincing.

Harley Earl's face was all squished up, and he was squinting through the reading glasses that he'd pulled from his pocket, trying to get a better look at the photo. "He don't look much like any kin to ya," he rejoined.

"Everyone says that," I replied, downcast. "I only met him once. I didn't know who he was until later."

"Damn, that's one bad piece of work, son," he replied, handing me back the license. "Best put that someplace safe then."

"Thank you, Mr. Earl," I said, slipping the license into the inside pocket of my new coat. The pocket had a zipper, unlike my other jacket, which only had snaps. Harley Earl opened the top of the trash can near the counter and dropped the brown Salvation Army coat inside. He brushed his hands and smiled after the coat had vanished for good.

"That's that then, I guess," he stated, picking up his Styrofoam cup and lifting it once more to his chin to spit.

A moment later, Marcus appeared, walking up the hallway and running a comb through the thin beard that was forming around his face. "Nothing finer than a hot shower," he remarked. He noticed my new jacket and gave it a closer look.

"Hey now, I didn't see that for sale in the gift shop. We really gotta get you on that Greyhound payroll."

"Mr. Earl ... I mean Harley gave it to me. Said I can keep it, fit so nice," I replied.

"It's a step up, that's fo' sho', Sebastien ... I mean Hank!" Both Marcus and Harley laughed a little.

"I don't look like a Hank though, do I?" I asked.

"We got a little more time. What say you about getting a quick bite to eat before getting back on?" Marcus asked. Harley looked at the clock above the counter and interjected.

"Between us," he spoke low, "I'd probably pass on anything from that damn Grey Café. You might get yourself a bad case of the

Hershey squirts. Not fun when you gotta hit that cold steel toilet over an' over." It was just before eleven a.m., and he gave a second look to the clock.

"If y'all hurry, just round the side of the building you can catch the Roach Coach. The food's a damn sight better and a whole lot safer," he advised us, rubbing his stomach.

"What's the Roach Coach?" I asked.

"Nothin' to worry 'bout," Harley replied. Marcus got the exact directions for the best way to get outside quickly, and then we said our goodbyes. I thanked Harley one more time for the jacket and shook his leathery and muscled hand. We found our way around to the side of the building, where we spotted the Roach Coach parked where Harley said it would be. It was still raining, and several men in Greyhound uniforms were sheltered under an awning connected to the truck. Another group of men was huddled next to the building under the lip of the roof, keeping dry, smoking cigarettes, and drinking coffee. The two of us slipped beneath the truck's awning as a few other men shifted over and made room.

"C'mon now," Marcus hurried.

We both examined the menu. It was all Mexican food, and I didn't have a clue as to what I wanted to order. Marcus ordered almost immediately.

"*Dos tacos al carbon, por favor.*" He spoke to a man inside the truck through a small window above us. The cook was Mexican, and it seemed that his wife was the one who handled the money, as she approached us wearing an apron, a change belt, and a big smile.

"The same for you, honey?" she asked me. I didn't understand it at all. Marcus spoke to her for me.

"*Sí, sí.* No hot sauce *para el niño, por favor.*"

"What did you just say?" I asked.

"It's all good, partner. I got your back. Ever have tacos before?"

"Only from Taco Bell."

"What's Taco Bell?" Marcus wondered, slightly bewildered. The woman looked at him strangely after hearing his response. I tried to figure out a quick answer, maneuvering myself under the awning, trying to keep dry at the same time.

"It's like McDonald's, only they serve Mexican food," I explained. Marcus seemed surprised about the whole concept. He was unaware of Taco Bell.

"Is it any good?" he asked. The Mexican woman snickered.

"It's alright," I answered. "My mom likes it a lot."

He laughed. "Well, from what I know, that's really not the best endorsement, is it?"

"No, I guess not," I laughed.

"Maybe we'll pass one before we get to Pittsburgh. We can check it out."

"I'm surprised you've never heard of Taco Bell, Marcus," I replied. "They're everywhere!"

"Not where I've been, kiddo," he laughed. The world seemed perfect for a few minutes. Maybe it was the smell of food, or being clean, or just being somewhere completely new. I realized that when we got to Pittsburgh that would be it, and we'd have to say goodbye. I couldn't help but feel a little sad about it.

"Cigarettes, *por favor*?" Marcus asked the lady. When the tacos came, he handed me two of them. They were wrapped side by side on a piece of tinfoil and warm to the touch. I watched Marcus open his, pick up the lime wedge hidden inside, and squeeze it all over the food. When he looked over at me to see if I was eating yet, I did the same. They were good. I could've eaten four more. He paid the woman and never even asked me for money. I couldn't object with a mouth full of food. I felt bad for not paying my own way so many times. Marcus really was looking out for me, even though no one had asked him to.

"We better head back to the bus before we get left behind and made permanent residents," he stated. *"Gracias,"* Marcus told them, as we dashed out into the rain, leaving the safety of the awning behind us.

"Right behind ya," I rejoined, as we quick-stepped it back inside the terminal. After almost two days, I'd been through the routine of making quick stops and immediate bus reboardings so often that I tried to block out the monotonous but headache-inducing boarding calls that crackled out of the public address system above us.

The forty-foot Buffalo rumbled in its place against the platform. A few more seats had been vacated, and the bus was now the emptiest that I had seen it yet. The two Native American men were still riding with us and were in the same seats in front of us. The older man smiled and greeted us as we came up the aisle.

"Aho!" he cried out. His son joined him by raising up his McDonald's coffee cup.

"McDonald's, eh?" Marcus commented.

"We found the place down the block. I didn't think my father and I would've survived whatever it was they killed and were serving in that café," he joked.

"Yeah, we got something off the Roach Coach instead. I just didn't have the courage for that place either," Marcus replied.

"Roach Coach!" they both announced loudly, like a toast, raising their coffee cups into the air. I didn't say a word and took my seat next to the window, but I had the feeling that they had more than coffee in their cups. My grandpa often put brandy in his morning coffee. I suspected it was the same for them. Marcus and the younger Navajo man kept making cracks about the food they were serving in the café.

"I've smelled dead horses that were more appetizing," the old man added.

"Well, I'm sure someone on the bus ate at the café," the younger man admitted. "It's just a matter of time now," he laughed. I couldn't help but raise an eyebrow to the obvious pain that they were alluding to.

"Looks like we have front-row seats to the show," Marcus added, leaning forward and motioning toward the toilet.

"That's what I'm afraid of," began the old man. "I may not have brought enough sage." They all started guffawing as the bus started moving. The back-up alert sounded, and the bus began its slow rolling out into the lane for one more safe departure. Soon Albuquerque would be just another memory, reduced to a few lines in my note-book. The face of Harley Earl would be gone, but I'd always have his kindness and the jacket. Maybe I wouldn't remember how good the tacos were, but I would remember that it was the first time I ever ate from a lunch truck.

The weather outside looked ominous, and I had to settle in for another full day's worth of driving. Thankfully, the seats weren't as uncomfortable as they looked. Our new driver turned on the fan but not the air-conditioner, as it wasn't needed.

"Good afternoon, welcome aboard the 1364 continuing to Amarillo, Springfield, and Saint Louis. No alcoholic beverages, loud music, or standing in the runway. Thank you for choosing Greyhound."

I was shocked at the heavenly quality of the old bus's overhead address system. It didn't click, pop, hiss, or create unnecessary static. The driver's voice just floated down to us from nowhere, like warm water. Her message was ordered and polite. She was the first driver to call the aisle the runway, and she thanked us for "choos-ing" Greyhound, as if there was some other choice of transportation that I wasn't aware of. It was interesting enough that I felt obliged to make a few more notes.

"You writing a book over there?" Marcus uttered softly. I was fixed firmly against the raindrop-strewn window glass.

"Nah ... just taking some notes, y'know?"

"No. I don't know," he smirked.

"It will be good to talk to my grandma," I said.

"That's right," he remembered. "You're going to call her when you get to Amarillo?"

"What time do we get in?" I asked.

"Later today, sometime around supper ... maybe four, five o'clock," he estimated. "You got enough change to make the call?"

"Thanks, Marcus. I've got enough money," I replied firmly.

"I know you've got enough money, Sebastien. But do you got enough change? You can't just start stuffing dollar bills into the telephone. It ain't a burlesque girl, y'know?"

I checked all my pockets, rounding up and counting all the

dimes, nickels, and quarters in my possession. "Three twenty-five," I answered.

Marcus calculated the phone call in his head. "Should be about four minutes, maybe five if you're lucky."

"That's it?" I guffawed.

"Ain't cheap, man," he replied, stretching out.

I thought about what I was going to say in the few minutes that I would have her on the phone. She was the only person I really wanted to talk to.

"I don't think I've told you, but I might have to get off the bus tomorrow morning," I said to Marcus darkly. He just stared at me strangely, squinting with a half smile and half something else. I hadn't seen that expression on his face before.

"Why would you be getting off the bus? You're supposed to go all the way through to Altoona. Is there something that you're not telling me?"

"My mother's family," I blurted out. I didn't know how else to say it.

"And ..." he replied, waiting, his face now showing concern.

"My mother's family is going to meet me at the bus stop in Mount Vernon, Missouri, early tomorrow morning."

"Wait, are these some of the same people who were supposed to meet you back in Los Angeles but left you just danglin' in the wind?" His voice had a tone of incredulity.

"Yeah," I answered sheepishly.

"So what ... they're coming down to the bus station in the morning? What time?"

"Five in the morning." As soon as the words left my lips, Marcus burst out laughing.

"Really? I've got to see this. You mean to tell me you've got some family that's going to crawl out of bed at four a.m. just to get a quick glance at a passing twelve-year-old in the rain? Who are these people? And don't say 'my mother's family,' " Marcus replied, riled up, excited, and laughing. He was grabbing his side and shaking his head he was laughing so much.

"They're my grandparents ... my mother's parents, actually," I answered. My words must have hit Marcus hard as he quieted.

"Your grandparents?" he asked. I nodded. "Have you ever met them? You guys tight or anything?"

"No, I can't say that I have. What I've heard about them from my mother was that she didn't really get along with them and that they were always arguing on the phone."

Marcus contemplated my dilemma silently for a while to himself. After a few minutes, I spoke up, needing to break the silence.

"I don't want to get off the bus in Missouri, but I have to call my grandma in Altoona and tell her that I might have to stay over for a day and visit with them. If I get off, though ... that'll be it, won't it?" My voice broke apart. I didn't have the words to say what I was thinking again, but I guessed Marcus already knew. It wouldn't be the same without him.

I became distracted by the old man as he started singing the same song as earlier and waving his green plant in front of his face again. This time, a light amount of wispy smoke was coming from it. It wasn't on fire, but it was smoking. It smelled damp, earthy, but not nearly as bad as the constant billow of cigarettes from the bathroom that now smelled worse and was doubling as a death trap. I caught the eyes of the driver looking up at us in the long mirror. She didn't seem pleased by it all but just kept on driving without making any announcement. She had probably seen this type of thing before and knew better than to interfere.

Marcus leaned over and whispered a few words to me. "I spoke to the old man earlier. He said the bus told him that the spirit was getting ready to pass up to Great Grandfather and be free of the machine that held it." Marcus was smiling as he told me this.

"Are you serious? He said that?"

"He said the bus talked to him earlier this afternoon in a dream. The bus told him that its job of carrying people was no longer necessary."

"Uh, what did you say?"

He punched me lightly on the arm. "What the hell was I

supposed to say?" I did my best not to make a sound, but the pressure to giggle was intense.

"I'll tell you what. I'll get off the bus and wait with you, just to make sure someone's watching out for you. No sense getting off alone if they forget about you. Agreed?" It sounded like a fine idea as I listened to his explanation, and I wouldn't have to be standing by myself in the cold rain either.

"Besides, it'll only put us off schedule by two hours," he added.

The thought of having to meet older, more bitter versions of my mother was intensely unappealing and honestly the very last thing that I wanted to do. I didn't know them, and I didn't want to. If they did show up at five in the morning, they wouldn't be happy about it. Who would? My mother had once told me that they said I was a "bastard child" and that she should've gotten rid of me a long time ago because I was nothing more than excess baggage in her life. My brain kept repeating everything I knew or had ever heard about them, and I could tell that there just wasn't any room for happiness in there. I crammed into the back corner of the bus, obsessing about it.

"You doin' alright?" Marcus asked me, after about an hour of complete silence and barely a movement. "I thought you'd turned into a statue over there," he continued. His words were much darker to me than how he had meant them. My head pivoted mechanically on my neck to face him.

"You're serious about getting off with me tomorrow morning?" I asked, obviously petrified and hoping it wasn't showing.

"You betcha, kiddo," he asserted. "I'm not going to leave my man hangin' in Farmersville, U.S.A. Assed out in the cold all by his lonesome. You should know me better than that." He was doing a lot to make light of the situation for my sake.

"Thanks, Marcus," I replied, quieted.

"It's cool. Just don't blow a gasket over it. Understand?" he smiled, slipping on his headphones.

I reached inside my bag and pulled out my Walkman and my Simon and Garfunkel tape. I spent the early morning and better part of the afternoon staring blankly out the window at the passing world that was getting drenched in rain. The two Navajo men in front of us had mentioned that it was going to flood and that we might get to see an accident on the highway. The old man said that he was going to sing a song to protect us and keep the old bus spirit company.

Just after two in the afternoon, the old coach stopped very briefly in Tucumcari and refueled. No one got on or off, save Marcus. We were stationary just long enough to fill the tank and for the driver to smoke a cigarette next to the ticket window of the depot. Marcus ran to use the pay phone, but I couldn't see if he had finally gotten through as he'd stepped inside the depot, which was doubling as a simple gas station and a detached bathroom building. Only a few moments had passed when Marcus appeared up the steps almost soaking wet from briefly crossing through the downpour. He stood near the door and tried to brush off as much water as possible. He was holding two cans of soda.

"Damn!" he announced, coming up the aisle. "It's coming down like hammers and nails out there!" The old man thought his comment was funny and laughed.

"You got pounded?" he cracked, under a chesty laugh. When Marcus got to the back, he handed both of the cans of Coke to the son.

"Here ya go. Thought the two of you might enjoy a cold one." I was shocked that he gave the soda away, but I realized that his gesture meant more.

"Thank you, Marcus," the younger man responded.

"*Aho!*" cried the father again in delight. It was his trademark call now. Marcus laughed and then thrust his hands into the pockets of his leather jacket and produced two more cans of cold soda.

"You were beginnin' to wonder, huh?" he remarked, catching the look on my face.

The cold soda was refreshing, and we both drank it slowly listening to our Walkmans, mentally hundreds of miles away. I knew Marcus was thinking about getting back, and I didn't ask about his phone call for a change. I just hoped he'd been able to get through. I realized that if he had, he wouldn't have had time to buy us all soda.

By three o'clock in the afternoon, we had crossed over the border into Texas. A large sign, shaped exactly like the state itself, welcomed us to *the largest state in the Union*. Marcus shook his head in disgust when we both caught a glimpse of it. The old man actually flipped the bird with his middle finger at the sign.

"You'd think they'd take that relic down. It's offensive," Marcus spat.

"Why's that?" I asked.

"Well, first off, Alaska is now the largest state in the 'Union.' And the connotation of the word *Union* only serves as a symbol to rednecks far and wide, and people like that fool back in Gallup, who maintain 'Southern Pride,' if you catch my drift. God only knows what kind of road signs we're going to see driving through this next stretch."

"Well, it is the Wild West, right?" My mind locked onto a few fleeting images of Clint Eastwood standing in the middle of a dusty street, wrapped up in a poncho, chewing on a cigar.

"No. It's not the Wild West, Sebastien. Hell, we ain't even in the West!" he admitted, laughing. Marcus spoke loud enough that the old man had heard our conversation. He lifted himself up and leaned over the seat, jokingly beating the palm of his hand against his mouth, making that whooping war cry that all the Indians make in movies. I couldn't help but laugh at it, and the old man smiled at me.

As we drove across the unending asphalt and rolling plains toward Amarillo, I kept thinking about the conversation I had with Marcus back at the Woolworth's diner. He had told me bluntly that there didn't have to be any guarantee on a parent's love for their child. I wondered if my sister, Beanie, had already figured this out. Maybe that was why she had refused to leave Altoona or my grandmother's house ever again. If she knew, why didn't she bother to tell me, or stop me from leaving last summer? Looking back on it now, I was just being foolish. I was wrong for believing that everything was going to work out and be different. I was actually mad at Beanie for not coming with us. At the time, I thought I had to give Charlotte one more chance. I heard her words from the night before echoing in my head.

"It just wouldn't be fair to Dick, having to raise another man's son. Can't you understand?" I couldn't understand, and nothing around me made any sense. Having Leigh Allen's driver's license in my inside coat pocket kept my brain bouncing around angrily. I kept asking myself how she could have put me on the bus by myself without any thought for my safety. It seemed that both my sanity and my happiness only extended to the edge of the glass window that I was leaning against and no further. I wanted to scream out at the top of my lungs until I either turned blue in the face or was lying in a crumpled and exhausted heap on the floor. I knew I couldn't make a scene, and I wouldn't embarrass myself like that. I just sat perfectly still without saying a word and listened to Simon and Garfunkel. Maybe that's what "The Sounds of Silence" was. I would do nothing about it at all ... just as Marcus had said in Woolworth's. I didn't understand why, but he had also told me to always be respectful toward women, which I didn't see as related. Maybe at some point I would understand. Maybe it was important.

"Yo," Marcus tapped me on the shoulder, trying to get my attention. I took off my headphones and hit stop on the Walkman, ignoring the hot-line button altogether.

"Hey, Marcus, what's up?" My voice sounded hollow again.

"You alright? Deep in your head somewhere?" he asked.

"I was," I answered honestly.

"Are we cool?" he asked with a worried tone.

"Of course. You're not upset with me, are you?" I wondered. I'd had my headphones on all afternoon, essentially blocking out everything around me. The old man, his singing and his strange plant, the groaning of the bus, the toilet and its strange smells, all of it. Marcus had spent a good part of the afternoon talking with the old man and his son.

"When we pull into Amarillo in about twenty minutes, I'm going to go inside to the gift shop to buy some batteries. You going to come along or hold our seats?" he asked.

I pulled out my wrinkled bus schedule and examined it carefully for a moment before giving an answer. I ran my finger slowly down a long list of stops that we had already passed.

"It says that we're going to be here for thirty minutes. I have to call my grandma, but we can go to the gift shop first. Maybe they can give me some phone change," I finally replied.

"Works for me. Must be another fuel stop. We'll probably get ourselves a new driver as well."

"Time flies on the bus."

"Smooth sailing from here out, hopefully."

Amarillo was apparently the twenty-second bus stop on my route between Stockton and Altoona. I counted from Stockton down to Los Angeles and then out to Amarillo. When we merged into the city—the freeway drove directly through it—we very abruptly slowed and pulled into a small, blue-painted station that looked not just out of place but unlike any of the other buildings around it. The Greyhound Terminal resembled a converted church, with painted stucco and a neon sign, but no cross. A large rotating elongated greyhound dog turned above us.

"*Amarillo. Thanks everybody,*" was all the driver announced after she turned the key into the off position. She grabbed her clipboard and thermos and opened the door. Everyone on the bus got up to get off, as it was looking to be the last big stop of the day and probably one of the last places to get something good to eat. The rest of the stops would probably be just vending machines, if they even had those. We wouldn't hit Elk City until just before ten o'clock tonight, but the schedule said it was only another ten-minute stopping point. That usually meant that if the terminal didn't radio the bus that a passenger was waiting, we'd keep right on going. Oklahoma City was listed as a stop at almost midnight, with a forty-minute layover, and then Joplin, Missouri. Mount Vernon wouldn't have to be dealt with until five in the morning. The closer we got, the more I just wanted to get there and get it over with.

The lady driver smiled at me from under her umbrella as I touched down onto the ground and stood at the bottom of the metal steps. I was always the last person off, and after twelve hours of driving, she'd already figured it out.

"Nice jacket, honey," she said, admiring my would-be Greyhound uniform.

"Thanks," I answered, following close behind Marcus, heading for the terminal doors. As we crossed inside, the standard bus arrival call greeted us from above.

"1364 on aisle 1, to Springfield and Oklahoma City. Departure in thirty minutes."

I was expecting more Eagles again on the radio for some reason, but instead a song that I actually recognized came on. It was Hall and Oates, and it was the first time I'd heard the song not wearing my headphones. It was the second song on side two: "I Can't Go for That."

"They're playin' our song!" Marcus said with a grin.

"How appropriate," I answered.

All I really wanted to do was make my phone call and talk to Grandma, but I needed batteries. Standing with Marcus in the gift shop, I felt frustrated and just wanted the whole damn trip to be over. I'd seen enough, sat enough, listened enough, and talked enough. I was really missing being home and was feeling anxious about it.

I went through the slow process in the gift store of buying batteries and making sure that I paid for my own, not letting Marcus continually pick up the tab. I asked the girl behind the counter if she had change for the phone, and she gave me a dollar in quarters, which I had calculated on the bus would give me more than enough. Marcus brought a book down from a tall wire book stand next to the register and paid for it.

"Ever read this?" he asked. I craned my neck to get a better look at the title.

"What is it?"

"The Catcher in the Rye," he answered.

"No. What's it about?" I engaged him, looking at the books on the rack. They were all used and well read. The majority of them were Westerns or Harlequin Romances. I only recognized the romance books because my grandma read them nonstop. Even though I was looking over the book he had in his hand, my brain was disconnected and elsewhere again. On the way in, I'd seen the only pay phone, unattended. I felt magnetically attracted to it. I was just hoping Marcus wouldn't go into a long explanation about the book, but I knew I needed to act.

"I'm going to go make that call," I said quickly, interrupting what he was about to say. I headed for the phone in a mad dash, worrying that someone was going to step in front of me at the last moment and get in the way. When I picked up the receiver and put it up to my head, I was immediately slapped hard across the face by the lingering odor of cigarettes and beer. The phone looked and smelled heavily used and hadn't been cleaned in some time. There were several stickers for the same cab company plastered all over the sides of the metal housing. When I heard the hum of a dial tone, I dialed the numbers and then dropped in all my coins in a steady procession, listening to the clicking of them being registered and counted. After I dropped my last nickel in, the tone changed, and I waited. I thought it was about to ring. Instead, the line went dead and all my change dropped through the machine and deep into its bowels, not into the change slot like it should have. The machine had ripped me off and left me penniless. I gripped the handle and wanted to start beating on it, but I knew that was probably the worst thing to do, as the ticket counter lady was watching me with a grimace. I tried to stay cool, but I wasn't happy. I dialed zero.

"Operator?" a voice beckoned.

"Hello, I just put four dollars and twenty-five cents into the phone, and it took my money." I unfurled my tale of woe.

"I'm sorry, there's nothing I can do on this end of the phone line. Would you like to make a collect call instead?"

"What about my money?" I asked.

"You'll have to call a local number and get in touch with a technician where you're located."

"But I'm in a Greyhound bus station in Amarillo."

"I'm sorry, but I can't help you. Would you like to make a collect call instead?" she repeated.

"Yes ... I guess," I answered, dejected.

"What's the number?" she asked. I slowly and carefully read it off, doing my best not to stumble over it or chew on my words. I read it off like it was today's date or something from the Bible.

"And who's calling?"

That was the part that I stumbled and stuttered over every time somebody asked that question. My name. It was the absolute hardest phrase for me to speak clearly. Why? I didn't have a clue. But saying "Sebastien" paralyzed me.

"Uhm ... it's like, ah ... like ..."

"I'm sorry, what's your name?"

"Like, uh, Sebastien," I replied.

"Michael Devin?" she repeated.

"No! Sebastien," I spat back, annoyed. Dealing with the operator was quickly becoming humiliating, and I hated it, but it was something that I just couldn't escape, no matter how hard I struggled. Fighting an inner urge to stutter only made it worse. I always thought maybe it wouldn't be like this if I just changed my name.

"One moment, please," she stated. I heard noises in the background, and after a moment, the phone on the other end started ringing. On the third ring someone picked up.

"Hello?" my grandma answered. It was her, finally.

"Would you accept a collect call from Michael Devin?"

"Ah ... Whooooo?" my grandma's voice swayed over the line, confused.

"Grandma, it's me!" I interrupted the operator.

"Sebby, honey? Is that you? Yes, I accept," she said.

"Thank you," the operator responded and then clicked off.

"Who in the heck is Michael Devin, honey?" she asked me immediately.

"No, Grandma, she misheard me. It's good to hear your voice," I replied, speaking loudly into the booze-soaked receiver.

"Where are you, Sebby?"

"I'm in Amarillo, Texas, Grandma."

"Is everything alright? Are you having a good trip out so far?" she asked. I could hear the obvious concern for me in her voice.

"I guess," I replied, immediately seeing the error of saying that now. "Everything's fine. Just can't wait to see you, that's all," I added.

"How's your mother? Is she alright? Has she been feeding you?"

"I don't know. I guess she's alright?"

"Honey, whattya mean you don't know? Is she feeding you? Is she there with you now?"

I was confused now. "No, Grandma. She's supposed to be in San Francisco getting married to Dick Brown."

"Whaaaaaaat? Where's your mother? San Francisco? She told me the other day that she was coming out with you on the bus!" I could hear the terror on the other side of the line, and it wasn't what I was expecting.

"No, Grandma, it's just me," I supplied. It was the very last thing that she wanted to hear.

"Aww my gaawwd, Jesus, Sebby. Your mother's going to give us all a heart attack over here!" She was flabbergasted, and I could hear her talking with my grandpa, who was probably standing beside her in the kitchen. "He says he's by himself and that Charlotte's in San Francisco." I very clearly heard my grandpa swearing in the background, calling my mother names.

"Sorry, Grandma. I didn't mean to call and upset you."

"Awww, honey!" she cried out. "Don't you feel bad now. When are you getting into town here?"

"Day after tomorrow, real early I think, but it depends ..." I started.

"On what?" she asked, really beginning to worry now.

"I think my mother's family is going to meet me at the bus station in Mount Vernon, Missouri. They might want me to stay a few hours and catch a later bus. I don't know."

"Oh my gawwwd, Sebby. You do know how to make your

grandma worry, don't ya, sweetie?" She chuckled a little at the mention of my mother's family. I could hear her smiling on the other end, trying to make me feel better.

"Will you call me from their house if you stop?"

"I will, Grandma. I promise," I shouted into the plastic handset.

"I love ya, honey," she said. It was the one thing that I needed to hear the most. I paused, unable to respond right away.

"I love you too, Grandma. I miss you."

"Don't you worry ... you just hurry on home now."

"Alrighty," I answered, and then got off. I could hear my grandpa in the background still stringing out the expletives. Even the barest mention of my mother upset him. My heart sank with the release of the receiver. My chest deflated, my head spun, and my legs got weak. I was still over a thousand miles away and would have to just suffer through the rest, trying to stay positive.

I was thankful that I had Marcus to wait with me in Mount Vernon. My secret hope was that my mother's family wouldn't show up and we'd keep right on going. With the way things already were with my Aunt Sharon in Los Angeles, anything was possible.

I found it disturbing to realize my mother had outright lied to my grandmother, tossing me on the bus and hightailing it away. I knew she never had any intention of coming, as I'd been subjected to listening to wedding plans for months. I also knew she was just appeasing Dick by sacrificing me to the wolves. I was her loose end, and she would do whatever was necessary to get rid of it. As I walked back out to the bus, I knew I couldn't hate anyone more than I hated my own mother.

7.

OUTSIDE OF ELK CITY, OKLAHOMA

As soon as we left Amarillo, the world started to change. The bus pivoted toward the north and slowly began twisting between hills and climbing in elevation. Traffic thickened, and more people, more semi trucks, more everything was all around us. The two men from the Navajo Nation had drifted off, but the old man kept talking in his sleep. At times I couldn't tell if he was talking or singing. Slowly, the red desert gave way to modest vegetation, trees, and the return of sprawling farmland. Huge barns dotted the landscape and could be seen rising from the horizon over great distances. Truck stops, roadside diners, small burgs with hay and grain warehouses with painted advertisements all became more frequent in the few short hours of driving through the northern portion of Texas and into Oklahoma.

Marcus reclined in his seat, leaning against the bathroom wall with his head stuck in the book he had picked up in Albuquerque. Langston Hughes was somewhere deep in his backpack. I felt an urge to ask if I could read it for a while. He hadn't said a word in almost two hours and only listened to his Walkman for a total of twenty minutes. A few times I wanted to make my way up the aisle and ask the driver to turn on the air-conditioner. I had gotten hot and had to peel off my new jacket and sweater. When I put my hand over the metallic vent below the window, I was surprised to feel the ice-cold air blowing up. It carried with it an odor of toxicity and charcoal. For some reason, it was definitely getting warmer in the back of the bus.

Behind us, and only separated by a metal wall that had been covered over in cheap wood laminate, the grinding and groaning of the engine became louder and made noises like an overworked farm tractor.

"How's the book?" I asked.

"Good," he responded in a daze, miles away.

"I thought you already read it once before," I interjected, trying to provoke him into talking.

"Mm-hmm," he answered. "A few times," he uttered, as he kept on reading. Outside, the sun was setting on the end of my second day traveling by bus. Although it had been a little less eventful than it was earlier, I was thankful. As the afternoon passed, we covered a lot of ground and breezed through place after place. I had already made this same trip twice now, and each time I thought it seemed different but it probably wasn't. In this instance, I could say that it was. The year previous, traveling with my mother and my sister, Beanie, I had foolishly managed to trap my left hand in a set of automatic doors in Washington, D.C. Concerned that my hand was broken, the terminal manager had called an ambulance and rushed me to the nearest hospital, forcing all of us to miss our bus. We were waylaid for a night waiting for X-ray results that never showed up. I felt an urge to tell Marcus the whole story, but looking over I could see that he was still heavily engrossed in *The Catcher in the Rye*.

"Is that book about baseball?" I asked.

"No," was all he said.

"What's it about?"

He finally pulled himself from its pages, giving me a long, thoughtful look, and smiled.

"It's about a young man who has trouble fitting in."

"Is it interesting?" I continued, digging.

"What do you think? Obviously, if I've read it more than once."

"How many times have you read it?" I wondered aloud.

"Man, you must really be bored," he laughed. "A few times," he admitted, flipping the corner of the page over marking his place. He quickly shoved the book into his jacket pocket.

"Are you warm back here, or is it just me?" I asked him. He glanced around, assessing the climate. The look on his face seemed to confirm my suspicions. I watched him take off his leather jacket, fold it up, and put it on the seat between us.

"Feels hot, huh? I'm gonna start sweatin' if they don't kick up the air-con."

"It's already on," I replied, running my hand over the vent again.

"Don't be messin' with me, now ..." he stated. "Is it really on?"

"Feel for yourself," I answered, pointing a finger at the chrome air vents next to me. He leaned forward, reached out, and held his hand just above the vent.

"You ain't lyin'!" he admitted, a little surprised.

"Told ya."

Marcus got up and made his way to the front of the bus to have a word with the driver. I peeked out of the seating section and down the aisle to see him kneeling next to the new lady driver, who had replaced the previous lady driver. She had both hands on the steering wheel and was looking straight ahead. I thought Marcus was going to just say a few words and then come back, but he stayed gone for some time. I saw him sitting on the floor at her feet, just past the thin white line that was painted on the floor where a sign said: *No passengers beyond this line while in motion.* Neither of them seemed to mind as they were still chatting away twenty minutes later.

The heat in the back was like a warm cocoon around me. The vibration of the engine rattled the seat, slowly putting me to sleep. Having gone almost three days without any real rest, my body felt like it was shutting down and warping my thoughts while I was awake. I didn't want to think about what it was doing to them while I slept.

* * *

I didn't have a clue as to where I was when I opened my eyes. All I knew was that I was standing somewhere in an awkward position

and unable to move my arms or legs at all. I didn't know what registered the loss of movement first, the moment I couldn't feel my
legs or my arms, or the stiff muscle in my neck locking into place. It
was dark, but not entirely black. It was difficult to see. All around
me the lights were off, and somehow I knew it was night outside,
but I knew I was inside by the feel of the air-conditioning breezing
by my ears and blowing across my motionless face. Strange shapes
and other figures were all cast in dark gray. When I tried to turn my
neck but couldn't, I panicked. Not having control over any portion
of my body was massively disconcerting. As my eyes adjusted to the
light, I became horrified when I recognized the surroundings.

Large circular racks of clothing evenly spaced across a vast and
well-ordered department store only pointed out the obvious. It was
after hours, and I was inside of Macy's, JC Penney, or some other
department store. In the far distance, against a wall, a red illuminated sign near the ceiling read *exit*.

My eyes darted through the darkness, landing on other human
figures. They were elevated above the racks of clothes and merchandise, well posed and casually staring down from the lofty displays.
Unmovable and nicely dressed. I was able to gain control of my
head and neck slowly and looked down at my wooden arms stuck
out in front of me as if I was holding some invisible object; my leg
was stepping forward, but I wasn't moving. My brain relaxed when
I realized that I was dreaming that I was a mannequin.

But the dream seemed as real as the pin-striped suit and tie that
I could feel against me. My only thought was the desire to move, to
step off the elevated stage I'd been placed on and get the hell out of
there. I tried to convince myself that it was just a matter of moving
quickly enough to the exit.

I was frustrated and betrayed by my own body, even though I
began to regain slight movement in my limbs. I felt wooden. I could
feel the metal rods embedded in my hands, as I kept them clinched
in tight-fisted, agonizing balls. The sensation of long, metal rods
shooting up through my legs, locking my knees, and forcing my hips
into an immovable position filled me with terror. As I looked out

across the department store, I thought I saw one of the other figures jump down from his platform before disappearing into the sea of clothes and slowly start heading in my direction. I was frightened, and my throat was tense and constricted. I struggled even harder to move but couldn't. I was sweating now, and I wanted to scream, but it felt as if my head was under a glass jar. I looked down and saw a hand reaching out for me from below. I had no air in my lungs or strength in my body for any type of necessary reaction. Brittle and beginning to buckle, I felt myself splintering from the inside out.

* * *

"Sebastien ... wake up, wake up!" I was being shaken force-fully with a tight grip around the bottom of my jacket. "C'mon, man ... the bus is on fire!" Marcus's face was panic-stricken, and the bus, although slowing, was still moving. I snapped up from the seat, rubbing my eyes and seeing that the lights were all on and the cabin was quickly filling with smoke. My eyes were burning from the chemical fumes. We were reducing speed and pulling off onto the shoulder. People were scrambling in their seats to grab all their stuff. Several people who had their whole lives in plastic trash bags, because they couldn't afford anything in the way of luggage, were struggling to get all their stuff together.

The old Navajo man was wide awake and standing up in his seating section, ready to go. It was the first time he smiled at me and nodded.

"That was quite a dream you were having," he announced loudly. His voice was deep and easily penetrated the smoggy air, the buzzing overhead alarm, and the wailing old ladies who were all coughing and choking from the acrid haze.

"Well, old man, you did say that this bus was getting ready to keel over and head off for the New World. You weren't kidding," Marcus commented.

The old man remained calm, as did his son. "Don't worry,"

he said. "We're all going to make it off in one piece." The bus screeched to a long halt on the shoulder, and the lady driver threw open the front door and yelled for us to get off quickly and safely. Dazed passengers moved with purpose and efficiency. The lady driver told everyone to step down the embankment and get clear of the motor coach.

Within a few minutes, we were all off the bus and standing approximately thirty feet in front of it. A fire had started in the engine compartment while I slept, and there wasn't anything that could've been done to prevent it. The fire burned out of control and escaped from the engine compartment in bursts. The driver, Marcus, and several other passengers decided to salvage as much luggage from the storage compartments on the bottom side of the bus as possible.

The sky was black, and the sun had set hours ago while I slept. The flames grew taller and started to spread. Soon the bus was fully engulfed, and we were stranded in the middle of nowhere. I stood as close as I could to the old Navajo man, who was singing, or rather chanting, with his son loudly. Their gaze was fixed on the bus, and both held one palm upward, possibly calling to the spirits. We watched bags being hurled off into the ditch. The backseats of the bus, where I had been sleeping only moments prior, were now completely engulfed in flames. White and black interlaced smoke billowed out the front door, and the putrid stench of the toilet cooking blasted us in the face with frequent bursts of warm air. Cinders rose up into the darkness, spread out, and floated back to earth like a massive swarm of fireflies being released from the soul of the bus.

No one else was driving on the road as we stood on the gravel shoulder watching our transportation quickly turn into a fiery nightmare. The few cars that were going in the opposite direction slowed, but they didn't stop. The spectacle of the flaming Greyhound bus against a clear and moonless night sky was both engaging and distracting. Listening to the two Navajo men singing made it less frightening but other-worldly. They were both bobbing around as they sang, and the old man had one hand on my shoulder the whole time. I didn't know if he was leaning on me or telling me something that I just couldn't understand. At times he was singing directly into my ear. He was singing in his own language and keeping the rhythm with his son. My mind was fixated on the moment. They were also laughing periodically between the long phrases of the song, as if they knew there was a joke that no one else understood. In a strange way, I thought it was funny too. But I just couldn't bear to laugh.

After all the bags had been saved, the passengers stood motionless along the ditch, watching the bus burn, mesmerized. Ahead of us, far in the flat distance, flashing lights were heading our way. The closer they got, the larger they looked. Wherever they had come from, it looked as if a whole battalion of emergency vehicles was speeding toward us. I felt a sense of relief watching them approach. I knew we'd all be okay, but the bus was a complete hulking waste. Everyone's face along the roadside shoulder was cast in a golden light that wavered gently as the flames struggled out of the cracking windows, which were breaking from the intense heat, and escaped up into the dark night sky.

"Should've brought marshmallows!" the old man announced in a singsong voice, mixing it in with his song. He was probably just trying to settle me.

I stayed with the two men from the Navajo Nation during the entirety of the blaze. We watched a steady stream of vehicles pull up, long after the bus was too far gone. We kept waiting for a fire truck, but none came. The first few flashing vehicles were several State Police from Elk City, followed by three ambulances, the fire chief in a red sedan, and then three school buses.

Flares were set out on the highway farther back to slow any passing traffic that had difficulty observing a bright ball of flaming metal and seat cushion in complete darkness. The old man and his son kept laughing about the emergency vehicles and thought it was fitting that no fire trucks from Elk City or anywhere else had responded.

"He must be the fire chief!" the son pointed out in a quiet tone, just for the three of us. They were both laughing heartily about that most of all. The old fire chief was wearing sweatpants and a button-down shirt. He had the look of someone who had already turned in for the evening but was forced to make an appearance.

"The spirit is free now. No longer a prisoner here. We should be so lucky. *Aho!*" the old man spoke.

"*Aho!*" the son answered back.

The police officers who had gotten to us first were a bit on the young side and busied themselves checking out all of the passengers for injuries. They took a head count, then grouped us together farther away from the flaming inferno and quickly loaded us, like cattle, onto school buses.

"You'd think that they'd gone through this before," the old man's son remarked. They both must have been really enjoying themselves, being there to catch the last moments of the old bus. Marcus and several other men, and the lady driver, had all volunteered to load up the second school bus with luggage.

I waited for Marcus, holding a seat for him in the back. He was one of the last people to board, and I heard him coughing as he got on. He made his way up the aisle, looking a little exhausted, and had ash and gray powdery dust in his hair and covering his jacket. I thought he would've been upset, but he didn't seem bothered by the incident at all. He had the same expression that the two Navajo men had and was laughing when he finally sat down next to us.

"You wouldn't believe it, but I spoke to an ambulance driver, and he said that this was the third Greyhound that's burned up on the freeway in the last year. All in the middle of the night too." The two Navajo men thought this was hilarious. I didn't understand it at all.

"I don't get it. What's so funny?"

Marcus responded incredulously to my question. "Are you kidding me? We're lucky to be alive, man. We could've been roadside casserole back there. That place is like the goddamned Bermuda Triangle." He was shaking his head, laughing about the whole thing.

The school bus started up, and we pulled out of there without further ado, or any overhead notice. I looked back out the rear window and got a long glimpse of the smoldering and smoky remains of the old forty-foot Buffalo. The thought occurred to me that Monty probably would've loved to have seen the bus burn just as much as Marcus and the Navajo Nation men did. As we sped away and closed in on Elk City, Marcus turned in his seat as if he had just remembered something important. He asked me about my luggage.

"Oh yeah ..." he started, clearing his throat and coughing. "Are you going to tell me what's in your suitcases? I couldn't believe how heavy they were. It felt like they were packed with bricks."

"What luggage?" I feigned ignorance.

"Oh no ... c'mon now, don't bullshit me. I saw your name on the tags. You're the only Sebastien Ranes on this bus as far as I can tell. What the hell you got in those bags? Car parts or something?" he asked, bewildered.

"Something, I guess," I finally admitted.

"No, no, no," he said, not giving up. He wanted to know. I felt up against the wall but just couldn't bring myself to tell him. Explaining it would be too much.

"Ask me later," I gave in. "I'll tell you if you just ask me about it later."

The two Navajo men were listening in on our conversation with rapt attention. After so much excitement, most of us sat quietly, as we were being driven by a man who looked as though he might've been a hundred years old. He peered through Coke-bottle glasses into the night, hunched over the wheel, taking us to our destination at fifty-five miles per hour.

Once we got to the depot, we noticed that a lot of people turned out to get a good look at us. It was as if the whole town had been alerted and had decided to converge on the Greyhound stop, which in itself wasn't much to look at. The tiny depot couldn't hold everyone inside who had gathered.

"Do they always greet the buses like this?" the old man joked.

"Maybe we should move here. At least our nights won't be boring."

"I don't think so, Dad," the son responded, absently but not amused, surveying the crowd with distrust.

For a half hour, I quietly shadowed Marcus and the two men from the Navajo Nation. The biggest problem, which was taking the most time, was getting another bus to take us all into Tulsa, where we could be handed over to yet another Greyhound coach. The lady driver was locked in the terminal office and on the phone with someone, reporting the situation and trying to work it out. We went through a luggage inspection to make sure that everyone still had all their belongings. Several people had lost their bags, either in the fire or on the side of the road. I still had my two cases, which had mud smeared and caked on the edges and compacted on the handles. Two Greyhound porters were busying themselves by brushing off the bulk of the mud from everyone's luggage, one by one. I was probably the only person who wished his luggage had been sacrificed in the fire. But standing next to the bags on the platform outside, I realized that I would have a lot of explaining to do once I got to Altoona, regardless of whether they had burned up or not. I knew my grandma wasn't going to be very happy with me, and she probably wouldn't appreciate the kind of phone call my mother would engage her in.

I kept pivoting around to watch the continual stream of people making phone calls at the kiosk behind us. It didn't look as though anything was about to happen immediately. When a phone freed up, I told Marcus I was going to make a call.

"You going to call your grams again?" he asked.

"No, not till tomorrow," I answered, walking toward the phone stand.

Not having anymore change, I knew I was forced to make another embarrassing collect call.

"Operator?" the voice answered, after I punched zero.

"I'd like to make a collect call, please." Weary and tired, I spoke calmly into the receiver.

"Number?" she answered. I gave her the phone number to our

house in Stockton, California, on Mendocino Street. Maybe someone would be home.

"Thank you, just a moment," the operator responded. On cue, I
heard the dialing of numbers, then the silence.

"*I'm sorry ... but the number you have dialed has been disconnected and is no longer in service. Please check the number and dial
again.*" An annoying tone followed, and then the recorded message
began to repeat. The operator interrupted it.

"Are you sure you gave me the correct number?" she asked.

"I am," I replied. We verified the phone number and tried again.
I thought that it must have been a dialing mistake, but the recorded
message began to play again.

"Is there another number that you would like to try?"

"No, thank you," I responded. She hung up without another
word. Dial tone formed in my inner ear. I hung up, momentarily
confused. The thought occurred to me that the phone was purpose-
fully turned off and that Charlotte and Dick had moved, but she
hadn't mentioned anything about it to me, and I hadn't *accidentally*
overheard anything regarding a move either. It just didn't make
sense, or I didn't want to believe it.

"What happened?" Marcus asked, when I got back to the bags.

"The phone was disconnected at my mother's."

He cracked a smile and started laughing. "It's been a long day,
now. Don't be bullshittin' me again."

"I'm serious," I said. He gave me a stern look, taking a deep
breath.

"You've gotta be joking, right? Maybe the phone got cut off for
not paying the bill?"

"No, I saw the bill get paid on the first of the month. I watched
Charlotte write the check. The thing said '*This number has been
disconnected.*'"

"That's cold. Not only did your moms drop you on the bus, she
gave you the okey-doke and then the slip."

"Okey-doke? What's that?" I queried naively.

"The okey-doke, y'know ... '*Okey-doke, baby, everything's gonna*

be fine. I'll see you in a few days.' That's the okey-doke." He had
raised the pitch of his voice to imitate a woman. Once again, I knew
what he was saying now was the truth.

"She gave me the slip too." I confirmed my thoughts out loud.

"That's some real ghetto behavior, man. That's a straight dope-
fiend move. Don't you got a social worker or something?"

"I don't know?" I was drawing a complete blank now. She'd
vanished into the night with Dick. I should've seen it coming, but I
was too trusting. I should've been happy about it, but I wasn't. I felt
strong earlier about deciding to never leave my grandma's house
again. But now I just felt dumb, as if I had been beaten to the punch
line of a really bad joke.

"Dope-fiend move ..." I repeated under my breath, as a statement, not a question, standing there quietly, staring off into space.

As I stood there burning time, trying to better understand my
mother, a bus finally pulled up. At first, I didn't think it was for us,
because it wasn't a Greyhound Lines motor coach. The outside was
painted red and white, and the logo along the side read *Trailways*.
When the door opened, a driver stepped down and dismounted. He
quickly waved at us to come forward.

"Are all of you from the Greyhound bus that caught fire out
on the 40?" he asked. The lady driver emerged quickly from the
terminal office and confirmed it. We'd be continuing forward on
Greyhound's main competitor. Now, having seen it, I knew they
actually had one. Before, it was just a myth to me. The compartment doors were unlocked, our luggage was stowed beneath the
behemoth before anymore time was lost, and we all boarded and
pulled back out into the night for Tulsa and Oklahoma City.

It was an odd thing, but even though we were on a different bus,
everyone sat in the exact same seats. Maybe with the entire world
shifting so intensely around us, everyone just naturally sought
a little bit of order. The tension and tired feelings were palpable.
Nerves were shot, some of the older women had broken out into
tears a few times, and if someone had decided for whatever reason
to switch seats, there would've been a fistfight. I was thankful to

have the back row with Marcus and the two men from the Navajo Nation. It felt like we were a team. Perhaps we were. Riding was the sport, and successfully getting to your destination was the goal. With everything that had taken place thus far, we had experienced more than enough obstacles, several delays, and an ample amount of frustration and anger. Traveling on a Greyhound bus might've looked like a simple thing from afar, but it wasn't. One of the first things that I had figured out at the start of the trip, which felt like so long ago, was to avoid looking at the schedule and not to follow the journey on my watch. I still had the paperwork with the route schedule that I'd picked up at the ticket counter in Stockton, but it was now crumpled, folded, and creased from being jammed in my back pocket and sat on endlessly. I hadn't glanced at it since Albuquerque, and I knew it was better to just leave it be.

The Trailways bus interior bore a striking resemblance in color to the forty-foot Buffalo, except for the lack of curtains. The bus had recently been cleaned and smelled of oranges instead of Pine-Sol, but the toilet had a sign on the door that read: *Out of Order*. The door was secured and put into the locked position. The small *occupied* light just above the handle was lit.

The ride to Oklahoma City apparently wouldn't be long—an hour and fifteen minutes at most. A few people really needed to smoke and ignored the no-smoking curfew. No one complained, and the majority of the passengers just slept, including Marcus. The two Navajo men were lightly snoring and slumped over in their seats. The old man was huddled against the window, buffered by his jacket. This was a position that almost everybody on the bus would eventually succumb to. Even though I felt sleepy, I sat there awake, staring out the window at the passing lights and the shadowed landscape. My eyes were tired and heavy, but I knew that I wouldn't be at ease until we transferred buses again and got back on schedule.

Greyhound management agreed to pass one of the stops altogether. In Elk City, we were asked if anyone was getting off in Tulsa. When no one responded, the lady driver got back on the phone, and

I watched her through the glass shaking her head no. A panic had struck when the reality had set in that bus 1364 would be at least an hour to an hour and a half behind schedule for the rest of the trip. Whoever had been on the other end of the phone wasn't very happy and had given her some explicit instructions. We were now driving in the leftmost lane and moving at a speed I hadn't seen since the evil Frank Burns was behind the wheel. But anyone waiting for us in Tulsa was going to be out of luck.

By the time we pulled into Oklahoma City, it was twelve twenty-five in the morning, and the lady driver, who was now a passenger and sitting in the front seat, looked frustrated and exhausted. She just grabbed her stuff and walked off the bus in a huff with absolutely no announcement, no thank you, no "sorry about the burning bus in the middle of nowhere," nothing. The Trailways driver followed close behind her, vanishing into the terminal.

I grabbed my Greyhound coat and my bag and peeled myself up off the seat, determined to do my best to secure a pillow without having to pay for it. I couldn't afford one, but I knew that if there was one lying around in the overhead bins, I was going to grab it.

As I started down the aisle, the last one off again, I quickly did my best to search all of the overhead compartments. I had to step up on the seats, one by one, to either pry open the lids or peer inside the few that were either left ajar or didn't have a door. I was feeling pretty stupid by the time I got toward the front of the bus and still hadn't found anything but empty potato chip bags and lint balls. A few seats from the front, sitting unused in a still-sealed plastic bag, was what I was looking for. Without hesitation, I grabbed the pillow and shoved it under my jacket.

Just as I was stepping down the stairs, I saw the Trailways driver coming back with the porters to unlock the luggage hold. Two ladies in janitors' outfits met me at the bottom and smiled. They were armed with mop buckets, brooms, and cleaning supplies and, to my astonishment, pillows. A feeling of uselessness washed over me for stealing what I could've gotten just by asking.

"You the last one?" the woman asked.

"It's empty, all yours," I replied. "Can I have a pillow?" I asked, wondering if it really was that simple.

"Sure, baby." She picked a small Greyhound pillow from her cart and handed it to me with an extremely seductive look. I wondered if she'd actually looked at me that way or if it was just me.

When I caught up to Marcus a few moments later, he was sitting at a table in Grey's Café with the two men from the Navajo Nation.

"I wondered where you had gotten off to. I saw you searching the overhead bins when we got off."

"I got you this," I answered, as I handed him the Trailways pillow.

"Alright, a souvenir!" he replied, happy with the gift. The two Navajo men were stoic, both grasping their coffee cups. The way they both had fixed their gaze on me made me feel nervous.

"Nice gift," the old man noted, nodding his head yes.

Marcus shoved the pillow on the seat beside him and continued staring at the menu and stirring his coffee.

A man in a white shirt and black pants came over to the table and set a menu down in front of me.

"You want something to drink?" the man asked me. "Juice, milk, something in a toddler cup?"

I didn't know what he meant by that or even if he was serious. They were all looking at me now, waiting to see what I was going to say.

"Coffee." I didn't even say please. The old man must have caught all of it, because he chuckled under his breath, bobbing in his seat a little.

"That stuff will either keep you up all night or close to a toilet," he informed me, concerned.

"No one ever let me drink coffee before. I kind of like it."

"It will make you into a man, fierce and alert. It is a gift from our Grandfather in the far away South," the son spoke earnestly.

"Well, you'll definitely be alert, that's for sure," Marcus remarked. "What time does your bus leave?" he continued.

"We pull out of here in thirty minutes," the son replied. "We should be in White Earth by tomorrow afternoon."

"Are you taking a different bus?" I asked naively.

"We must all take our own paths," he said.

"There's such a place called White Earth?" I wondered.

"There is such a place. My sister is getting married the day after tomorrow to a Chippewa. There will be a lot of good food and dancing."

"I've never heard of White Earth," I said, fascinated by the name. It sounded mystical, like the center of everything or where another world might exist.

"We are all living on a White Earth," the old man replied with a sort of halfway grin. "A land where real magic is pushed into the ground and forgotten. When you're a man, they'll sell you back your dreams that they're about to steal from you now."

"You can say that again," Marcus remarked.

"We're all living on a White Earth," we all repeated in unison like a knee-jerk. It was late, and we were all partially delirious. When the waiter came, I ordered a BLT and fries. The coffee was stone cold in my cup, and after one sip I had no desire to finish it.

"What's wrong?" the younger man asked. He was sitting directly across from me and had noted my grimace when I sipped it.

"The coffee's cold and I think it's burnt."

"For someone who's not allowed to drink coffee, you sure have a good tongue for it," the old man spoke. They were all looking into my coffee cup for the answer.

"You're not going to drink that, are you?" Marcus asked.

"I don't think so ..."

Marcus raised his hand and got the waiter's attention. Within a minute he appeared at our table with the same pot of cold coffee.

"Is everything alright?" he asked.

"Coffee's cold. Have you got any hot?" I spoke just above a whisper. I thought he was going to ask me to repeat myself, but he just stared at me. He looked thoroughly annoyed and made a sound. Marcus nudged me under the table and cleared his throat.

"Can you make some more?" I asked.

"Okay, I'll make a fresh pot," the waiter whined, turning away and taking his cold, burnt coffee with him.

"Good job," the son praised me. "You're paying for it. Make sure it's worth it." The old man grunted something and agreed. No one was drinking their coffee now. I thought maybe I was just being picky and difficult.

When the waiter appeared the third time with our food, not only had he brought fresh coffee out, but he had four new cups as well. After he had put everything down and poured everyone a cup, the old man told the waiter that he was very thoughtful for replacing the cups.

"It's okay, just doing my job," he replied. "Besides, it's not often we get a visit from the United Nations," he said. They all laughed together, but I didn't get it. At least not right away. I got the distinct impression, watching the whole thing unfold in front of me, that maybe what had happened was supposed to have happened. It was something that I was supposed to see. Had someone served Charlotte and Dick cold, burnt coffee, they both would've flown into a rage. Instead, everyone stayed calm and it was easily remedied.

Traveling made me hungry. I had been eating more food than ever before. I wasn't prone to eating so much, so often. I wasn't complaining, though. It was a nice change being able to eat whatever I wanted and not having to worry about going without, or only ordering a peanut butter and jelly sandwich because someone wanted to buy cigarettes with what little money we had. It was always that way whenever I ate with my mother and sister. I ate my fill and wasn't afraid to eat something different every time. I paid with my café vouchers and slowly sipped my coffee as we all waited for our buses and digested our food. Listening to the overhead music in silence was more than enough.

When the first boarding call went out for the 2326 to Minneapolis, the two men got up to leave and headed out to the bus platform. Marcus said he wanted to smoke, so we all got up together and drifted back outside. We were met once more by the sprinkling of rain on our faces and the chilly night air. It didn't feel like May at

all. I looked up and saw the light rain passing by the overhead lamps
that hung down from the awning, illuminating the fine misty spray.
Nighttime on the bus was easily the best time. Everything slowed
and became quiet. The world became dark and didn't seem to exist
past what I could see. Everything felt smaller, safer.

I stood staring up the platform at the long row of buses that
were all simultaneously in the terminal. It was the most buses in
one place I'd seen thus far. Signs in the top left portion of the wind-
shield listed their destinations or the next major terminal. We were
standing next to a bus that was going south to Dallas. You could
read the lit signs easily from the platform: *Minnesota, Tallahassee,
Omaha, Columbus*. Columbus was our bus; from there, a change
was necessary to get us to Pittsburgh, which was only a few hours
later. After leaving Los Angeles, our bus had periodically changed
its sign—from Phoenix to Albuquerque and then to Oklahoma City.
Finally seeing Columbus like that gave me a sense of relief. Home
was no longer out of view, at the other end of the world. It was
somewhere a lot closer than before and getting nearer. Oklahoma
City was well past the halfway point, and we were already into the
third day.

As the three men stood there conversing and smoking cigarettes, I took notes and busied myself with my thoughts. A feeling
of dread overtook me as I began to worry once more about the luggage. I wished the cases had burned up in the fire, but I wasn't destined to be so lucky.

"*2326 to Minneapolis. Now boarding aisle 11.*"

"You two have a safe trip, and enjoy the ceremony."

"I'm just looking forward to the food," responded the old man,
stomping out his cigarette butt on the concrete platform below.

The son straightened his hat and looked around, taking a final
assessment of the rain. "Should stop by tomorrow," he said. "Good
luck on your journey to your grandmother's. Go safely," he spoke to
me, concerned and thoughtful. The thought entered my mind that
maybe that was how a father spoke to his departing son.

"I will. Thank you," I answered. He shook my hand and grabbed
my shoulder at the same time. He looked directly at me, bent down

a little to face me, and said *"Aho!"* loudly. The old man said the same thing, almost as if it was an answer or an echo.

"Aho!" the old man repeated.

"Aho!" I stated.

"You're learning," he said again, nodding his head. They both headed off down the platform and disappeared up inside the bus to Minneapolis. After they had left, I realized that I had never once asked their names. I forgot to ask the old man how he knew about the bus as well. I never got the chance, but every time there was an opening in the conversation, I felt too intimidated to bring it up. I had never met anyone like them before, and I never would've guessed that I would have been eating dinner with them in the middle of the night either. So far, the majority of the people that I'd met on the trip had all been very good to me. The conversations with my mother were very different and often ended in her getting upset or angry, and arguing was always her way of explaining everything.

When the boarding calls for the 1364 began again, I was happy to get back on the road and continue putting down miles. For the first time, the bus started to fill up, and a lot of the seats were now occupied. Even being after midnight, it was a lot noisier and even a little warmer, despite the air-conditioner going full blast and it being a new coach. Marcus and I had been the first to get on, and yet again the driver gave our tickets the once-over.

"You the boy traveling alone?" he asked.

"Yeah, I am."

"Well, sit up front like you're supposed to so I can keep an eye on you. Regulations."

"No, thanks. I'm sitting in the back where I've been the whole trip," I answered, defiant. I even shocked myself.

"Fine, get on," he replied curtly. Maybe he meant well, I don't know. I didn't have any desire to be bossed around or babysat. After we reclaimed our seats in the very back, Marcus started laughing.

"You sure weren't going to take any funny business from him, huh?"

"No way am I sitting up front. No thanks." I was adamant about it. As far as I was concerned, Marcus and I were traveling together from now on. The new Greyhound man could go to hell if he didn't like it. Maybe I was supposed to feel this way now that I was twelve. I knew that I had different responsibilities to myself. Being bossed around by strangers had ended.

"Welcome to the 1364," the driver announced. His voice crackled loudly over the PA system, brutishly interrupting my thoughts. *"Service continuing through to Columbus, Ohio. Please respect the no-smoking curfew on the bus. No drinking alcoholic beverages, no fighting or playing loud music. Please keep all children restrained and quiet at all times. No illegal substances of any kind. A violation of this policy will get you removed anywhere along the drive. My name is Germaine, and I'll be your driver between Oklahoma City and Saint Louis. Enjoy the trip."*

Marcus rolled his eyes at the length and volume of Germaine's message. "Germaine, huh," he commented. "I've never met a 'Germaine' before," he spat.

"Me neither," I parried, siding with him in earnest. We both placed him in the category of Greyhound drivers we disliked. We were both well past rookies.

Once more, we pulled off into the night and out onto the highway. The rain immediately intensified. The sound of it crashing down on the roof and coursing past the windows obscured everything and fogged up the glass.

I did the only thing I could do and closed my eyes, hoping to get some sleep and possibly to oversleep, missing Mount Vernon in the process. I wasn't looking forward to the morning. I sure wasn't looking forward to meeting John F. Kennedy.

8.

MAY 13, 1981 ...
MOUNT VERNON, MISSOURI

The bus pulled off the main highway, twisting around the narrow, tree-lined streets leading directly into a small town square that was surrounded on all sides by ominous-looking red brick buildings. Each one had darkened windows and fading signs. The cast-iron streetlamps dotting the sidewalks still shone down a semi-visible glow as the sun started to rise somewhere off in the distance in the dark morning sky above.

The bus stopped in front of a small coffee shop, which was at that hour the only open business. The driver stepped down onto the pavement below and buttoned his yellow raincoat. The rain was sheeting down in buckets.

"This is it?" Marcus queried, peering out the window, trying to stir me from my seat. By the time I came around, he was already standing in the aisle, buttoning his jacket and slipping his backpack over one shoulder.

"Time to face the music," I whispered, as I got up and followed him down the aisle of the bus. Most of the passengers were still sleeping, but a few people were awake and trying to figure out where they were.

As soon as we were off, we hurriedly stepped closer to one of the buildings and under an awning. I'd never seen it rain so hard before. The driver was under the compartment lid and reaching for my two suitcases. I hadn't seen them since Los Angeles in the daylight, but seeing them again on the sidewalk gave me butterflies in my stomach.

"You're disembarking as well? I only had the boy in the notes," he shouted over to Marcus. The driver was a little flustered trying to avoid the rain and get the bags out lickety-split.

"I'm getting off here. Don't worry, I don't have any other luggage," Marcus answered. The driver nodded and slipped away to secure the storage compartments. He slipped his key in the round locks, closed everything up, and moved with purpose. He stepped under the awning next to us and offered Marcus a cigarette.

"Smoke?"

"Thanks. It's early, it's cold, it's wet." Marcus listed off the various obvious complaints.

"It's Mount Vernon," the driver joked. "Rustic, quaint, and, well ..." He just shook his head.

"Do you usually stop here?" I asked, trying to shield myself from the downpour.

"Only for five minutes. This is just a place I usually pick up some old granny either going to Springfield for the weekend or to Joplin to go buy another cat."

"Is there another bus coming through here?" I rejoined.

"There's a bus 'passing' in almost two hours, but he won't stop here unless he's instructed to. Someone getting on or off, that is."

"Can you radio back and have him stop for us?" Marcus chimed in politely.

"This ain't the end of the line for y'all, is it?" the driver asked.

"No. My family has a way of forgetting about me. I guess I shouldn't be surprised that no one's here yet." I had to speak loudly to be heard over the intense downpour. I looked around the street for anyone at all, any sign of life. There was nothing but the cold and damp in the half darkness. "Are we late?" I asked.

"No, right on time. We picked up all our lost time slingshotting past Tulsa. I had to do eighty most of the way. I'll get gas in Springfield and try to get ten more minutes ahead of schedule if I can, just to be safe." The driver inhaled his cigarette like it was a piece of candy. He finished in a few short drags. Even Marcus watched him suck it back with gusto, a little shocked.

"We are both getting off in Pittsburgh. If you could holler back to the other bus, we'd be grateful," Marcus announced.

"Will do. I'll make sure he knows," the driver announced. Marcus and I thanked him and watched as he climbed back aboard and closed the door. We stood there unmoving as we watched our old bus pull away into the cold morning without us.

"Well, I guess we had ol' Germaine figured wrong, huh?" Marcus considered.

"I just hope he radios the other driver," I answered.

Beside us, the neon sign of the coffee and donuts store blinked off and on in rhythm. A small metal sign with the blue-and-red Greyhound logo painted on it was attached to the brick wall above my head. It was the only thing that noted the location as a stopping point. Marcus and I each grabbed a case. I hefted mine with two hands and went inside, escaping the downpour.

"Good morning, boys," spoke an elderly lady with dark curly hair and large glasses that made her eyes look wide and large like an owl's. She was happy to see us and greeted us warmly.

"Nothing like the first customers of the day," she continued with a beaming smile.

"Morning, ma'am," we answered. I dropped my case against the wall just inside the door. The store had room for only a few seats, as the bulk of the floor space was taken up by glass display cases. It was intended just as a place to purchase coffee and donuts to go. A sign next to the cash register read *No Checks, No Credit, No Trouble*.

Marcus ordered two cups of coffee and a half-dozen assorted donuts. Still aching and tired, we eased into chairs next to the front window. It was hard to let my eyes rest because of the busy décor surrounding us. The walls were covered with strange oil paintings of several different churches. None were the same, but they all had the distinct feeling of being painted by the same hand. They looked like paintings done by a child. The only problem was that there was something about them that made me feel compelled to stare at them. I scanned each one carefully.

"You like my paintings?" the old lady asked, as she set our coffee and donuts on the plastic gingham table cover.

I shook my head, nodding yes. "There sure are a lot of them," I said, mesmerized and trying to figure them out, as if they were a puzzle.

"They're all for sale," she replied in an upbeat tone. "You two boys live near here?"

"No, ma'am. I'm supposed to be meeting my grandparents here this morning. They should've been here already," I answered. Her curiosity was piqued.

"Oh, really? Who are your grandparents? Perhaps I know them. Mount Vernon's not that big."

"My grandfather's John F. Kennedy. Do you know him?" I asked. I looked over to see Marcus smiling. He turned his gaze out the window and stirred his coffee.

"Well, not *that* John F. Kennedy, Marcus." I laughed a little, seeing the humor in it.

"Old John? Sure, I know him. He's a bit of an old buzzard. Is he your grandfather?"

"Mm-hmm," I replied positively, with my face connected to my coffee cup.

"My, my," she said, half under her breath. "Have you ever *met* your grandfather?"

"No, I haven't. Why do you ask?" I responded. Marcus didn't say a single word. He just sat quietly, taking it all in and biting into his donut.

"He knew you were coming too?"

"He does ... or they do. My grandma as well," I answered again. She had a lot of questions, but since she knew him, I was trying my best to be polite.

"Well, your bus was on time and he's not here. You just want to wait for a while, I suppose?"

"Is that okay?" I questioned.

"Sure." The old lady slipped back behind her counter and into the kitchen to continue sliding donuts around on trays. The whole exchange was a bit strange, but maybe she knew something I didn't.

"She didn't say anything good about your grandfather. You did notice that, right?" Marcus responded to her comments pointedly, and in a very low tone.

"That thought just occurred to me, actually," I admitted. I wasn't smiling, and I was beginning to be a little afraid of the prospect of actually having to meet John F. Kennedy. The clock on the wall said twenty-two minutes after five, and there wasn't another soul to be encountered anywhere.

Marcus was gazing out through the huge window and trying to get a clue on our surroundings. "Is that a graveyard?" he asked under his breath.

"Well ... our bus should get here just after seven if Germaine radioed back to the other bus," he continued. My mind was already leaving town, even though my body was still firmly fixed in Mount Vernon.

"You didn't have to get off, Marcus. I don't think anyone's coming, and I feel a little silly for even bothering," I responded apologetically.

"No, don't feel bad. I told you I wouldn't leave you hangin' in this place all by yourself. It's a little too quiet." His eyes darted to the sides, trying to be both funny and spooky simultaneously. I nodded in acknowledgment. Outside, the world was getting a thorough rinsing. The rain had been unceasing since Blythe and had followed us across the last four states. The thunder made its presence known somewhere off in the far distance. Almost six seconds later, lightning strikes cracked the earth. I didn't know if I was supposed to count the thunder or the lightning. Either way, it probably didn't matter.

"So, are you going to tell me what's in those cases that are so damn heavy?"

"Clothes," I answered, without missing a beat.

He laughed out loud. Not as loud as on the bus earlier, but loud enough that I knew he wasn't going to be satisfied with such a simple answer.

"No, no. I want the real story about what's in them cases. Clothes? C'mon, man. Be straight with me."

"They are pretty heavy," I admitted with a grin. I stared into my coffee cup, fiddling with the handle. "I don't know what to say, but I wish they had just burned up under the bus. It would've been easier."

"Just tell it like it is," Marcus prodded. "That's all."

"If I tell you, you're not going to be mad?"

"You just asked me a question and put a condition on it. I can't guarantee you how I'm gonna feel, but I'm probably not gonna lose it," he answered. I hadn't thought about it like that before, but I guess I was just afraid of what he was going to say.

"Both of those cases are filled with women's clothes. Dresses, shoes, stuff like that." It was better to just put it out there than sit there and fuss over it.

"Pardon me?" Marcus responded.

"I filled those suitcases with my mother's dresses before I left. They had left the house for a couple of hours the night before they put me on the bus. I switched everything out then."

"And why would you do that?" he asked, more confused now than before.

"She cared more about her dresses and her damn shoes than she ever cared about me or my sister."

"Beanie," he replied, still seeing the humor in her name. "It just seems a little strange that you would empty out your momma's wardrobe and haul it across America."

"I'm not gonna wear it," I said. "If that's what you're trying to say."

Marcus put his hands up in the air, backing away from the subject. "Take it easy, now. It's not like that. You'd have to be pretty messed up for that. But what are you planning on doing with all of it?"

I scratched my head and didn't respond. I stayed quiet as the old lady skirted the counter and approached us one more time with hot coffee. She very carefully refilled our cups, giving Marcus a long look.

"Thank you," Marcus replied, motioning toward his coffee cup.

"Ain't nowhere to go until Ben Franklin's opens up just after nine, but you'll probably be gone by then. Did you want me to call up to your grandpa's house? His name is listed in the phone book."

"What's Ben Franklin's?" I asked, still trying to catch up, distracted.

"It's a department store that sells odds and ends, crafts mostly. It's located just down the street and across the square. It's the biggest store in town. You want me to make that call? You should let them know that you're waiting," she crowed, just above my shoulder.

Marcus seemed a little disengaged, as if he was watching me every step of the way to see how I was going to handle it, like it was a test.

"She's probably right, big man. It's all you now."

"Ain't no 'probably' about it," she said, interrupting and chiding Marcus. "The phone book's sitting right there on the side table."

The pay phone stuck to the wall in the corner across the small café looked old but well taken care of. On a wire-rack table beside it stood a neat stack of phone books. One yellow and one white—both were about as thick as a *Reader's Digest*. I took a seat on the stool next to the phone and thumbed through the white pages, looking for the name John F. Kennedy. I wondered as I flipped the pages if he got a lot of prank calls in the middle of the night. *"Hello, is this the President?"* I imagined it would probably start. I slowed as I got to *Keller* on the bottom of the page and turning, discovered the same exact name on the top of the next one. I ran my finger past several other names and settled on *Kennedy, John F., 24 Brooks Street*. I found a quarter in the pocket of my jeans and dialed the number. The storm was strong enough to hear the swooshing of the static as the phone seemed to idle in silence for an eternity. I thought the line had died, but as I lifted my hand up to cancel the call, it rang. The sound of the ringer was different and seemed far away. Not the probable five or six blocks that it was in real life. I felt my body freezing up inside, knowing I was required to speak. As it continued, the sound of the ringer became the loudest sound I'd ever heard. I thought my eardrum was going to pierce from the pain with every ring. I wanted it to stop, even if someone picked it up, but it just rang.

I looked over at Marcus and shrugged. I replaced the handset back on the metal casing in relief. I heard the quarter flop through the guts of the machine and meet an end at the coin slot. I collected myself and my money and went back to our table at the window.

"Maybe they're on the way or something?" I suggested.

Marcus smiled. "Maybe ... let's see if they show up."

"Let's just be clear, Marcus," I asserted. "I hope they don't show up. I'd have some explaining to do if they did." I motioned at the cases. "I'm sure my mother called them already and told them."

"What are you going to tell them when they get here?" he asked bluntly.

"I don't have any idea. Probably better not to say anything at all. I don't think they care too much for me or my sister. Whatever happens, it's not going to go well."

"Well, you can say that again. But I can only help you so much, buddy."

"I know."

"So what are you going to do with these cases full of women's dresses and shoes? You were never really planning on taking them all the way back to Grandma's. That much I do know."

"No, I just thought that the first chance I could get to ditch them, I would. Maybe give them away. Burning up under the bus would've been cool."

"Well, we do have to change buses in Columbus later tonight. Maybe during the layover we can think of something. If it's not in Columbus, it'll be in Pittsburgh."

"You'll help me get rid of them then?"

"I'm here, aren't I? It's not like I need them, that's for sure. Your moms is gonna blow a gasket when she finds all that stuff gone." The look on Marcus's face seemed to be him imagining my mother's surprised expression as she opened her closet door to find the back of it empty.

"I just felt like it was something that I had to do. I'd thought about it for quite a while. I also thought about setting the place on fire, but someone may have gotten hurt, and I wouldn't have wanted that."

"How thoughtful," he replied sarcastically. He shook his head at me while chewing on a pink-frosted donut with sprinkles. The old woman turned on a radio that sat on the counter above the register. The music wafted out at us, barely audible, but we both listened to it intently. It sounded like the same stuff my grandma listened to on her AM radio in the kitchen every morning. It was the "Tie a Yellow Ribbon Round the Old Oak Tree" song. I didn't know the title, but I'd heard it lots of times and knew most of the words.

"Wow, he was on the bus too," I remarked on the lyrics.

"Just got out of prison as well," Marcus added with a laugh.

"Was it wrong of me to take that stuff?" I asked Marcus, concerned.

"Well," Marcus began, just as he always did, "I wouldn't necessarily say it was wrong, but I would say that stuff like that happens. If all she lost was a handful of pretty dresses and a few pairs of shoes, she got off easy."

I scanned the street out front nervously, looking for any signs of life. The only person who came into view outside was the local sheriff. He parked his truck directly in front of the shop, left the engine running, and slipped inside under the protection of his umbrella.

A bell attached to the top of the door jingled as it opened. He shook off and adjusted the plastic cover on his cowboy hat. "Whew, it sure is coming down out there, Lilah," he spoke, as he dabbed his face with a white handkerchief, sorting himself out. He looked a lot like my grandpa in Altoona. He had well-combed white hair and a bushy white mustache. He finally saw us out of the corner of his eye and turned toward us.

"Morning, boys. I didn't see ya there. Coffee hot? Hopefully you left me some," he said. He was peering at us, perhaps sizing us up.

"Good morning, Sheriff," Marcus responded cheerily, like he was welcoming the conversation. "Coffee's good. How are ya today?" The old sheriff made a step toward us, holding his hat in his hand, and leaned on a chair from the other table.

"Not bad so far. A little wet, but thankfully it's quiet. Hopefully, it'll stay like that."

"Keeps raining like this, it just might be the slowest day of the year," Marcus remarked coolly.

The sheriff laughed at his comment. "You just might be right. You never can tell."

"I hope not. I've got a business to run," the old lady chimed in. "Good morning, Sheriff. Everything is all ready." Her tone was familiar and snarky. She slid a hot cup of coffee in a mug across the counter and set down a big pink box of donuts beside it. She was filling out a receipt and listing off what was in the box, mostly under her breath.

"Four custard-filled bismarks, two old-fashioned, two chocolate rings, two regular rings with sprinkles, and two powdered jelly-filled. Comes to four dollars even. Here ya go," she announced, as she handed him the receipt, which he gladly accepted, folded, and put in his wallet.

"You both waiting for the seven o'clock bus?" he asked us, taking a sip of his coffee.

"Yes, sir," I answered. I didn't want to say too much. I didn't feel like telling my whole story again. My brain imagined the sheriff tracking down my mother's father and bringing him here. Hopefully, he wouldn't ask.

"This is John Kennedy's grandson," the old lady squawked, as she filled the sheriff's thermos.

"Old John? You're his grandson?"

"Yes, sir. We're waiting on him now. He's going to come down and see me while we wait for the next bus," I informed him. The sheriff's face went from happy to dour. The old lady handed him his things, which he took, never once looking away from me.

"John Kennedy, huh? Coming down here?" he bellowed.

"That's what my mother told me."

The sheriff just grunted and sipped his coffee. His steely gaze finally broke away from me. He brought a comb up to his mustache and brushed it contemplatively.

"Lilah ... how long has it been since Old John stepped foot in here?" he asked. It was the second time that he'd called him "Old John." I could only wonder how old he really was now.

"That old coot ..." she interrupted herself. "John Kennedy's never stepped foot in here once in the twenty years that door's been open. To be honest, I didn't even know he had children." She was still busy sliding donuts around from warming ovens in the back to the display case up front and brewing another pot of coffee all at once. They both had been speaking about me as if I wasn't even there.

The sheriff didn't say a word. I looked over at Marcus, clearly bothered. He was staring out the window at a car that had pulled up across the street. A man in a dark raincoat and hat sprung from the car and hotfooted his way across the street, shaking briskly as he came inside. My heart began beating faster as I wondered if it was him, Old John, John F. Kennedy, my grandfather.

"Morning, Judge," the sheriff announced, as the old-timer flapped his coat sides in the doorway. He slipped out of it and hung it on the coat tree against the wall, just above my cases. I collapsed at the table and rubbed my eyes, a little more anxious than I needed to be.

"Well, well, well," the rotund old geezer cheerily clucked. "Hopefully that coffee is fresh and hot, Lilah dear."

"It's all ready for ya, Judge," she answered back.

The sheriff used his coffee cup to motion in our direction. It was like a scene right out of an Old West movie, where everyone seemed fascinated by the outsiders.

"Judge, this here's Old John's grandson. Waitin' for him now to come down." The judge was surprised by this, and his whole demeanor shifted as he floated his huge hulking frame in our direction. He pulled his glasses from his face and tried to get a better look at us.

"Old John, ya say? Hell, I didn't even know that old coot had any kin, especially this young," he announced loudly. "Let's get a better look here," he continued, as he put his specs back on after cleaning the rain from them. He pulled up a stool next to ours, and I now had the feeling that we were both on display and being made a spectacle. Rather, I felt this way. Marcus seemed to be completely enjoying himself now.

"John Kennedy's grandson! I do say ..." The old judge put his porky hand on my shoulder and looked closely at my face. He just grunted. "Well, that's probably a good thing," he spoke, not really talking to me as much as he was about me.

"What's your name, son?" he asked me.

"My name? Sebastien. My name is Sebastien Ranes." I did my best to not stutter, moving around the words like obstacles.

"Sebastien Rayyynes?" He repeated my name, in shock. "You French, boy? Whoever gave you a name like that?"

"I guess my mother, sir."

"Your momma named you that?" he asked, literally dumbfounded. He took a deep breath and then took a big sip of coffee. "Lemme guess, no daddy. Bastard of the first degree, huh?" He gave Marcus a quick look but paid him no mind. "Don't worry, son ... I can tell these things. Your momma must be French. John Kennedy must've had children during the war and then abandoned them. That's it."

I tried hard to object, but he wasn't having any of it. He told me to calm down when I tried to set it straight and correct him. He seemed to have made up his mind about me as Old John didn't come across to him as someone who would have ever had a family.

"My mother's not French," I answered. The judge just laughed, and the sheriff just stood there watching and combing his mustache.

"Don't you fret, youngun'. No shame in being an immigrant. My great-great-grandpappy came over to this country from Bulgaria a long time ago. We's all a transplant at some point."

The sheriff finally interrupted. I thought he was going to clear it up for me. "He did say Old John was comin' over to see him too."

"Well ... now that's peculiah! Old John?" he called out, with a mild tone of sarcasm. "Up in here? I'll eat my hat, Sheriff. I will indeed. I will eat my hat."

I got the feeling that Old John, or rather my grandfather, was not a very likable person and had a foul reputation. The longer I sat there waiting, the greater the embarrassment I felt. I was praying to God, desperately, for him not to show. We'd already been there for close to an hour, so the pain of having to deal with Charlotte's family once again was already half over.

After the sheriff and the judge had left, both disappointed that they didn't get to see Old John stepping foot into the diner-cum-depot, Marcus and I slowly drifted back to our conversation from before.

"Your grandfather seems to be a delightful fellow, judging from how much everybody just *loves* him," Marcus pointed out.

"He's not my grandpa, he's my mother's father," I replied unhappily.

"Well, chief ... hate to break it to ya, but even if you're not too fond of him, he's still your grandpa."

"I wonder why they called him Old John?" I asked Marcus.

"Probably because it would cause too much of a scene continually calling him Old Asshole, which is about how it sounds," he responded. "But I guess we'll never know if he doesn't keep his appointment." Marcus checked his wristwatch again. His back was to the wall clock, which was in my direct line of sight. It was already closing in on six-thirty.

"Do you think it's good to have a reputation like that?" he asked me.

"No. That's pretty simple to tell."

"Well, to you and me it is, but Old John must either be oblivious to it or just doesn't give a damn about other people too much. I'd expect it to be the latter of the two, y'know?"

"Yeah, me too," I sighed. "Why is everyone in my family so messed up?"

"Messed up? Nah ... I think you mean selfish."

Marcus laughed out loud. He threw his head back and leaned against the back of his chair, lifting the front legs off the ground. "It does seem to be a pattern though, huh?" He spoke through his chortling, trying hard to be reserved, but not doing such a good job of it.

We sat there for another forty minutes, uninterrupted, until the bus finally showed a few minutes late. I was relieved when it pulled up in front and blocked out our view of Mount Vernon, almost as if it were a sign that the suffering was now over.

When I stood up and slung my bag over my shoulder, I glanced at my two cases and considered leaving them behind. The only problem was that the people here knew who I was. They would see to it that Old John got the cases, and he would then begrudgingly pay money to pass them on to my mother, and all would be for naught.

Marcus and I each grabbed a case and headed outside. Our new driver already had the storage compartment doors lifted and very adroitly took my luggage and stowed it. If Old John showed up now, I'd just say "sorry" and get on board anyway. I pulled out my ticket, and the driver gave it the once-over before handing it back to me. Before I climbed up, I gave a long look in both directions down the street just to make sure Old John really wasn't coming. Not a soul in sight. It was like the last day on earth, and Greyhound was collecting people for the rapture or something worse.

Once inside the bus, I felt happy again. I made my way toward the back of the bus, heading for my old seat, never even looking to see if it was open or not. As I looked around the seats, most of which were empty, I saw the usual collection of old people, fat people, young soldiers, an old woman with a sleeping child, and single men all headed back East. The back three rows were empty on both sides, and I knew that Marcus and I would stretch out a bit, looking to get a few hours' rest to unwind from the stress of our excursion into Mount Vernon. It had been a complete waste of time and two more hours on the journey for no reason. When my Aunt Sharon left me stranded in Los Angeles, I remembered how upset I had been about it. Now I was thankful to be forgotten. It shouldn't have made sense like that, but it did.

9.

SAINT LOUIS, MISSOURI

As we found our way quickly back onto the interstate, I busied myself by taking more notes. In close to three days of traveling, I had taken so many notes that the small cardboard-encased flip-ring notebook was now almost full. I had started off by jotting down only single words and phrases that stood out, along with prices and slogans that had repeatedly popped up, like *Go Greyhound* and *Have a Coke and a smile.* Now I wrote entire pages, one after another, about everything that happened. For the record, I had now done both, and while a cold can of soda always sounded good, I had had enough Greyhound to last me a lifetime.

The world outside was changing again. It was getting greener, denser, and more populated. The huge farmlands that went from one horizon to the next were getting smaller and fewer. Houses dotted the roadway, surrounded by restaurants, gas stations, and fast-food joints, which had a vested interest in changing the landscape permanently, one lighted sign at a time.

The passengers had changed as well. California had supplied a constant crop of men in military uniforms, and the desert had unending senior citizens traveling for a day to go see other senior citizens or shop at big-city malls or get their prescriptions filled someplace cheap. Now, the bus was mostly occupied by inner-city working black folks heading east. The volume of talking had gone up, as had the level of laughter in almost equal proportions. As I watched a lot of the riders conversing, it looked as if everyone knew one another and hadn't seen one another in a long time. Even Marcus was barely in his seat for a good part of the morning. Someone had a thermos of coffee and was kind enough to share a cup of it with him. A little while later, he returned with a small paper cup from the dispenser in the bathroom, full of hot coffee for me.

"He ya go!" he said. "On the house."

"Thanks, Marcus," I whispered, taking it. I could feel the hot coffee through the thin paper cup.

"Well, I think it's official now. You and the driver are the only white folks on the bus," he whispered back, as if letting me in on a secret joke or something I best keep quiet about.

"Too bad Monty isn't here," I answered, carefully taking a sip of the hot coffee. It tasted just like the stuff from the Roach Coach back in Albuquerque. No sugar really did make a difference.

"Yeah ... Monty was alright. Miss that old man already. Don't forget, we got to check and see if there's a message from him when we get to Saint Louis."

"I know," I nodded. I had thought about Monty and the secret pact we had made the day before. Two words went through my mind: *Daryl Hall*. The thought of being chased across the country by Leigh Allen didn't seem to compare to how I felt when I got off the bus in Mount Vernon. The only thing that bothered me about Charlotte's family was how I would've felt if I had been hoping to see them. If my hopes were up and they had let me down, I know it would've hurt and I would've been scarred. So naturally, sitting there in the back of the bus, taking more notes, the thought of them just burned me up inside.

"You want something to read?" Marcus asked, holding out his copy of *The Panther and The Lash*. "You can borrow it if you like."

I took it happily and thanked him. Even though I finally had something worthwhile to read, I stared at the back photo of Langston Hughes for some time. It was my first time getting such a close look at him. He had freckles around his eyes, which were deep set. I imagined he was on the verge of saying *"Hey now, Sebastien Ranes!"* It felt as if he was watching me just as much as I was looking at him. I smirked when I saw the background of the photo. It

looked like an airport or the outside of one of the many bus terminals that I had already passed through.

Marcus slipped away and was now sitting next to a woman. She
was probably the one with all the coffee. I flipped through the book,
not knowing where to start, but abruptly stopped on a blank page in
the back. Someone, maybe Marcus, had neatly written out a poem
in pencil. I read it slowly.

Tomorrow

We have tomorrow
Bright before us
Like a flame.

I interrupted myself in midsentence, pulling quickly away from
the page, and flipped to the back photo of Langston Hughes, and
stared at the square ring on his finger, contemplating that tomorrow
was going to be like a flame. I took another look down the aisle for
Marcus, who was sitting in the frontmost seat on the aisle, reclin-
ing with his legs crossed and talking. I could see his hand moving in
small gestures as he spoke to the woman beside him.

Flipping back through the book, I opened upon another short
poem that caught me with its hook. I stopped in the middle of it,
realizing exactly what it meant. I thought of only one person.

Out of love,
No regrets—
Though the return
Be never.

It felt like a message from Mr. Hughes directly to me. Maybe this
was what drew Marcus to keep reading this stuff. It was immediate
and direct. I felt uncomfortable about it and put the book down on

the seat next to me. I felt surrounded by both Langston Hughes and my mother all at once. *Though the return be never* reverberated in my head, calming me.

I dug my Walkman out and put on the Hall and Oates tape. I had already listened to it several times and knew most of the lyrics of every song. A few songs I didn't like at all and had to repeatedly fast-forward past them. Sometimes I just turned the volume down for a few minutes instead, so as not to waste the batteries. "Everytime You Go Away" and "I Can't Go for That" were my favorite songs. I remembered hearing "I Can't Go for That" over the lobby radio back in Albuquerque and had made a note about it in my book.

The bus meandered around downtown Saint Louis for some time, going down side streets and sitting at red lights. It was a sprawling and fast-moving city. A few people actually jumped off the bus as we sat at a couple of long red lights. The driver wasn't bothered by it at all, and as they were luggage-free, it was just a matter of pulling the handle to let them off. Maybe it was just easier to let folks do as they needed to rather than arguing about it. The rules clearly stated that there were no "unscheduled stops whatso-ever." But I could testify in court that most of the rules I'd read on the bathroom door had so far been ignored, more of them violated by the Greyhound drivers rather than the passengers themselves.

Watching the huge Arch of Saint Louis from off in the dis-tance slowly getting closer was the most impressive sight so far on the trip. The top of the big silver giant was enshrouded by nim-bus clouds that drifted past it continuously. Rain was still falling, making traffic slow, but the people in the streets outside moved around under a throng of black umbrellas, skirting the sidewalks, skipping over puddles, and darting in between the cars. The pedes-trians seemed to stretch out and bound across the crosswalks in packs, like it was an Olympic event. I watched several people mak-ing huge strides to get clear of the intersection and slip into a shop or an unmarked building.

Just before one-thirty, a few people commented that we were close, and several folks got their stuff ready and started to button up and pull on hats. The majority of the passengers were already standing when the driver pulled into the terminal and read off his message.

"Welcome to Saint Louis, everybody. It's almost one-thirty in the afternoon, and as you can see outside, it's wet and rainy. Be careful disembarking after we stop, and all those continuing east, you'll need to transfer to the 1684 to Pittsburgh, Philadelphia, and New York. Thanks for riding with us, and stay safe."

Yet another style of delivery in the overhead announcement, I thought. His message was full of caution and genuine-sounding concern, but I did notice that he never once mentioned the word *Greyhound*. Pulling around the massive stone structure that was doubling as a terminal, we sat and waited for a moment for another bus to pull out before taking its parking space.

"You gonna get over to the information counter and check that message?" Marcus wondered.

"Yeah, I guess I better," I replied.

"I have to make a few phone calls, so I'll be a bit busy. You alright?"

"Yeah, don't worry," I said. "I'm not going to take off with any strange police officers. Besides, I have to call my grandma and let her know what time I'm getting in tomorrow."

Marcus dug into his pocket, counted his change, and then gave me eight quarters.

"It's okay, Marcus. I've got money."

"But you don't got any change, do you?" he pointed out.

I searched my pockets. All I had was thirty-five cents and some lint.

"You can give me two dollars if it makes you feel any better," he said. I quickly pulled out the cash and handed it over.

"Thanks, Marcus."

"No, thank you, Sebastien Ranes. You doin' alright? Are you still rattled about stopping in Mount Vernon?"

"Nah ... I'm over it," I answered quickly. "I'm actually relieved. At least I won't fall for the 'let's go live with my parents in Missouri' when that one comes up."

"Don't wanna fall for the okey-doke? That's my boy," he smiled.

"My thoughts exactly."

Inside of the Saint Louis Greyhound Terminal, everything was bigger, much bigger. It was easily the largest terminal I'd been in so far. It was the size of a museum or an airport terminal. The high ceiling was decorated, ornate, and painted. Large columns rose up both sides of the brightly polished marble-floored depot, supporting it. The air-conditioner pumped out chilly air. Everything didn't just appear to be clean and well cared for—it looked like it up close. It was one of the nicest Greyhound stations thus far. The gift shop was massive in size, and from only a passing glance, it looked as if they sold anything and everything a person traveling might need, including a huge assortment of Greyhound paraphernalia, which probably no one needed.

A long bank of metal-and-glass telephone booths, with black plastic seats and sliding doors for privacy, sat in the middle of the lobby in front of a large seating area. Marcus waved at me as he shut himself inside of one and picked up the receiver to call. I made my way across the lobby to a small office against the wall. Two ladies were busy working, answering the telephone and typing. I stood at the tall counter, barely visible, but one of them saw me and raised a hand, indicating it would be a minute as she was talking on the phone.

I stood there for a few moments listening to her give someone directions. When she finished, she got up and came my way.

"Can I help you?" she asked, leaning forward against the dark wooden counter to get a closer look at me. Her well-shaped bosom heaved forward as she crossed her arms in front of her on the counter and smiled at me. The other lady was still busy at a typewriter in the back, but I could only tell that from the sound. My eyes were locked on the woman in front of me in the white polka-dotted blouse.

"Yes, I'm checking to see ..." I began, hoping to get the whole thing out of mouth cleanly. But I hesitated.

"Yes ...?" she queried me, unflinching. My gaze went down to her chest again, and I probably blushed.

"I need to see if I, I, I have a message? A message?"

"What's your name, sweetie? You're awfully cute," she said. I was terrified inside to answer for all the usual reasons. My body was constricting and turning into wood as I stood there.

"Sebastien," I answered, disguising my nervousness through some coughing. "Ahem ... Sebastien Ranes."

The lady turned to the woman at the typewriter. "Are there any messages for Sebastien *Ranes*?" she asked. I watched her as she turned and took a few steps away from the counter toward her desk. She was lovely to look at from any direction. She carefully placed a hand on her hip and canted her rear end. Her close-fitting black skirt drew the lines of her body like a roadmap I'd never thought to follow before.

"The message book is on your desk, Jackie," the other lady responded, never looking away from her work. When she bent over her desk and lifted up on her tippie-toes to stretch for the message book, my eyes became as big as teacup saucers. My mind stopped working, and I only hoped I wasn't drooling. If I was, I just hoped that it wasn't visible. She whipped her head around and caught the expression cemented on my face. Now I knew for sure that I was blushing, because she giggled.

"One second, let me look through the book," she announced, turning back to her desk. I thought I was dreaming when she ran her hand down her backside, smoothing the fabric of her skirt, but the thought did occur to me that she was going to lift it up for me as she touched the hem. It was an absurd and fleeting fantasy, and it hit me that, before this trip, I didn't used to look at women and feel like this. She turned back to me and approached the counter one more time with the book, going down the pages, looking for my name. There must have been a lot of messages.

"Sebastien *Ranes*. No, I'm sorry, honey. I don't see anything here for you. Can I help you with anything else though?" she asked politely. She once more rested herself against the partition between us and met my bewilderment with a smile. She was pushing herself forward again, and I was trying desperately not to look.

"If only ... too bad I have to leave ..." My words were more like fragments as they left my lips. I didn't believe that I had actually said them either, as much as thought them. I was magnetically attracted to her in every way. She must've been having a slow day, because she just stared at me. I didn't have a chance in the world with her, but she laughed at what I said regardless.

"Why don't you step to the doorway to your left?" she suggested. I immediately wondered what I had gotten myself into. It was then that the typing in the background suddenly stopped and the other lady looked up with a smirk.

"Okay," I replied. The door she had mentioned was the same dark wood as the counter but had a frosted pane of textured glass and gold letters that read *Private Office*. I stepped lightly over to it as it opened. Jackie stood there with the door ajar, holding the knob and beaming at me. She motioned at me with her index finger to come closer. When I did, she noticed my Greyhound jacket and brushed the sleeve. I was very thankful that I had bathed back in Albuquerque and didn't smell.

"Nice coat. You worked for Greyhound long?" she asked, moving her hand across the fuzzy collar. She was standing so close to me now that I could smell her perfume. I had never been this close to a real woman before. It was exhilarating, and I thought my heart was going to stop working. Her dark chestnut hair was wavy and long but was held back with a clip. I was trying to look at her completely but was easily overwhelmed.

"Somebody gave it to me," I replied, almost in a whisper, transfixed.

She looked past me out into the lobby for only a brief second and then leaned down and kissed me on the cheek. I was breathless and couldn't blink. She grabbed my hand and put it on her hip, which was soft and warm and everything I always thought a real woman would feel like. She then moved in again and kissed me on the lips. Her other hand had a firm hold on my collar, and I was lifeless under her control.

I felt her lips peel away from mine and her hot breath exhale across my face. I momentarily worried that my breath smelled like coffee.

"Are you French, Sebastien Ranes? That sure is a nice name." Her words hit me like waves on a beach, and I noticed that every one of them slowly began to get farther from me as she pulled away. What I was feeling now must have been longing, because it was painful.

"Everyone always asks me that. Sometimes I wish I was."

"You sure are a strange boy, but you sure are something to look at."

"So are you," I replied.

"A strange boy?" she joked. "Don't worry ... I know," she answered back with a wink. "Sorry you didn't have a message. Was it important?"

"No, not really," I answered.

"Alright, sweetie. You have a safe trip home, okay?"

"Thanks, Jackie," was all I could manage. When she closed the door, the words *Private Office* took on a whole new meaning for me. I stepped away slowly and back toward the phone booths in the center of the lobby. I turned back to see Jackie watching me from the corner of her eye as I left. She waved. I thought she was going to blow me a kiss, but she didn't. I felt like a zombie from a late-night movie as I floated across the tiled marble floor toward the bank of pay phones, without a single thought in my head but the smell of her perfume and the memory of her figure. I stopped outside of the one Marcus was in and rested against it, semi-bewildered.

He was talking into the receiver but paused when he saw my face on the other side of the glass. He pulled the phone away, rested it on his shoulder, and slid open the glass door.

"I just want you to know, I witnessed that whole damn thing ... and I'm proud of you," he laughed. His eyes seemed to examine my face for some reason. "You seen yourself lately?" he asked, closing the door again, going back to his conversation.

I caught my bare reflection in the clear glass of the open booth next to Marcus. It was hard to tell, but my lips looked red and smeared. What was completely obvious, though, was the red lip print that Jackie had left on my cheek. My face was covered in lipstick, and I didn't have any way to get it off. Marcus was now completely engrossed in his conversation and would most likely tell me to go into the bathroom to wash it off.

Looking up at the large clock affixed to the marble wall, I could see it was closing in on two o'clock, and I still hadn't called back to Altoona yet, or gone to the restroom, or got a snack from the gift shop. I rationalized that if I walked away from one of the only open phone booths to go wash up, I'd probably miss my opportunity. I slowly slid the door closed and parked myself on the triangular bench with the receiver in my hand. After listening for the tone, I dialed the numbers and waited for the automated payment response to come on.

"Please insert ... one dollar ... and seventy-five cents ... for the first ... five minutes." The line began beeping after the message ended. I dropped in the entire two dollars in quarters and waited.

"Thank you ... you have ... twenty-five cents credit," then the line started ringing.

"Hey-loww?" Unexpectedly, it was my grandpa. I was glad that I hadn't decided to call collect.

"Grandpa ... it's me, Sebastien," I announced.

"Well, hello, Sebby. Are you all right? Your grandmother tells me you're traveling the country solo these days."

"Yeah, what can I say, Grandpa?" I responded back in kind. "At least the coffee's been good." He laughed at the remark.

"Hopefully not better than what I make. I usually like a bit of whiskey in mine, but don't tell your grandma." I knew he was just joking with me.

"Me too. Don't worry, though. The last place I was at they burned the coffee pretty bad."

"What time you getting in?"

"The schedule says 6:45 a.m. We were a bit late coming into Saint Louis this afternoon ... so probably a little later."

"You in Saint Louis? Did you get to see that Arch?" he asked.

The automated operator cut in, *"One minute remaining. Please insert more coins ... now."* I had to wait a second before the line came back on.

"Only from the window, Grandpa," I answered.

"Probably better that way. I wouldn't go up there if they paid me," he commented.

"Me neither," I remarked.

"Well, you be safe and hurry on home," he urged.

"Will do, Grandpa."

"Okay, I love you. See you in the morning." It clicked back to dial tone and all the change dropped through the torso of the phone and into its hollow belly. I made my way through the lobby and into the men's restroom to wash up and try to make it to the gift shop before getting back on the bus. I had a strange feeling now going into the men's room by myself that I didn't have before. Overhead, the music stopped and made way for my boarding call.

"First call, first call ... now boarding the 1684 to Columbus, Pittsburgh, Philadelphia, and New York on aisle 20. Departs 2:15. First call ... first call."

There it was. I had to hurry and get out of the terminal if I was going to make it back on the bus to grab the backseat and hold it. Marcus had vanished while I was talking on the phone. I stood at the sink and washed my hands and face. The water was blistering hot, and the cold wasn't working at all. I did my best with the paper towels and lack of soap. I had to step carefully as I made my way around the bathroom, as it was covered in half an inch of water coming out of the toilet stalls. Not wanting to wait around to see what was blocking the toilet, I got out of there, not seeing any reason to press my luck.

Outside, I stood by myself on the platform, watching business as usual unfold around me while waiting to get back on the bus. Saint Louis was an interesting place. As far as big cities went, it had an entirely different look about it that wasn't easy to define. It felt different too. The air was cleaner, and there seemed to be constant movement everywhere I stood. Maybe it felt heavier, more dense, something unexplainable. I was mystified by the Arch that loomed up into the sky at an odd angle. No matter where I stood on the platform, I could see it either directly or in the reflection of something like a newspaper machine or a plate-glass window. The closer you were to it, the stranger it became. It gave me the creeps as the clouds eerily slipped around it, engulfing it and grabbing at its sharp edges. The Arch looked like an artifact from another world or something that was being used as a transmitter to make intergalactic phone calls. I laughed to myself, realizing that I would rather be lost on earth somewhere and not know my place rather than be lost in the universe, trapped in some strange city with only this peculiar object to call home or keep me company. But at least the Arch would tell me that I wasn't alone. The more I contemplated it, I realized that there just wasn't much difference in the two. From longer distances though, the Arch looked normal. It gave you the feeling that it was something designed by the same guy who devised the golden arches for McDonald's, but that he only gave the city half the supplies needed to construct it. Maybe two arches would've just looked silly. No one else on the platform seemed bothered by it. Everyone else was too wrapped up getting from one bus to the next or collecting their luggage from the porters and struggling to get out of there as fast as their crumpled bodies would carry them. Everyone looked wounded.

I waited alone, blending into the concrete along the terminal wall, watching the porters load all the bags into the underside of the bus. Some people were carrying suitcases, some people had boxes, and one man only had a guitar. Several people though, more than most, had all their belongings stuffed into black plastic garbage bags with stickers on the outside of them, identifying who they belonged to. The trash bags were the first things loaded and were tossed hard, bag by bag, into the rear compartment in an obvious attempt to save space. Next, the duffel bags and the musical instruments, then the heavier luggage and boxes, were all placed carefully in the midsection. My two cases were some of the last bags loaded. I stared at them the whole time, contemplating their demise and how that was going to come about. They still had mud caked along the bottom corners from the night before and now had multiple tags hanging from the handles, which weren't there when they were loaded back in Stockton. Someone had even gone so far as to slap a red Trailways sticker on the outside with the word *PITT* in bold black letters just below the famous white logo.

Several passengers had already boarded. So far, no one with kids had gotten on, so I hoped that Marcus and I would once more, and for the last time, have the backseat to ourselves. I hadn't seen him since the phone booth earlier and began to wonder where he was.

I decided to board early, as the overhead call had already sounded. Once I got up the stairs, the driver was seated and expecting me to show him my ticket. I dug into my pocket for the stub. He was carefully examining my Greyhound jacket with a grin.

"You Sebastien Ranes?" he asked.

"Yes, sir," I responded mechanically, as I found my ticket folded in the back pocket of my jeans. After a cursory glance, he gave it back to me.

"Nice jacket. Where did you get it?"

"It was a gift from someone in Albuquerque. No one was using it anymore, so he said I could have it."

His face tightened, wondering if I was lying to him. "A gift from whom?" he asked bluntly.

"A man named Harley Earl," I said. Just the mention of Harley's name changed everything about the man.

"Wow ... old Harley gave that to ya? Man, I should've guessed it. I haven't seen him in a while. They switched me off the 1364 a few months back. How is old Harley?"

"He's a really nice man," I answered, minding myself carefully.

"Yeah, kid. He sure is. Alright, you seem to be in the right place. Go have a seat."

As I made the long walk back, I began to recognize a lot of the faces from the bus that Marcus and I had gotten off earlier in Mount Vernon this morning. We had caught up to them due to the extra-long layover in Saint Louis. Several people recognized me and smiled. A few people even said hello. There were some passengers who had been on the bus since Los Angeles and were continuing on to Pittsburgh. But so far, no Marcus, and nobody was yet sitting in the back three rows. It was the Greyhound Wasteland for sure. I felt an incredible sadness not seeing him there and hoped that something hadn't gone wrong. Maybe the police were looking for him but hadn't said anything to Monty about it.

When the driver started the bus, I panicked. I wanted to run back up to the front to tell him to wait, but I reluctantly sat down in Marcus's seat knowing that it was futile, that he wouldn't listen. I was a kid traveling alone. Maybe the driver would get mad and make me sit up front next to him or just take me off the bus for causing problems. Just as I was starting to boil in my frustration, I saw Marcus's figure running through the terminal, dodging people and cars, running along the busway, coming for us. He was carrying something in his hands and trying to wave at us all at the same time. The driver was going for the handle to close the doors.

I launched from my seat and stepped down the aisle. "Driver, wait!" I yelled out excitedly. I caught his concerned gaze first in the long mirror. Annoyed, he turned around to address me. I was waiting for him to tell me to sit down, shut up, and not interrupt him.

"Look, someone's coming!" I pointed out the window. The driver turned and looked outside, trying to spot whatever I was making such a fuss about. Marcus was sprinting through the outer terminal several buses down, clearly visible and trying to wave for us to wait. He was having trouble gesturing with his hands full. Once the driver saw him, he pulled the doors back open and watched him run to get on.

When Marcus appeared at the top of the steps, a few people clapped that he had made it, and Marcus tried to smile through several out-of-breath pants. He was clutching his ticket beneath the white-and-red paper bags in his arms, which were covered in raindrops. The driver examined his stub and let him on.

"Thank you," he replied.

I smiled from ear to ear once he saw me. "Wow, that was too close!" I said.

"You ain't kidding!" he agreed. He lifted up the two bags, showing me where he'd gone and what it was that almost made him miss the bus.

"McDonald's!" he announced. "I thought you might be hungry. I was trying not to spill the drinks the whole way back. Someone in the terminal said that it was only a block over, but it was more like two."

"I can't believe it!" I responded, shocked. I was surprised, but found it funny that he'd gone for McDonald's. "I'm starving to death, Marcus. How did you know?"

"Buddy, that makes two of us."

We ate the food as the bus pulled away from the Greyhound Terminal and out of downtown Saint Louis. Like clockwork, the driver came on the overhead and addressed us.

"Good afternoon, ladies and gentlemen. Welcome to the 1684 to Columbus, Pittsburgh, Philadelphia, and New York. We have an approximate drive time of eight hours and fifteen minutes. This is the afternoon express, so we'll only be stopping in Indianapolis long enough to refuel. There will be an adjustment to time as we cross into Indiana and the Eastern time zone of one hour. According to the latest reports, the rain should slow this afternoon and finally break by this evening. With any luck, we should be pulling into Columbus with clear skies. Other than that, all posted rules apply. Thank you for riding with us."

Both Marcus and I listened with rapt attention as we ate our cheeseburgers and drank our ice-cold soda.

"That was informative," he said.

"Easily the best yet. Weather report, time change, schedule announcement, and no rules."

"Yeah, I think I'm pretty clear on what not to do on a Greyhound bus at this point," he replied sarcastically.

"Well, they never said anything about half the stuff that we've seen in the last few days." My words came out in between bites and chews of French fries and hamburger.

"This is it, buddy. The final stretch. You're almost home," he pointed out. My mind could now see the distance between Pittsburgh and Altoona. It was a matter of continually dwindling hours before I'd have to switch to the last bus, taking me into Altoona. The schedule said five-thirty tomorrow morning in small black numbers.

"Thanks for the lunch, Marcus."

"Don't sweat it. I'll let you pick up dinner tonight in Columbus with your vouchers. You still got some left?"

"Sure do," I answered.

"Alright. Then we set," he affirmed, enjoying his French fries. "I've gotta say, that was the coldest May rain that I've been caught in in a long time," he continued.

"Eight years," I said thoughtfully, or rather without thinking.

Marcus stopped his eating and looked over at me without saying a word. "That's right, eight years. A long time." His words were a little darker now, more contemplative.

"Were you able to get a hold of anyone back home?" I asked. We hadn't spoken about our phone calls, but it seemed like a good time to ask.

"I did. I've spoken to my moms. She said she'll be glad to see me." His voice trailed off behind his words. Anyone paying attention, including myself, could've been able to tell that something was wrong. Marcus's expression altered. He drank his soda and looked away from me. He was making slurping sounds as he got to the bottom, finishing it.

"Some people don't want to see you anymore because you were in prison?"

He sighed. "Something like that. For me, my moms is the only person who ever stuck by me. She sent me packages all the time when I was on the inside. Letters, pictures, candy, magazines, cigarettes, even though she don't smoke herself," he said, leaning in closer. "She kept my spirits up, helped me to remember that there was always still something for me outside of that place, that life would always be there and that folks thought about me and cared. Prison would've been very different without her." He looked at me closely. "That's what a moms is supposed to do."

"Life would've been different without her," I repeated. Marcus looked at me carefully, understanding what I meant as if it was crystal clear.

"That's absolutely right, partner," he agreed with a grin.

"Did you get in touch with your grams?" he asked.

"No, she was out when I called."

Marcus was a little shocked. "Uh-huh, nobody was home?"

"I spoke to my grandpa. He said he'd be there to get me in the morning."

"Okay ... that's a good thing, then. Let me ask you though ..." Marcus's face was serious. "They're gonna be there, aren't they? I won't be able to get off and stay with ya."

I laughed about it, making light of what he'd already heard and witnessed for himself. "Thanks, Marcus. They'll be there. I'm sure of it," I answered.

"Okay, but I'm just sayin' ... y'know?"

"I appreciate it, but I know that they'll be there to get me. She's my grandma." Even the thought of my grandma letting me down or not being there to get me seemed completely out of the question. She had never given me a reason to doubt how much she loved me, and it was probably why I was just glad to be getting back. Even though I knew that Altoona wasn't my home, and probably never would be, being with her and my grandpa at their house, with my bedroom up in the oversize garret room, felt more like home than any I had known thus far.

I hadn't thought about my room in the attic the whole trip, but I remembered how much Beanie always wanted it for her own. She probably took it after I left, leaving me the small bedroom on the second floor with the wood-paneled walls and narrow windows near the ceiling, which no one ever slept in. The room in the attic was well lit, spacious, and airy. I used to lie in the huge bed near the front windows that overlooked the street and watch the rain fall on the rooftops of the other houses. The attic was always warm in the winter and cool in the summer. During hot days, my grandpa would pull out the fans from the garage and put them up there to circulate the air, making it even nicer. He used to tell me to not play with the plug and electrocute myself, as if I was a baby, but I knew he was just kidding around. I'd spent hours sitting in the bed reading alone and listening to the radio, happy all by myself.

Part of the attic was used for storage. Walls had been built going in all directions, making three different rooms from the space the attic provided. It was like a maze. There was over thirty years of storage in the attic and always lots of interesting stuff to look through. I got in trouble a few times for digging through some of it, but it never stopped me, as I always thought it was the most fascinating place in the world.

Altoona was a place I knew like the back of my hand. I'd spent entire summer days from sunup to sundown riding my bike through all the different neighborhoods. My grandma's house was connected to a rolling churchyard and an old stone church that never had a Sunday service and whose bell rarely ever rang. I'd spent more time on church property playing ball in the grass than people probably spent praying inside. The church tower, with the foreboding bell enclave, could be seen from a long way off, which made it easy to find my way back.

A small deli and market called Miller's Corner was usually the first stop for soda and gum. Just past the Weiss Grocery Store in a different neighborhood was a community swimming pool and a few baseball diamonds. The climb up the hill was so steep, I usually had to get off the bike and walk. The farther I went, the stranger and more run-down the houses got. The house that I had been born in, that my mother had once rented, was several blocks in that same direction. I would often bike over just to get another look and see who was living there now. All I knew was that it wasn't me, and judging by the shape the house was in, I was thankful. But maybe I shouldn't have been so quick to judge.

My aunt lived next to the baseball diamonds, and we would all pile in the car and drive over to see them every few days and watch Little League baseball. My grandpa always drove us, and it seemed to be farther than it was because of how slowly he drove. I would usually get carsick in the backseat, as it was the only car I had ever been in that was upholstered in black velvet. It was a white 1977 Chrysler Cordoba, and my grandma loved it. I loved it too, whenever I got to ride in the front seat, but I hated it whenever I got penned in the back with Beanie. It was stifling, soft, and everything the backseat of a car shouldn't be. It was a long way from the backseat of a bus as well.

I was going to listen to my Walkman, but the driver had turned on the overhead radio, which was tuned to the oldies station that played long blocks of the Beach Boys and Elvis Presley. Marcus was reading his book, and his face was stuck in concentration. We had pulled away from Saint Louis entirely now, and all my thoughts were focused on being back. I couldn't think of much else, and I imagined it was the same for him too.

When Marcus finally put the book away, he gave all the usual signals that he was about to have a cigarette. As I watched him light up, it occurred to me that I didn't have the same ill will toward Marcus and his smoking habit that I had for my mother and her habit when she would light up. Maybe it was because he didn't chain-smoke. He didn't have endless fits of coughing until his face and head exploded or fill up drinking glasses with cigarette butts and only ever rinse those same glasses in lukewarm water. Maybe it was all those things and the fact that he didn't reek like a wet ashtray all the time, or rather at all. That's what made me have no concern about his habit. He was sparing with his cigarettes, often had people openly offering him one, without having to ask, and always seemed happy, relaxed, and in good spirits. He could've been in a television commercial advertising Marlboro cigarettes, he was so calm and relaxed. Not the frantic, hacking, red-faced mess that my mother was. She was fit for the funny farm and looked like someone in front of a firing squad every time she had a cancer stick hanging haphazardly from her lip. I wondered if I would ever smoke cigarettes but quickly hoped not. Marcus said people never seem to learn from the mistakes of others, no matter how many examples they're given. He said you could probably test it in a laboratory and prove it every time. This stuck in my mind and resurfaced as I thought about whether I would smoke cigarettes or not.

For a few hours, we both sat quietly, listening to the radio. Marcus had spent a good portion of the afternoon reading *The Catcher in the*

Rye and was now more than halfway through it. I found it exciting that he could read that fast. When I asked him if there was a special trick to it, he just laughed and kept right on reading.

After a pause, he said, "Once you've read a couple hundred books, you'll figure it out as well. It ain't hard."

"You get to read a lot of books in prison?"

"You get to read constantly," he continued, still absorbed, flipping another page methodically in time, like the beat of a drum.

"Food any good?" I asked.

He laughed. "Mine was, being the head cook. I ate better than all the prisoners and most of the employees. I only ever ate what the warden ate."

"Did you fight a lot in prison?" I asked. "People in movies about prison always fight a lot."

"Some do, some don't. I rarely ever did," he answered. He put the book away, folding a corner over. "Rarely," he emphasized.

"Were you ever in prison with Al Capone?" I wondered aloud. He was someone I'd heard about in school who had gone to prison.

"Al Capone?" He laughed out loud. "Man, he died a long time ago. Long before I showed up." He shook his head and kept right on chuckling. "What's your latest interest in prison? You planning on making a visit? I hope not."

"No ... me neither," I answered sheepishly.

"I was in the same prison as Charles Manson," Marcus noted aloud.

"Who's he?" I asked.

"You've never heard of Charles Manson?"

"No," I replied meekly. "Who's Charles Manson?"

"Don't worry. If you don't know who he is, you will. He's on TV enough," he stated.

I began to mentally drift. "Maybe my dad was in prison. Maybe that was why he never called or came around," I suggested.

"What makes you say that?" he rejoined.

"I don't know. Maybe ... I ... just ..." I couldn't find an explanation for what I was thinking about.

"Look, sometimes there is no answer or reason. Some people

don't want to be fathers, y'know? Not everyone's cut out, see. I'm not making any excuses for the sorry piece of trash, but he doesn't have to be in prison to not come around. Besides, you know what the truth is, and it has nothing to do with prison." I looked at Marcus silently for a moment.

"Sorry I called your birth pops a sorry piece of trash. I was just trying to be real with ya, that's all."

"Cowards and men."

"That's right," Marcus acknowledged. "Soon, you'll come to grips with the fact that deep down we're all the same, but some folks will work overtime to not act the same. It's real life."

"Deep down, we're all the same ..." I repeated quietly, contemplating what he said. I didn't feel the same, not by a long shot, but I think that I understood it.

"Deep down ... we are all the same, and don't you forget it," he reaffirmed. "But it doesn't mean to turn your back on them or let your guard down."

Marcus and I continued talking for the bulk of the afternoon. The conversation shifted around from getting home by tomorrow, to music, to all the waitresses we had met, specifically the black waitress back in Gallup. I admitted to Marcus that I thought she was the most beautiful girl I'd ever seen. He just laughed out loud and told me I'd feel that way about a lot of girls in the next few years and that it was perfectly natural.

"If I can tell you anything about girls, the one thing you need to remember—and never forget," he emphasized, "is that you can't choose who you'll fall in love with. You may *think* you can choose, but it just gets more complicated. Things get weird when you mix women with your own expectations."

"I think you may have lost me," I rejoined, but he made me write down what he said, word for word, in my notebook.

"File that under '*incredibly important,*'" he remarked, pleased with what he had said. During the afternoon, I found myself looking out of the windows on the opposite side of the bus. We had passed lots of semi trucks on the road in the past few days and even seen a few convoys, but what we were seeing now was different.

We kept passing large convoys, one after another. The line of trucks at times was so long that it blotted out the view as we slowly crept past. Marcus and I counted a few lines and were surprised every time we would break twenty.

"There's no way this convoy's gonna break twenty," he'd say, but we just kept counting. The record was thirty-two trucks in a row. Once, the driver even came on the overhead, a little overwhelmed and amused.

"That's the biggest convoy I've ever seen."

Trucks filled the sides of the highways at rest stops and weigh stations. Pieces of blown-out rubber tires seemed to litter the roadway across the entire landscape and could've been a healthy food source for any animal that would eat them. Numerous times we passed lone tractor-trailers on the soft shoulder changing a tire. Once we even passed a truck that had gone off the side and into a field, spilling boxes of fruit everywhere.

When we had talked about almost every subject I could think of, Marcus finally asked me the question.

"You gonna tell me about what happened two years ago?"

"Why do you ask?" I deflected it unknowingly.

"Stuff like that is usually best let out of the darkness. It's usually like a poisonous snake that someone might put inside a black box, and then you're always afraid to open the lid."

"Maybe it's better that way. Not to ever look, you know?" I stated.

"Well, it's all well and good, but eventually the snake in the box is going to die and turn to dust, and the person who put it in there to begin with goes on being afraid to open the lid for no reason."

I knew what Marcus was driving at, and he was right about that as well. "You learn about all this stuff in prison?" I asked.

"Maybe ... maybe not, but you'll be the one with a dead snake in the box if you don't lift the lid."

"Where do I begin?" I asked.

"Just start off anywhere you like. It'll be easier than you know."

"Two years ago, my mother ..." I coughed, clearing my throat, "... my sister and I all lived together in an apartment. She was dating this sleazebag named Roger McDougall-Daggett," I began.

"Are you messin' with me? Roger McDougall-Daggett? What kind of a sissy-ass name is that?" he asked, almost at the point of laughter.

"I don't know, but everybody he met, he always introduced himself that way. He was even more annoying about it on the phone because he would spell it out. *'Capital em-small-cee. Capital Dee! Oo-you-gee. Ayyy. Double ell. Hyphen! Capital Dee! Ayyy. Double Gee, E. Double tee. McDougall-Daggett, just like it sounds!'* " I imitated from memory.

Marcus couldn't help but laugh hysterically now. "Man, I didn't think your story was going to be like this," he rejoined, laughing.

"He was always drinking, and he talked nonstop about his great-great-grandpappy being a Civil War hero in the history books. I didn't like him at all, nor did Beanie, but my idiotic mother was in love with the guy and laughed at all his stupid jokes and dull stories." I was breathing bitter disgust as I thought of Roger.

"Civil War hero, huh? North or South?" Marcus asked.

"South. It was all he ever carried on about. How the South would one day rise again. He said he was a descendant of Stonewall Jackson too."

"Stonewall Jackson ... wow, that's rich." Marcus seemed to be taking mental notes, pressing his lips and leaning in to hear better.

"Anyway, he was always drunk and on something. One day, when I came home from school, our dog, Gorilla, was nowhere to be found."

"You had a dog named Gorilla?" he interjected.

"It was a little black poodle and always made strange grunting sounds all day and all night, even when it slept. Beanie named him that. Our neighbor said the dog probably had asthma."

Marcus made the sound of a wheezing gorilla as quiet as he could without making a scene. "Man, your story just keeps getting weirder," he added.

"Roger was passed out in the bathroom drunk, but before I could wake him up, the police came and were knocking on the apartment door. Someone had seen him outside in the parking lot of the complex beating the dog to death with his bare hands. They arrested him and took him away in handcuffs. He struggled with the police and tried to get away. He was yelling at me the whole way out the door."

Marcus's face cringed when I mentioned Roger beating the dog to death against the hot cement like a madman. "What the hell did he do that for? Sorry. Did you see the guy again?"

I paused for a moment and stared out the window, watching the traffic. "When my mother found out that he'd been arrested and had killed the dog, she broke it off with him and refused to post his bail. At the time, she had been saving money for us to move into a house or buy herself a different car ... something. She had almost a thousand dollars, and Roger knew about it. Four days later, I came home from school, and no one else was in the apartment, but the door had been kicked in."

"He broke into the apartment to get the money," Marcus surmised.

I nodded yes. "Did I mention that my mother also had a loaded shotgun in the hallway closet? My uncle gave it to her after someone tried coming through our bedroom window one night."

Marcus's eyes grew wide. "Damn" was all he said.

"Roger was angry and looked strange. He was raging and pissed off that my mother had quit him and left him to sit in jail." I took a huge breath of air. Marcus just watched me without interrupting.

"I'd never seen him like that before. He was holding the shotgun and loading it with shells when he saw me. He pointed the shotgun at me as I stood in the hallway. He started screaming, '*Where's the money? Where's the money?*' When I tried to run, I ducked from the hallway into the kitchen. I didn't think he was going to fire at me, but his first shot hit the air-conditioning unit in the window. The gun sounded like a loud explosion going off in my head. He fired a second time and hit the kitchen cabinets above me. They splintered everywhere. I was crouched down on the kitchen floor against the refrigerator door in the corner. He screamed again about the money as he got closer, but my head was ringing. I remember I was crying. He put the front end of the shotgun against my forehead and pushed me back into the refrigerator door. When I looked up, all I could see was the bottom of the barrel of the shotgun rising back up toward his face. He was smiling on the other end. He told me to quit crying."

"Holy shit ... say what? What an evil son of a bitch," Marcus said, squirming around in his seat.

"It wasn't a good moment for me. When he pulled the trigger back, all I heard was this loud metallic sound, like a dry snap, but nothing followed. I looked up at him, and he was confused. He thought he was going to kill me. As soon as he took the gun from my head and began to lift it upright, it fired. He blew a hole in the kitchen ceiling, and plaster showered down on us from above. My ears were ringing so loud I could barely hear anything else. Before he slammed the butt of the gun to my head, I heard him say that if he ever saw me again, he'd pull the trigger and I wouldn't be so lucky. After that, I don't remember much. It's kinda blank. "

I sighed and sat still for a moment and stared blankly into the nowhere that I was surrounded by.

"I couldn't hear very well for weeks. I had a ringing in my ears for almost a month. Once the ringing faded, I began stuttering all the time. It came on gradually, but it might as well have been there the whole time. I was teased about it a lot. Saying my own name is *still* the hardest thing for me to do."

"That's a really messed-up story, Sebastien. My heart goes out to you, bro. Did you ever see that fool Roger McDougall-Daggett again?"

"No. He drove off with the shotgun before the police got there, but he didn't get the money. Beanie and my mother were downstairs in the parking lot when they heard the shots go off. They were terrified, but they both ran upstairs to help me. I think it was the one time my mother may have cared. After that, she was mad about

Roger not working out, and was upset and seemed to blame Beanie and me for the whole thing. Beanie and my mother argued about it, and within a few months we were finally sent to go live back in Altoona, which was last year."

"Your mother is a cold-ass piece of work, man. Animals in the wild take better care of their kids."

"If you ever listen to her talk, all she ever talks about is 'all the sacrifices she made for us' and all the things she had to do without because of us. She likes to lay on the guilt and doesn't listen to anybody else."

"That's some tragic-ass shit. I don't know what the hell to say. I've been through some hard times my damn self, but my moms and pops were always close—they were always together, no matter what. I saw some messed-up stuff in prison too, but you're just a kid. No offense. You shouldn't have stories like that for another fifteen years." Marcus's tone seemed to rise as he began to get angry thinking about it. Even though he had never met her, I could tell that Marcus had had just about enough of my mother.

"And let me say this," he spat, now furious. "Some people will tell you that they make, or have made, sacrifices for you, but don't buy it. The truth is simple: everything they ever did was for themselves, and what they did had little bearing on what was best for you. You were just a ... hostage, along for the ride. You were just furniture, luggage, window dressing, dead weight to them. At least it's a good thing that you're hip to it now."

As I watched Marcus going off on a rant, I listened, because he was more serious than he had been. "People like that are toxic and will do everything they can to ruin your life. And if they can't do it alone, they'll find others to help them, no matter how long it takes." What he said got to me and crept under my skin, giving me a chill. It was a disturbing thought. She was doing it all again with Dick and didn't care on any level about Beanie or me. Everything she was doing was for herself, and she'd never change.

Marcus and I both sat quietly for quite some time after I told him my story. Feeling the urge, I stood up, excused myself and went inside the bathroom. After I closed the door behind me, I slid the small metal knob to the right, locking the door, which activated the *occupied* light on the outside.

I sat down on the closed stainless-steel lid of the toilet. The whole bathroom, four feet by four feet, was stainless steel, including the floor. Part of me wanted to cry, and another part wanted to scream and break something. Both options at that moment seemed out of the question. A slight breeze was filtering in through the small window that had been left open by someone else. I could see the sun setting one more time in the sky outside. It was my last Greyhound sunset, and I watched it locked in the bathroom. After the final sliver of light had fallen below the horizon, I got up and washed my face and hands in the sink. Seeing myself in the mirror, I realized that even though I felt older, I was still twelve years old. I couldn't quite recall how I'd felt getting on the bus, but I knew getting off that things would have to be at least a little different.

Just as I reached up for the knob, somebody rapped loudly at the door. I emerged with a surprised look as a young man with a beard was waiting to use the toilet. Slipping out and back to my seat, I looked over at Marcus, who had hit the hot-line button on his Walkman.

"You alright? I thought you might have fallen in or something. I was about to call the cavalry," he joked.

"Just as long as it wasn't Stonewall Jackson," I responded.

"Feel better?" he asked.

"I guess I do. I think I understand the snake in the box thing a bit better."

"I knew you would, kiddo."

"Thanks," I said.

"It's cool. It's your life, my man. Just don't feel too wounded about it, and you'll be cool."

I nodded in acknowledgment. After I checked the time and my schedule, I estimated we were only a few hours out from Columbus and we'd probably get in early. I slipped my headphones on and faded away to Hall and Oates again. My favorite song on the tape, after listening to it so many times, was "I Can't Go for That." It had a beat and catchy lyrics, which I had almost completely memorized.

I thought about what I had told Marcus, and while it did feel a little strange telling him, I knew on some level I would feel better. He said it would change me by telling "my story," as he referred to it, the way I saw it. I knew better than to expect any type of dramatic shift in my personality or to stop stuttering tomorrow. I had been told many times already that I would eventually grow out of it. Maybe this would help me to grow out of it just that much faster. Marcus had a way of making me feel more included in everything around me than I had ever felt before, but by myself I still felt as if I was separated from everyone else. It wasn't hard to understand, or reason why, when being noticed was equivalent to a "ghost sighting." Usually when people took notice of me, they'd follow it with the sentence "What are you doing here?" or "How did you get in here?" I was always in the way. Maybe the biggest thing I had in common with Marcus was staring me in the face the whole time. While he knew what it was like to be imprisoned and freed, I knew what it was like to be taken hostage mentally and imprisoned inside myself.

The problem with being trapped inside your head all day is that it's difficult for others to notice it. Most people will just say, "Ohh ... he's so quiet and well behaved."

Sitting in the darkness, I could feel another level of anticipation and frustration peel away like an invisible layer. The interior lights were on, illuminating the ceiling and the floor. Almost all of the small overhead lights above each passenger were shining down, even my own.

Early evening on the bus was just another set of routines. People began pulling out food, snacks, drinks, leftovers they'd brought from home, and sat enjoying whatever company was around them. One man who had gotten on the bus back in Blythe had been sleeping almost the entire time. I only saw him awake twice, and that was only for a short bathroom visit. It was as if life on the Greyhound was too much to absorb, and thus shutting down was the only option. A long rotation of bathroom visits and smoke breaks ensued, and the driver would usually turn on the radio to the evening news so folks could get a sense that the world hadn't actually ceased to exist, even though everything on the bus typically pointed in that direction.

You could also hear the shuffling of cards, and a few people would get up and move seats to have conversations with other riders. For the most part, everyone tried to be as pleasant as they could. One bad seed was all that was ever needed to spoil the bunch, but people like Leigh Allen and Frank Burns were incredibly rare.

It was just after ten-thirty when we got into Columbus. The rain had stopped just as the driver said it would, and the streets were all wet and puddle-strewn from the same heavy storm that had been following us across the country. Neon signs hung in shop windows everywhere as we drove toward the depot. Downtown Columbus had so many neon lights burning, they could've doubled as streetlights. We drove past a church with a neon sign that said *Jesus Saves*, but it definitely wasn't the first sign like that I had seen. I'd probably seen that same sign more than any other. *7-Eleven* was a close second. Even though it was already quiet and hardly anyone was out, the several 7-Elevens that we did pass along the way all had people standing around just outside the door and under the building's green awning. The pay phones were never lonely either. It was something you could count on.

"You need to stop at the gift shop?" Marcus asked, as he shoved his paperback book back into his jacket pocket. He was almost done with it now. It looked as if he was on the last few pages.

"Yeah, I wanted to buy some gum," I answered.

"Cool, I'm going in too. I need to get some batteries and a bag of chips."

I started to think that all the terminals would begin to look the same, but it just wasn't the case. Every so often the Greyhound stations would be these odd streamlined-looking blue-and-chrome museum-style buildings from another era, and other times they were just a window in a shop or a part of some other structure like an afterthought. The Columbus station was a giant gray cube with a rotating sign outside the building, possibly to let airplanes know to avoid it or to try to land out front on the main street because they had a twenty-four-hour café. I meandered around the gift shop, bored stiff and stuck in my head. I was numb from traveling. Marcus had to tap me on the shoulder, as he had called out my name several times and I didn't respond.

"Sebastien, you alright?" he asked. He was looking at cassette tapes next to me at the counter.

"Yeah, I'm fine. Why do you ask?"

"I called your name three times and you didn't hear me. You look stuck in your head."

"I didn't?" was about the most I could manage. I looked up at the cassette tapes and examined the titles. More names of people I had never heard of and probably wouldn't want to. The name *Engelbert Humperdinck* made me smile. Turning the racks, I saw Petula Clark, Charlie Rich, Roger Whitaker, and Merle Haggard. I saw nothing I would've wanted to buy right off the bat. As I turned the rack a little more, two names caught my eye: Three Dog Night and Cat Stevens.

"You ever listen to Three Dog Night?" I asked, looking over at Marcus, holding up the tape.

"Nope," he stated succinctly, bringing over an Al Jarreau tape and paying for it.

"How about Cat Stevens?" I followed up. He looked as if he was concentrating.

"You going through a list of animals first to help you narrow down your choice? What's the title of the cassette?" he asked. "Is it *Tea for the Tillerman*?"

"It says *Greatest Hits*," I replied.

"You seem to have a small collection of Greatest Hits building up, don't ya?" I hadn't thought about it before, but I did. My other two cassettes were both greatest hits compilations. I liked both of them and made my decision to buy the Cat Stevens. A sign above the rack read *fifty percent off*. All the tapes were a dollar seventy-five. My money situation was getting tighter, but it would be gone soon no matter what I spent it on. At least I could listen to music all summer long.

After I paid for the tape and gum, we made our way over to the diner. It was the first diner I had seen that was called something other than Grey's Café or The Grey Café. This one was just called The Road Grill. The smell wafting through the air didn't make me feel in a hurry to eat there, but I knew it was the last chance I would have to eat with Marcus, and I wouldn't want to eat once we got to Pittsburgh, as it would be close to three in the morning.

A young waitress in the signature gray-and-blue uniform walked us over to two seats that looked through the window to the outside world. Looking around, I could see a constant throng of bodies that were heeding the warning of *"final boarding call to Amarillo on aisle 3."* I couldn't imagine making the trip backward now after everything that had happened. I didn't envy any of the people running to catch their bus. If they knew what was good for them, they would miss it entirely. The image of the wildlife mural on the wall back in Blythe went through my head again. If they only had a clue that a bear in a stream full of salmon was patiently awaiting them, they might've had second thoughts.

I sat and read the menu, occasionally glancing around the restaurant or outside at the neon sign across the street that read *Same Day Dry Cleaning*. It was blinking off and on methodically, which kept me looking at it. Marcus ordered a bowl of French onion soup and a corned beef sandwich. He never ordered the same thing twice and was still happy about how good it all tasted. Every time he took a bite, I'd stare at his face and watch him eat. He was ecstatic. I'd never seen anyone enjoy eating as much as Marcus did.

I ordered a glass of iced tea and a patty melt with a salad instead of fries. I hadn't eaten any vegetables in days. The last time I saw lettuce was on the tacos in Albuquerque, and we had eaten them so fast, I barely noticed it. For all I knew, it could have been pocket lint or shredded paper rather than lettuce.

"What time does your schedule say we get into Pittsburgh?" Marcus asked. I took a sip of iced tea and dug it out from my back pocket, carefully unfolding it.

"Three-ten in the morning."

"Any stops in between here and there?"

"No, it's an express. The small *e* after Columbus means no stops until the next terminal," I answered.

"You got that thing pretty much figured out, huh?"

"I've been trying not to look at it too much, but I think I've got it completely memorized at this point."

"How long is your layover in Pittsburgh?" Marcus asked.

"I switch over to the 4692, which leaves at three-thirty."

Marcus nodded. "Doesn't leave too much time does it?" he asked thoughtfully.

"For what?" I wondered.

"To get rid of those bags, what else?" he replied. "We'll have to do something drastic. You'll have to get your bags from the porters before they wheel them over to your new bus, and whatever we do with them is gonna have to be quick, or we just might end up missing our connection."

"The next bus from Pittsburgh into Altoona doesn't leave until seven a.m. I have no way to call my grandparents and tell them I missed the bus. I can't miss it."

"Don't worry, you'll make that bus, buddy," he promised. "Was this trip everything you thought it was going to be?" he asked me.

"It's been a lot different than what I expected, that's for sure." We both laughed out loud as we dug into our food. I was beginning to feel a little sad again about the prospect of having to say goodbye to Marcus.

"Y'know ..." I started. "You saved my life. I just wanted to say thanks." I felt the need to tell him that one more time. I was actually unsure if I had previously thanked him at all. He kept staring into his food and balled up his face into an expression as if it was nothing at all.

"Ahh ... you don't need to thank me, man. We're cool, y'know?" he sputtered.

"No, Marcus. I'm serious. If it hadn't been for you, I wouldn't be here right now," I stated firmly. He looked up at me, carefully weighing my words.

"You're welcome, Sebastien. Sometimes you just got to look out for people. That's all it is," he rejoined. "Y'know ... if I can impress upon you one last thing to remember, it's this," he pointed at my jacket pocket. "And you can take notes too, if you want," he suggested with a grin.

"Always try to be good to people, don't always put yourself first, and don't always expect things to be fair, because they won't be. You do that ... and I doubt you'll end up *anything* like your folks. Got me?"

It took me a few seconds to write down everything he had said. I had to use a napkin because my notebook was full and somewhere in the bottom of my bag.

"I hope I don't end up like them," I asserted honestly. Marcus raised his eyebrows and got a crazy look across his face as he bit into his sandwich. I couldn't tell if it was what I had said or the food.

"I wouldn't wish that on anybody!" he answered back.

"What's going to happen to me, Marcus?" I asked bluntly. I thought it was a question I needed to ask, and it was mostly out of desperation.

"I have no idea what's going to happen to you, partner. Nobody does. I don't have a crystal ball, and folks that talk like they do, don't listen to them."

I watched him carefully, and he seemed uncomfortable with what he had said. He put his glass down, wiped his face, and exhaled nervously. I looked away and drank my iced tea as I felt the tension rising. He wasn't mad, but he wanted to say something else.

"Look ..." he started again. "If I had to take a guess, all I could say is that you're going to spend your life looking for friends and continually coming up short. That's what happens when you don't have a real father. You're going to have to be careful about people and know that they often have very selfish motives and will rarely be honest with you about them ... but it doesn't mean not to trust anyone either."

"I'm not going to have any friends?" I repeated, somewhat stuck on that part.

"No. That's not what I said, now," he spoke back quick and sharp. "I said you're going to be looking for friends and won't find many. It's a big difference, understand?"

"I don't know. I guess," I answered, a bit flummoxed.

"Hmm ..." he laughed quietly to himself. "I guess," he repeated, all while watching me.

We sat talking for another five minutes before the waitress came with the bill. I gave her two café vouchers, but she looked puzzled when she picked them up.

"What's this?" she responded angrily. Marcus and I both failed to answer her tone right away. We just sat quietly watching her. A moment later, she became uncomfortable and looked down at the café vouchers. She didn't seem pleased at all.

"Where did you get these?" she snapped. I pulled out Mr. Hastings's business card and handed it to her. She gave it another quick glance.

"I'll have to talk to the manager and make sure we can even take these, but don't count on it."

"Just m– m– ..." I couldn't get it out in one piece.

"What?" she growled hurriedly.

"The card. Just make sure I get that back. Mr. Hastings is my friend."

She looked at me as if I was pathetic, turned around, and left to go check with her boss.

I looked over at Marcus who wasn't bothered by the girl's rudeness at all. He was watching her figure as she walked away. I was surprised. He smiled broadly, his eyes fixed to her rear end.

"Hey, even angry girls need love too, buddy. Don't forget that either," he laughed, pointing at her as she slipped away.

I pulled out the rest of my café vouchers and slid them across the table. "Here, you might as well have these. I won't be needing them at my grandma's house. They gave me a bunch of them back in Los Angeles when our bus got hijacked."

Marcus was immediately shocked by this revelation. "Say what? You never told me about that." His hand slapped down on the table, and all the silverware bounced in unison, making a loud noise.

"Yeah, what can I say? It's been one of those weeks," I confessed lightly. We both found it funny.

"Thanks, man. I appreciate it."

"No problem, Marcus."

"Hey, you going to go see if there's a message from Monty at the information booth? We only got a few minutes left."

"I almost forgot," I rejoined.

"I'll handle the waitress. You go check it out, just in case," he suggested.

I'd almost forgotten about Monty's message. I walked quickly out of The Road Grill and through the long stretch of lobby toward the information counter, which was on the other side of the terminal. I had seen it on the way in but had dismissed it completely.

A smell of cigar smoke and body odor emanated from the doorway of the small office that was marked *Information* by a small brown plaque jutting out into the hall. An old red-faced man with a bulbous, bright-red nose was telling a story to another Greyhound driver. I knocked on the half-size door, but neither of the two men acknowledged me. The second time, I knocked firmer and much louder.

"Hello!" I announced. They were both a little taken aback that I had interrupted them, but they didn't budge. The old man just swished the cigar around in his mouth.

"I'm looking to see if I have a message," I spoke. The two men went stale and silent, staring at me. I felt like I was being examined; it was disturbing.

"A message? What's your name?" he barked. I knew he was going to ask, but it didn't make a bit of difference.

"My name? It's uh, like ..."

"What the hell's your name, kid. Stop the goddamned mumbling and spit it out. This isn't a goddamned petting zoo," he yelled. The other man laughed and leered at me, creeping me out.

"Ranes," I squeezed out through my hardening vocal cords. "Sebastien," I continued in a truncated fashion.

"Ranes? Sebastien?" he groaned. "Which is it, punk?"

"My name is Sebastien Ranes." The words came out of my mouth like huge pieces of rusted metal. My gums and lips were dry. I was sweating and nervous.

"Got problems with the English language, huh?" he commented unsympathetically. The other man just sipped his coffee.

"Lemme just check the books," the old man growled from behind a continuous puffing of smoke. He flipped through two pages slowly and seemed surprised as he came across something. He finally looked back up after a brief hesitation.

"What the hell ... you do got a message." My heart started racing even faster now, and I felt hot underneath my thick Greyhound coat.

"I do?" I responded, stunned. The old man didn't say anything at first. He put the log book down on the small shelf built into the flimsy Dutch door affixed to the office wall. He thrust a pen at me and pointed with his thick digit to a blank line in the book.

"Sign it and date it first," he ordered, sharply.

"What's today's date?" I queried, not looking up.

"May thirteenth," he replied, annoyed. Hung on the wall, beside the man's head, was a small paper flip-calendar with dark numbers that took up the entire square. Thirteen was the size of his red face, and the word *May* was harder to read but still visible. I wished I had looked up before asking, rather than the other way around. I quickly signed and dated the register, then handed him back his pen.

"All it says is: *Message for Sebastien Ranes. John Oates and Sara.*" The old man read it off aloud, never letting me see the original in the book. After he read it a second time, realizing that it wasn't much of a message, he grew confused and a little bewildered. "What's the matter with you now? You look like someone just walked over your momma's grave." I stood still, as it felt as if every ounce of blood had just dropped out of me through my shoes. I was probably as pale as a sheet.

"Thank you," I replied, quickly making my way outside. Marcus was smoking a cigarette on the platform when I caught up to him.

"Well?" he asked, as he watched me quickly making my way up the parking island. "Was there a message?"

"Yeah ..." I rejoined gravely. His face immediately shifted to show concern.

"John Oates *and* Sara," I whispered, still heading for the bus.

Marcus quickly stomped out his cigarette underfoot and pointed at the open door of our transportation. "Hurry up and get back on. Let's just get the hell outta here, if we still can." His tone was urgent. We were both nervous during the last five minutes in Columbus as we waited to pull out and get back onto the road and deeper into the world. I had intended to listen to my Cat Stevens tape on the way to Pittsburgh, but the never-ending barrage of bus fumes, coupled with sheer exhaustion and raw nervous tension, knocked me out cold. I drifted off as soon as we turned left and headed down the on-ramp, merging back onto the freeway and toward whatever was going to be waiting for us in Pittsburgh.

* * *

When I opened my eyes again, my head hurt and I felt absolutely awful. I was congested and had to wipe my nose on my jacket cuff to stop it from running. Overhead, my mind registered the words *Welcome to Pittsburgh* followed by a loud clicking noise, as if someone was cocking a gun next to the speaker. I looked over, and Marcus was still fast asleep, which was uncharacteristic, as he seemed to be awake and alert at all times. I had to nudge him back to life.

"Marcus ... we're here. Wake up," I said, pulling on his arm. He quickly came around and rubbed his eyes.

"Man, I'm dead-ass tired," he announced, sitting up quickly and yawning. The bus was already in the terminal, and people were pouring themselves down the metal stairs.

"I guess this is it," I said, looking over at him, waiting for a response. He just smiled, grabbed his stuff, and started slowly down the aisle.

"C'mon, kiddo. We've got one more thing to get done before all that."

Once we were off the bus, we both waited with everyone else on the platform for my bags. One of the porters came over to us.

"Name?" he queried.

"Ranes. Two cases," Marcus replied, interjecting with expedience. I didn't say a word, but I was thankful that I didn't have to speak. A moment later, the man came back with my cases and set them down on the pavement in front of us.

"The tags say that we're supposed to transfer these to the 4692. You still traveling on to State College or Altoona?"

"My bags are traveling separate," I announced. I gave the man the two stubs that I had been given three days before back in Stockton and finally redeemed my luggage. As soon as we picked them up and moved a mere ten feet down the platform, we heard the overhead announcement.

"*First call. First call. Now boarding Greyhound 4692 on aisle 4 to Altoona, Hollidaysburg, and State College. First call.*"

We both stopped and looked at each other, unsure about what to do next. I looked up and realized that Marcus was obviously getting a kick out of this, judging by the ecstatic grin across his face.

"This is the most entertainment I've had in days!" he admitted.

"What are we going to do, Marcus?" I asked, now frantic.

"You got anything inside you need or that has your name on it?"

"Uh-uh. Nothing," I responded.

"Hurry up and take your Greyhound tags off the handle," he pointed out. The paper tags were being held on by white rubber bands that easily broke when pulled at with any amount of force. Marcus quickly peeled off the red Trailways sticker that had been slapped across the case he was carrying.

"C'mon, let's get to the front of the building. I've got an idea," he said. We hurriedly made our way around the terminal through an alleyway that opened out onto the main street in front of the bus station. Even for three-thirty in the morning, it was busy. The bus station sat on the corner of a huge intersection that was brightly lit by a barrage of streetlamps. People were coming and going from the terminal or hanging out on the benches, waiting for a city bus to come pick them up. Marcus was looking around for something or someone.

"Here we go," he exclaimed. "Follow me!"

I ran after him, dragging the suitcase with what little strength I had left, as we made our way down the sidewalk and away from the bus terminal toward an old homeless lady pushing a shopping cart a half a block away from us.

"Excuse me, ma'am!" Marcus called out to her. At first she didn't turn around, but as we got closer, she slowed and eventually turned her head and her whole body toward us. The old woman was dressed in multiple layers of clothes and rags, which were all filthy. She was hauling two baskets full of what looked like worthless and random junk. As I stood beside her, next to Marcus, I began to notice how badly she reeked. I never thought anything could smell like that, but it was awful. She smelled ten times worse than the man who had defecated in his pants back in Phoenix. I tried not to let it show on my face, but I was overwhelmed by the smell. When she saw me, she smiled, and her face lightened and relaxed.

"Are you alright?" she asked me. "Why are you out so late?" Her words seemed out of place, like she recognized us. She was talking to me as if everything was perfectly normal.

"Sorry to rush, but these are for you," Marcus informed her, putting the cases down next to her. "We both wanted you to have these and thought you might get some use out of what's inside," he added. She smiled, stared at Marcus, and then started to feel the outside of the cases with her hands.

"Ohh ... now these are really lovely," the old homeless lady pointed out. "Let me get you a receipt for these."

"We've got to get back. We have a bus to catch. Kind of in a hurry, okay?" We both scratched our heads as she fumbled around in her basket for a moment, looking for a "receipt." When she turned back around, she was holding two empty bags of pretzels and handed us one each.

"One for you ..." she said, giving an empty pretzel bag to Marcus, "and one for you," she stated, patting my shoulder and looking closely into my eyes.

"Thank you," I said.

"Alright, boys. Have a nice trip and don't miss your flight. Call me when you get in," she followed up.

"C'mon, we've gotta get back to the bus," he said, as he headed down the sidewalk. I felt a little strange as I turned away from the two suitcases and picked up into a full sprint after Marcus, racing to the bus in the middle of the night. We rounded the back end of the terminal and returned to where we had started. We took a second to catch our breath and watched people climbing aboard our buses, which were parked beside each other. Sweat beads were running down my face, and we were both panting for air.

"This is it, Sebastien Ranes," he said, sticking out his hand. I felt compelled to give him a hug.

"Thanks for everything, Marcus Franklin," I replied. I patted him on the back twice and then backed off, feeling odd. Even though I had only known him for three days, it felt as if we had been friends for much longer.

"Oh, here ..." I interrupted myself, distracted, and handed him a small piece of paper. "I wrote down my address in Altoona. Maybe you could write me during the summer, tell me how everything's going up in New York."

"Okay ... look forward to it, then. I'll send you word, alright?"

"*Final boarding call, 4692 to Altoona, Hollidaysburg, and State College. Final call. Final call.*"

"Damn!" I swore. "Gotta go."

"You be good, Sebastien. Stay safe," Marcus called out, as he stepped over toward his bus. It was an odd moment getting on the new coach without him, and it felt strange, bleak, and unsettling all at once. Everything had gone smoothly, and I was almost home. I would be there in a few hours, and I wondered how much of all this would begin to fade out and be forgotten. Nothing ever felt permanent. Sitting in the back of the bus for the last time, I looked over at my old bus and saw Marcus in the window, waving goodbye. He was standing up and had his palm against the glass, giving me the thumbs-up. I did the same and watched him smiling as we pulled backward, away from the terminal, beeping the whole way.

10.

MAY 14, 1981 ...
ALTOONA, PENNSYLVANIA

As tired as I was, and as early as it was, I should have just tried to sleep the next four hours away, but I couldn't. I was wide awake. My brain had fallen into the habit of automatically tuning out all the background noises, the groaning engine, the muffled coughing, and the endless pockets of people snoring. Now it was absolutely dead quiet, and it was disturbing. Most of these people were just making a short road trip to an out-of-the-way place in the middle of the state. They weren't road-weary, filthy, and exhausted like I was. I felt like a thoroughbred of travelers now. I was a real professional. Now that I was finally alone, just as I was when I had started out, the entire experience of the last three and a half days began to wash over me and sink in. I felt older, and I could sense that I'd probably feel like this for the rest of the summer. Or at least I hoped so. My thoughts shifted back to Marcus, and I knew that he was somewhere on this same stretch of highway, sitting in the backseat and wondering how I was doing, and if someone would be there to pick me up once I got to Altoona. It was a safe bet. In the past, every time we had moved, I had left behind a few friends, and sometimes it would hurt to leave. But after so many moves in such a short period of time, I had slowly become numb to it. Now I was feeling sad for not getting to spend more time in Pittsburgh saying goodbye, even though I knew it was something I was going to have to deal with all day long. No one had ever been a friend to me like Marcus, and no one had ever spent so much time talking with me as he had.

I stared out the window into the waning light of the morning, which seemed slow to come. The moon was now low in the sky, near the horizon and thin like a fingernail, getting ready to fall off the edge of the world, plummeting into daylight. Pulling away from Pittsburgh, the driver must've known it was too late at night for any announcement, as it never happened, and the runner lights on the floor and along the ceiling had been placed in the off position.

The majority of the passengers who had gotten on the bus were younger than the people riding on the previous legs of the trip, and a lot of them were wearing purple sweatshirts with a large cat head on everything. The weekend was now over, and they were probably all returning to school in State College. I really didn't have any hard evidence, but I assumed it by the name of the place.

The farther we got from Pittsburgh, the darker and more uninhabited the world outside became. Mountains rose up all around us, and thick rows of trees blotted out any views that might have been had. The bus slipped through tunnel after tunnel, forging through the innards of small mountains. The inside of the bus momentarily flashed with a brief amount of dim white light from inside the tunnels, illuminating the way. I relaxed and sunk into my headphones to finally listen to the Cat Stevens tape that I'd bought back in Columbus. I started to think that with as much darkness as I was surrounded by, I was bound to eventually fall asleep.

When I popped the cassette tape in and hit the *play* button, I didn't know what to expect, having never heard of him before. I turned down the volume just in case it was going to be loud. When a few seconds passed in complete silence, I turned the volume slowly back up until I heard the very faint sound of a guitar playing. Checking the back of the cassette box, I saw the title of the song was "The Wind," which seemed more than fitting. The music was very soft and similar to the Simon and Garfunkel tape, but more soothing. As the bus went on and Cat Stevens sang, the sun rose up from the front of the bus and very slowly, mile by mile, replaced every inch of darkness.

I didn't close my eyes the whole way in. When the bus finally came to a stop behind the large red-brick building in downtown Altoona, I was overcome by an immediate sense of terrible sadness knowing that, as the engine died, my trip had finally come to an end. I was home.

I filed off the bus behind everyone else, and as soon as I stepped down onto the platform, I saw my grandparents coming toward me, smiling. It was still a little cold out, and my grandpa was wearing a red flannel hunting jacket, which could have been spotted from several hundred yards out. I immediately thought back to the shop window in Gallup.

"Ohh my gawd!" my grandma cried out as she saw me and finally took a hold of me. "You had us all so worried for the past twenty-four hours, Sebby, honey."

"Sorry, Grams. I didn't know my mother told you that she was coming."

My grandpa was staring at me and sipping coffee from a white Styrofoam cup that had Dunkin' Donuts printed on the side.

"Let's get you back home and into the bathtub. You smell like you've been working on a dairy farm," my grandma said, as she continued to hug me. "And let's not talk about your mother right now, okay?" she suggested under her breath, motioning with her eyes toward my grandpa.

"You have any luggage, Sebby?" my grandpa asked, his voice booming across the platform against the cold morning air.

"No, Grandpa, just my bag here," I rejoined, slinging my small backpack over my shoulder. They both had horrified looks on their faces, thinking that my mother had sent me away without even a change of clothes. I could've said that Greyhound had lost my luggage in Pittsburgh, but I decided to just keep quiet and not complicate things. I didn't want to start off with an outright lie that I could very easily be caught in.

My grandma made me peel off my Greyhound jacket and put it in the trunk before getting into the car. The huge white Cordoba with the black velvet interior was just soft enough and just dark enough to put me to sleep on the ride back to the house. When I woke up, I felt my grandpa pulling on my arm, trying to get me out of the back-seat. I came around after a few moments and realized that I wasn't feeling very good. I now had a headache, and my nose was running like a faucet. When I told my grandma this, she chuckled and said that I'd feel a lot better after a hot bath and a long sleep.

We got up onto the oversize back patio that was connected to the rear of the house and covered with a large sloping roof. My grandpa had already disappeared inside to get everything started for the day. "Don't step a foot inside the house with any of those filthy clothes," he called out from inside. I very quickly, and without any protestation, stripped down to my underwear, leaving every-thing, including my bag, on the porch beside me. I made my way in a daze through the kitchen and upstairs to the bathroom to run the hot water. When I hit the sheets and closed my eyes, I had a vague recollection of my sister's face beside me and my grandma taking my temperature.

★ ★ ★

When I woke up, a full two days had passed. The sheets I was tangled in were soaked with sweat, and several bottles of medicine were sitting on the small bedside table. I found it difficult to focus my eyes and read the labels. Sunlight was filtering in through the window. Beanie was sitting in a chair on the other side of the room, listening to my Walkman. I watched her for several minutes before she noticed I was awake.

"Well, someone's returned to the land of the living," she announced, pulling the headphones away and stopping the tape. Beanie got up from the chair, crossed the room, and went down the staircase and into the hallway, calling out for Grandma.

"He's awake!" she bellowed.

"Nice to see you, sis. I missed you," I managed, when she came back over to the bed.

"Where did you get this Walkman? It's the coolest!"

"I bought it in Los Angeles," I uttered, clearing my throat and looking around the room, realizing fully that I had made it. I reached for the glass of water beside me, but it was empty.

"Grams is bringing you up some tea. She thought you'd get up late today. Good thing you woke up though. We thought we were going to have to put you in the bath again."

"Again?" I asked, blushing and a little embarrassed.

"Grandma, Aunt Jeannie, and me had to drag you into the bathtub yesterday because you had a fever of a hundred and five. You were limp and babbling insanely."

"Babbling? What did I say? What was I talking about?" I hurriedly questioned her, immediately worried, rubbing my eyes and trying to break all the sleep away that had collected in the corners.

"Dunno, something silly about you thinking that you were a mannequin and you didn't want to be put in storage or get taken apart? You just kept repeating it. You passed out at one point while you were in the tub and slipped under the water. It took us a second to get you out, but for a moment ..."

"Yeah?" I wondered, following her words as her eyes hit the floor.

"For a moment, when you were underwater, I actually thought you looked like a mannequin. It was creepy. You were pale and still like those figures over at Macy's. Once we got you out, it took you forever to breathe again. Grandma thought you were going to drown in the bathtub."

"Wow ... I would've drowned in the bathtub." I murmured her words aloud.

"I'm just glad you're awake, and I *cannot believe* that Mom put you on that bus like that!" she continued, her tone changing to bewilderment, "... and she also lied to Grams too. What's she going to do for an encore?" Beanie asked sarcastically.

"Disappear, I hope," I muttered.

"Don't count on it," she rejoined, narrowing her eyes. The door, which had been left ajar, swung open, and my grandma slipped through, carrying a large tray of tea and other stuff for me.

"Well, as usual you gave us quite a scare and had us all on the edge of our seats. You wouldn't wake up, and we had to have Dr. Michelson from across the street come over to check on you."

"Hi, Grandma. I missed you a lot," I blurted out, without waiting. "Good thing I made it home in one piece just to drown in the bathtub."

"Ahh ... she told you about that?" Grandma responded with concern. She smiled and sat down on the edge of the bed next to me, holding the tray in her lap. Beanie just shrugged it off and went on listening to the Walkman. I watched Grandma prepare a dose of cough syrup for me, and she forced a cup of hot tea on me.

"Here, drink this," she said, handing it over, not taking no for an answer.

"So where did you get the money to buy the Walkman?" Beanie asked, shifting her focus back to the tape player, already bored of me. "They're almost fifty dollars!"

"Where *did* you get the money for that thing?" my grandma followed up.

"Greyhound refunded my ticket money when we got to Los Angeles," I stated.

"And why would they do that?" she continued, without missing a beat. Beanie had the same look of incredulity on her face, wondering why.

"Somebody hijacked the bus when we were in Bakersfield."

"Sweet Jesus!" Grams announced loudly. "A crazy person hijacked the bus with you on it? Oh my gawd," she replied, looking absolutely mortified.

"No ... not a crazy person." I tried to clear it up, but it was no use. I fumbled over my words as they fell on deaf ears. Beanie was wrapped up in the Walkman, and my grandma was imaging God knows what. I knew I wouldn't be able to explain everything that happened. I drank the tea and tried to settle back into the bed, but I was ushered out and made to sit in the chair in the corner while they changed the sheets and handed me a fresh pair of pajamas.

"I spoke to your father yesterday. He said he was going to come down to see you in a few weeks. That should be something to be happy about," my grandma informed me, while stripping off the sweat-soaked sheets.

Glancing over at Beanie, I could hear the Hall and Oates tape playing loudly in her ears. She was gathering up the sheets and my old set of pajamas. I didn't say anything about what I was feeling in regard to my father to my grandma. She wouldn't understand and probably wouldn't want to. I wondered if she had ever lectured him for abandoning us. She probably didn't see it that way. I decided to change the subject.

"Has Charlotte called at all?" I asked.

My grandma glanced at me, disapproving of the subject and the use of my mother's name. "No ... not a word at all." She hadn't called, which I found a little surprising, seeing as I had taken off with her entire wardrobe in the middle of the night without her knowledge. I thought for sure that she would have hit the roof over the loss of her precious dresses. As I drank my tea, the image of Marcus and me handing over the suitcases to the homeless woman on the sidewalk brought me some consolation and a smile.

"Something funny?" my grandma asked.

"No, it's nothing," I concealed. I wondered to myself if it was just a matter of time before Charlotte finally disappeared for good.

It took almost a full week before I was let out of bed and declared recovered. They couldn't tell if I had pneumonia or something else. I began to get settled and was thankful I still had my room in the attic. Dr. Michelson, the neighbor, had told my grandpa that I had picked up something nasty on the bus being exposed to so many different germs while traveling the country. He also made a point of saying that I was most likely not washing my hands.

The weather had changed dramatically in one short week. Summer had taken over completely. It was hot every day, and I spent as much time as I could outside catching up with Beanie and everyone else in the neighborhood who had the luxury of never having to move. I rode my bike over to the community pool a few times, watched baseball games, and read comic books on the steps of Miller's Corner delicatessen. I quickly forgot about Charlotte and Dick getting married, and just as Marcus had said, my memory of being on the bus began to fade. I had read my journal a few times, thinking about all the places we went, everything we had talked about, and everything he had told me to remember. I even wrote all those things down again, as I thought they were important enough to repeat a few times to myself. In my head, I could still hear his voice telling me about "cowards and men." Those words floated across my consciousness like a billboard advertisement.

It was almost three weeks after I had gotten back when my grandma handed me Marcus's letter, postmarked from New York City. She hadn't opened it to search through it for money, as my mother undoubtedly would have.

"Who do you know in New York, sweetie?" she asked. "That's not your mother's writing, that's for sure."

"Oh ... just a friend," I rejoined sheepishly. I carefully opened the letter and sat on the edge of the porch outside and read it slowly. It was handwritten.

July 1981

Sebastien,
How's everything in Altoona? Feeling okay? Sorry I didn't write sooner, but I was feeling a bit under the weather after I got off the bus. You're not going to have many adventures like that one again. I can almost guarantee it.

New York is just as I remember it. It's just as crowded as it was when I was your age, when we moved out to California. I saw my mom and my pops, God rest them both. I didn't make it back in time to see my mom before she passed, as she was pretty sick the last few months with the cancer. I didn't want to say anything about it on the bus, as I didn't know how to tell you, but I guess you know now. Being on the bus and talking with you seemed to take my mind off things for a while, so I hope you're not mad at me.

It was a good thing that we separated when we did. When I got to

Philadelphia, the police questioned me about Leigh Allen and you, but they couldn't hold me, as they had nothing, and I denied everything. Sometimes you gotta do that with the law. I hate to say this, but you're probably going to have to keep looking over your shoulder for Leigh Allen for some time to come.

I'll never forget our trip together across the country, and Mount Vernon now seems etched in my mind forever. I heard that "Tie a Yellow Ribbon" song the other day, and it reminded me of sitting in that coffee shop at six a.m., watching it rain and waiting for John F. Kennedy. No one would believe it if I told 'em.

Anyways, remember what we talked about, and things shouldn't ever be that bad. You'll never need to look too far for friends if you just be yourself. And don't forget that it's easier to be a man than it is to be a coward. It's just harder to be an honest man than an honest coward. You can always lie to yourself, even if you never lie to others.

Have a good summer. I hope you like the book I left you, and stay safe.

Your friend,
Marcus

I laughed as I read and then reread his letter. It was unexpected, but good to hear from him, and unsettling to think about Leigh Allen. I still had his driver's license in my inside jacket pocket, which was now boxed up and stored away in the attic. His license was the only thing I had that would serve as a reminder to me. Maybe in the future I'd be able to do something about it, but for now there was nothing to do but bury what had happened away in the back corners of my mind.

Later in the middle of summer, my mother did call, rearing her ugly head. She had spoken very briefly with my grandma and told her that the house had been broken into when she was on her honeymoon. The television, a radio, some knickknacks, and the majority of her wardrobe had all been stolen. I was a little surprised by the turn of events, but I honestly didn't care, as I was now off the hook. All I wanted to know was if she was planning on coming to Altoona to uproot me or my sister again. Hopefully, she wasn't. It was the only time she had called, as they had most likely argued about putting me on the bus by myself. Knowing my grandma, she probably gave Charlotte the tongue-lashing she deserved. Knowing my mother, she most likely dismissed everything that was said to her and lit another cigarette with her nose in the air.

When I had gone through my backpack, I found the Langston Hughes book that Marcus had left. I read it several times from cover to cover, but once, when I was randomly flipping the pages, I caught sight of something that I had previously overlooked. On page sixty-seven, someone had put a pencil line through the title of the poem "Color" and boldly retitled it "Have Hope." It was the same handwriting in the book as was in the letter. I knew it must've been Marcus.

The book was more of a request than it was a present, and I was beginning to understand what these small things meant. Even though he was gone, he was still thinking about me and probably always would be. Sometimes a thought, though, isn't enough. A few kind words can carry you a little further. That's what Langston Hughes did. That's what Langston Hughes would do. The last message from Marcus was an easy one, and I understood it. He was worried enough about me to care, and it wasn't something that I would soon forget.

During the intense humidity of July, I sat on the porch playing Scrabble with Beanie and my grandma. I had been struggling with the letters, trying to come up with something better than *bus* for five points. The task of double and triple word scores was all I was focused on, even though we were, once more, waiting for my father. He was supposed to have come for dinner, but he was running late.

As the night wore on, clouds rolled in and lightning bugs swarmed the yard around the house. We sat watching the small lights floating in the darkness and listening to the building thunder approaching from the distance. When it was ten o'clock, it was time for bed, and my father still hadn't shown up. The only person who was upset about it was Beanie. My grandma and I had watched her sulking in her chair on the patio for most of the evening, even though she had successfully come in first place on the Scrabble board. The fact that he didn't show didn't bother me in the slightest. I guess it was what I expected. I went to bed that night and slept peacefully, happy to be where I was, and happy to be home. The last person I thought about before I fell asleep was my friend, Marcus Franklin.

GREYHOUND:

A FEW THOUGHTS ...

Greyhound Bus Lines was founded in Hibbing, Minnesota, in 1914. For most Americans, traveling by bus was the preferred mode of travel for almost seventy years. Greyhound, and later their main competitor, Trailways, built up a large infrastructure across the continental United States, replete with bus depots that were considered state-of-the-art, and even luxurious, by many standards. Many of the stops, often called depots, stations, or terminals, depending on where exactly you were in the country, had large lobbies with pay televisions, a full-service sit-down restaurant chain known as The Grey Café, Grey's Café, or The Road Grill, and many other amenities like gift shops, showers, vending machines, coin-op laundry, lockers, and other services.

Since that time, a lot has changed. In the late 1970s and early 1980s, Congress deregulated the transportation industry, which gave more people access to passenger airlines such as People Express and PSA. The airline industry offered lower rates to fly, putting both Greyhound and Trailways on the brink of bankruptcy and extinction. Both companies could not compete with the new lower fares for both short and long distances and thus saw the bulk of their patrons lifting upward into the clouds and away from the tradition of bus riding forever.

In 1981, Greyhound Lines had posted an almost $2 billion surplus for the year. In 1982, because of the deregulation and the launch of People Express and PSA in 1981, the company nearly folded.

ACKNOWLEDGMENTS

First and foremost, I both need and want to thank my close friend and editor Mark Espinosa for the many hours and days spent editing, questioning, revising, and "making another pass," as well as all the late-night phone calls, the wise words, and mostly the encouragement. Always number one in my books.

I would also like to thank Courtney Abruzzo and Bryce Lowe for their early edits when the book was in first draft form and for exhibiting a gracious amount of patience.

Many thanks also to Gene Nicolelli, director and founder of the Greyhound Museum in Hibbing, Minnesota, for all his help verifying some of the more important details and historical information that only he would've known. Thanks also to Debra Jane Seltzer for her unending obsession with photographing the ever fading American landscape.

Many thanks also go to Terry Goodman at AmazonEncore for waking me from that afternoon nap to tell me congratulations and for putting up with me, ever after. Thanks also to Sarah Tomashek, Shoshana Thaler, and Cheryl Della Pietra for marketing and editing.

Special thanks to Ben Gibson for his amazing artwork on the front.

I also need to thank U2. Thank you for saving my life and keeping me here long after I thought I had given up. You'll never know how grateful I am. People's hard work does have meaning to others.

I also want to thank all the readers, including you. The point of this book was to give something beautiful to the world and to whomever sees themselves within these pages and to know that you're not alone.

ABOUT THE AUTHOR

Born in Pennsylvania in 1971 and raised in England and various parts of Alaska. Attended school at the University of Alaska, Anchorage and the University of California, Los Angeles.

When Piper lived in Alaska, the mayor of Nome asked him to "leave and never return."

Steffan Piper currently lives on the outskirts of Los Angeles with his family. Most of his writing occurs in the dead of night unlike the bulk of his contemporaries.